Fun Favorites

Fun Favorites

THE WALT DISNEY PARADE
OF FUN, FACT, FANTASY AND FICTION

WITH ILLUSTRATIONS BY THE WALT DISNEY STUDIO

Golden Press * New York

Contents

Library of Congress Catalog Card Number: 73-116695.

Published by Golden Press, New York, a division of Western Publishing Company, Inc. Printed in the U.S.A.

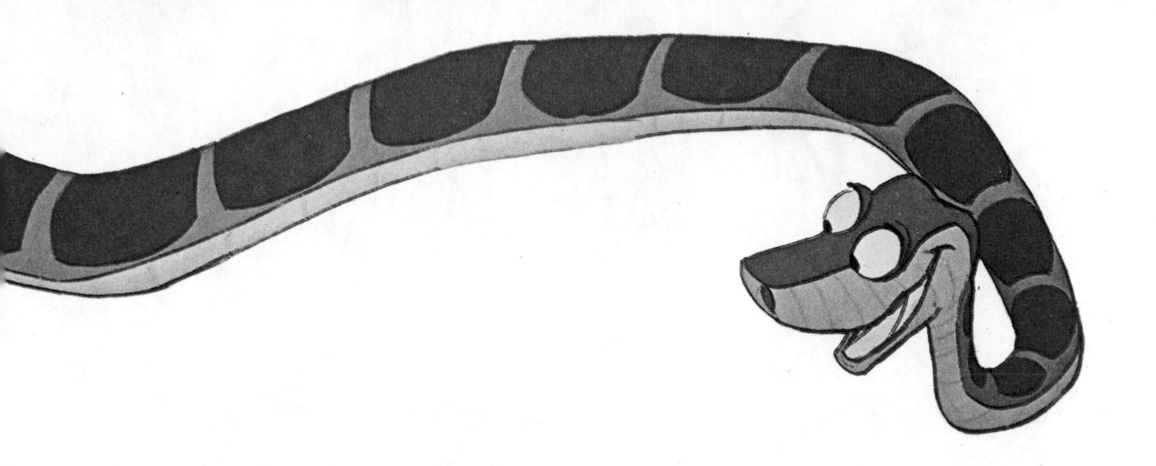

The Jungle Book

The Man-Cub

MANY STRANGE tales are told in far-off India. When the work of the day is over and the village people sit together in the dusk, they speak of Bagheera the black panther and of Baloo the bear. They tell of Shere Khan the tiger, the man-hater who once stalked the jungle. But no tale is so strange as the story of the small boy called Mowgli.

No one knows to this day where Mowgli was born or who his parents were. It was Bagheera the panther who found him in the jungle one warm spring evening. Bagheera was a night prowler, as are many of the jungle creatures. He was just waking from his day's rest, stretching the muscles under his sleek black coat, when he heard the cry.

Bagheera pricked up his ears and listened. Far away to the east the monkey people chattered as they raced through the treetops. Bagheera heard the comfortable grunting of a buffalo at the water hole nearby and the screech of a night bird leaving its nest. Then again the cry floated to Bagheera on the wind. It was a sound the panther had never heard before in the fastness of the jungle. It was the thin, outraged wail of a man-cub!

Warily Bagheera padded down a well-worn trail toward the river. There, where the grasses grow tall at the edge of the water, he found the thing which the folk of the man-villages call a boat. Bagheera watched from the shadows until he was sure there was no one about. Then he crept forward.

The scent of man was strong on the boat. One end had split away and sunk in the river current. The other end had struck upon a stone and was tilted sharply upward. It was in that end that Bagheera saw a basket such as the folk of the man-villages use to carry their belongings, and sometimes to bed down their young. A very tiny man-cub was tucked inside.

Bagheera's first impulse was to turn and walk away. The man-cub was not the panther's concern. Let those from the man-village come and tend to him.

Yet Bagheera knew in his heart that the villagers would not come. They could not even know about the tiny creature in the basket. His boat must have come from some village far up the river. And there was no doubt of it—whoever manned the boat must have perished in some mishap on the journey down the stream. No one would have left such a young man-cub alone.

The angry wails went up again. The basket rocked in the boat as the baby threw his legs and arms high in the air. Clearly the little thing was hungry. Without a mother's care, he would quickly perish.

Bagheera pondered the puzzle of the man-cub. It would be an evil thing to let the little one die. Yet it was a long journey to the man-village. Moreover, the villagers had arrows and guns, and a great fear of the jungle creatures. It would not be safe for Bagheera to approach them too closely.

Then a happy thought came to the panther. Not long ago the family of wolves who lived in a cave above the river had had a litter of cubs. Perhaps Raksha, the wolf mother, would be willing to feed one more hungry mouth.

Very gently, Bagheera took the handles of the basket in his mouth. He carried it away from the river and up to the entrance of the wolves' den. There he put it down upon the packed earth. The man-cub had stopped crying. He stared up at Bagheera with wide, dark eyes.

Bagheera retreated behind a screen of jungle brush and waited to see what he might see. But, except for the small sounds of the jungle, all was quiet. No wolf appeared.

Bagheera did not want to be all night on his errand of mercy. He slid out from his hiding place and gave the basket a hearty cuff. It rocked from side to side, and the man-cub protested with a shrill cry. Bagheera faded back into the brush as five yipping wolf cubs tumbled out of the den. They were followed by their mother. Bagheera held his breath.

The mother wolf sniffed at the small warm bundle inside the basket. Then she nuzzled it. So far so good, thought Bagheera. Then out of the den strode Rama, the father of the cubs. He was one of the swiftest hunters in the wolf pack. Sternly he nosed aside the cubs and stepped close to the basket.

The man-cub's wailing cry softened to a hiccupping, gurgling coo. A soft little brown hand reached up and touched the wolf father's nose. Rama hesitated. Then he licked the tiny hand. He lifted the basket gently in his strong teeth and carried it into the den.

From deep in Bagheera's throat came a purr of relief. The small man-cub had a home. All was well.

Bagheera stole away from the wolf den and set about his night's hunting.

The Law of the Pack

Ten times the rains came and went while the man-cub lived with the wolves. The mother wolf named the child Mowgli, which means little frog. She was very proud of her man-cub. Sometimes, truth to tell, she was more proud of him than she was of her own cubs. He was cleverer than the others. He was always thinking of new games to play and new things to do.

Raksha's cubs were more than willing to accept the man-cub as their brother. They reveled in the games he taught them. And his nimble fingers could always remove a thorn from a paw or a burr from an ear.

The wolf cubs, of course, grew much faster than Mowgli. They were full-grown hunters while he was still a small child. They left the den, and Raksha had another litter of cubs, and then another. Mowgli, at last, had many wolf brothers. They watched over him when they went on a hunt. From them, and from Rama, Mowgli learned the ways of the pack.

Bagheera the panther never forgot that it was he who had found Mowgli. He would stretch out on a branch near the den and watch Mowgli

at play with the wolves. And often, when he did this, he felt strangely troubled.

"Mowgli is more clever than his brothers," the mother wolf would tell Bagheera.

"See how quick he his!" the father wolf would exclaim.

"Perhaps that's because he is a man-cub and not a wolf," Bagheera would remind them. "He is different."

"He is my cub," the mother wolf would say, and Bagheera would sigh and hold his tongue.

Where would it all end? Mowgli might run with the wolf pack, but he was *not* a wolf. Even after the rains had come and gone ten times, Mowgli was only half grown. It would be many seasons more before he was a man. Would Raksha and Rama live to see this? And if they did not, what would become of Mowgli? "He should go back to his own people," said Bagheera to himself.

Then one night the cry of Akela, the leader of the wolf pack, sounded through the jungle. He was calling his followers to meet with him at Council Rock.

At Council Rock

Rama answered Akela's call, of course. He took his place at Council Rock together with the hunters of the pack. Many of Mowgli's brothers were there. And so was Bagheera. For many seasons the black panther had joined in the councils of the wolves. But Bagheera remembered always that he was a guest. He kept himself a little apart from the wolves, and he seldom spoke unless he was spoken to.

Akela the leader waited until all the wolves were ready. Then he spoke. "Shere Khan is returning!" he said.

A ripple of uneasiness swept through the pack.

"The tiger is coming back," said Akela. "The ravens have seen him journeying from the north. Today the monkey people were chattering in the trees of a bullock dead near a water hole not two days from here. Shere Khan pulled it down and killed it with one blow. Then he fed."

One of the younger hunters spoke up. "Why should we care?" he asked. "Bagheera hunts in our land and he sits with our councils. Isn't there game enough for all?"

"There is game enough," admitted Akela. "But Shere Khan does not hunt as we do. Shere Khan has hunted man."

There was a murmur among the younger wolves. To hunt a man was forbidden by the first law of the jungle.

"Once Shere Khan hunted in the fields on the very edge of the man-village," Akela told them. "The men came out with their guns. They carried their red flower blooming on the ends of long sticks. One of the men threw a stick which was all burning with the red flower. It struck Shere Khan in the face. The monkeys gossiped about it for days afterward. They said the tiger screamed. Then the men made a great noise with their guns. Shere Khan screamed again and his blood dripped on the ground. He ran away, and ever since Shere Khan has hated men and men's guns and men's fire."

"But we are not men," said the young hunter.

Akela looked beyond him toward Rama. "Mowgli is a man," he said.

Rama sprang to his feet. "Mowgli is but a man-cub," he declared.

"He will be a man," said Akela. "He can no longer stay with the pack. He must leave."

"Leave?" gasped Rama. "But he knows no other family or home. Surely he is entitled to the protection of the pack."

Some of the other wolves drew away from Rama. "The pack cannot protect Mowgli," one of the older wolves pointed out. "You know how bitterly Shere Khan hates man. He will sniff out the man-cub and destroy him. If he learns that we are hiding Mowgli, he will destroy our cubs."

"The man-cub must leave," rumbled another wolf.

"It is the only way," warned one of the elders of the pack—a wolf with a muzzle white with age.

"The man-cub must return to his own people," said Akela. "He will be safe with them." We have a day's time before Shere Khan comes. Perhaps, with great good fortune, we have two days. That is little enough. If the man-cub leaves immediately, he will be safe in the man-village before Shere Khan can learn of it. What does the pack say?"

The old wolf who had told of Shere Khan's hatred spoke up. "He must go!"

"He must go!" echoed the other wolves. "He must go! To the man-village."

The wolves had cast the man-cub out. Rama knew it, of course. And so did Bagheera.

"Wait!" cried the panther.

The wolves turned toward Bagheera. He rose from the tree branch where he had been stretched out. "It was I who carried the man-cub from the river to Rama's den," he said. He leaped to the ground and approached Rama. "It is because of me that the man-cub is here," he admitted. "Let me see the man-cub safely out of the jungle. I know the way to the man-village. Mowgli will be safe there. Let him go with me."

Rama did not answer. Instead, his great, shaggy head dropped almost to his paws.

It was answer enough. Mowgli's fate was sealed.

Mowgli Rebels

Mowgli had grown to be a night-roamer, like his brothers the wolves. He did not think it strange that Bagheera came to the den in the hillside by moonlight and invited him to come out. When else would Bagheera come? And Mowgli went with the panther gladly. Bagheera was more strict with Mowgli than his wolf father, but the panther could teach the man-cub many things.

So, long before the moon set, Bagheera and Mowgli were far from Rama's den, speeding along a jungle trail. To Mowgli's surprise, Bagheera did not attempt to lecture him.

"Bagheera, where are we going?" asked Mowgli.

The panther only coughed.

"I'm getting sleepy," said Mowgli. "Shouldn't we be starting home?"

It was a moment Bagheera had been dreading. But the panther knew his duty. He sat down and spoke very quietly.

"We are not going back," he told Mowgli. "I'm taking you to a man-village."

"A man-village?" Mowgli thought this was a funny idea. He laughed at the very thought of one of Rama's cubs in a man-village.

"Shere Khan the tiger has returned to this part of the jungle," Bagheera told him. "If you remain with the wolf pack, Shere Khan will try to kill you."

Mowgli stopped laughing. Bagheera sounded very serious. Being killed sounded very serious, too. "But why should Shere Khan do that?"

"Shere Khan hates man. You are a man-cub. Shere Khan will not give you a chance to grow up and become a man and hunt him with a gun and the red flower."

"But I wouldn't do that!" exclaimed Mowgli. "I'll just explain to Shere Khan that I . . .

"No one explains anything to Shere Khan," interrupted Bagheera. "All you can do is stay out of his way. You must leave the jungle and go to the man-village."

"But I'm not afraid," insisted Mowgli.

"Now, that's enough!" said Bagheera sternly. "We're going to the man-village."

The panther looked around. The night was far gone. It was time to rest. Bagheera selected a tall, stout tree with a straight trunk. "We'll sleep up there for a while, eh, man-cub?" suggested the panther. "It'll be safer."

Mowgli looked up. Thirty feet above him a limb jutted out from the tree trunk. Mowgli had learned many things from his wolf family, but climbing was not one of them. He could manage fairly well on a small tree where he could get his arms around the bole. A tree with branches reaching low to the ground was possible. But one like this was too much for the man-cub. He took a short run at the tree and jumped, trying to dig into the bark with his toes and his fingers.

"It's too big around," protested Mowgli. "Besides, I don't have any claws to climb up with."

"Well do I know it," sighed Bagheera. The panther put one paw under Mowgli's rump and pushed. "Up you go!" he said, climbing easily as his claws took hold of the bark. He generously overlooked the fact that Mowgli was kicking him in the ears.

When they had reached a high branch, Bagheera watched Mowgli settle himself against the bole of the tree. "Now get some sleep," advised the panther. "We still have a long journey ahead of us."

Bagheera yawned and stretched out, kneading the branch with his claws. Then he put his head down on his paws and closed his eyes.

"I don't want to go to the man-village," said Mowgli. "I want to stay in the jungle. I can take care of myself."

Bagheera's whiskers twitched, but he didn't open his eyes. "You wouldn't last a single day by yourself," he advised.

"I'm not afraid!" insisted Mowgli.

Bagheera didn't answer. Mowgli leaned back. He was about to close *his* eyes, too, when Kaa the python uncoiled part of his great length from a branch above him and swung down to stare at the man-cub.

"S-s-say, what's this-s?" hissed Kaa. He gave Mowgli a snaky smile. "Why, it's-s a man-cub! A delicious-s man-cub."

Mowgli was in no mood to exchange the time of day with a snake. "Go away!" he snapped, rather rudely. "Leave me alone!"

Kaa continued to smile, but Mowgli's careless words echoed in his cold brain. A springy column of muscle thirty feet long, with a head like a battering ram, Kaa was a creature worth fearing. In the jungle none knew for certain the limits of his powers, but he was said to perform deeds of magic. Few could look him in the eye without feeling their senses reel, and fewer still had felt his cold coils and come out of the embrace alive.

Now Kaa looked straight at Mowgli. "Go to s-sleep, man-cub," he hissed.

Mowgli felt his head grow heavy. Kaa came nearer and nearer until his gleaming yellow eyes filled all the world. "Go to s-sleep!" he crooned. "S-sleep, little man-cub. S-sleep! S-sleep!"

Cool, smooth coils of muscle began to settle around Mowgli.

"Bagheera!" The man-cub just managed to get the word out.

Bagheera did not even raise his head. "No use arguing," he muttered sleepily. "Go to sleep now. We'll talk later."

Kaa chuckled. "He won't be here later."

That brought Bagheera wide awake with a snap. He sprang up and whirled around. "Kaa!" he roared, and his huge forepaw caught the python a heavy blow on the head.

Kaa hastily let go of Mowgli. His head swayed with the pain of the blow. Then the python turned his eerie gaze toward the panther, and wise old Bagheera tried to shrink away from those strange eyes.

"Look at me!" demanded Kaa.

"Now, Kaa!" Bagheera pleaded.

"Look me in the eye!"

Bagheera did, in spite of himself. And he felt himself falling into the power of the serpent.

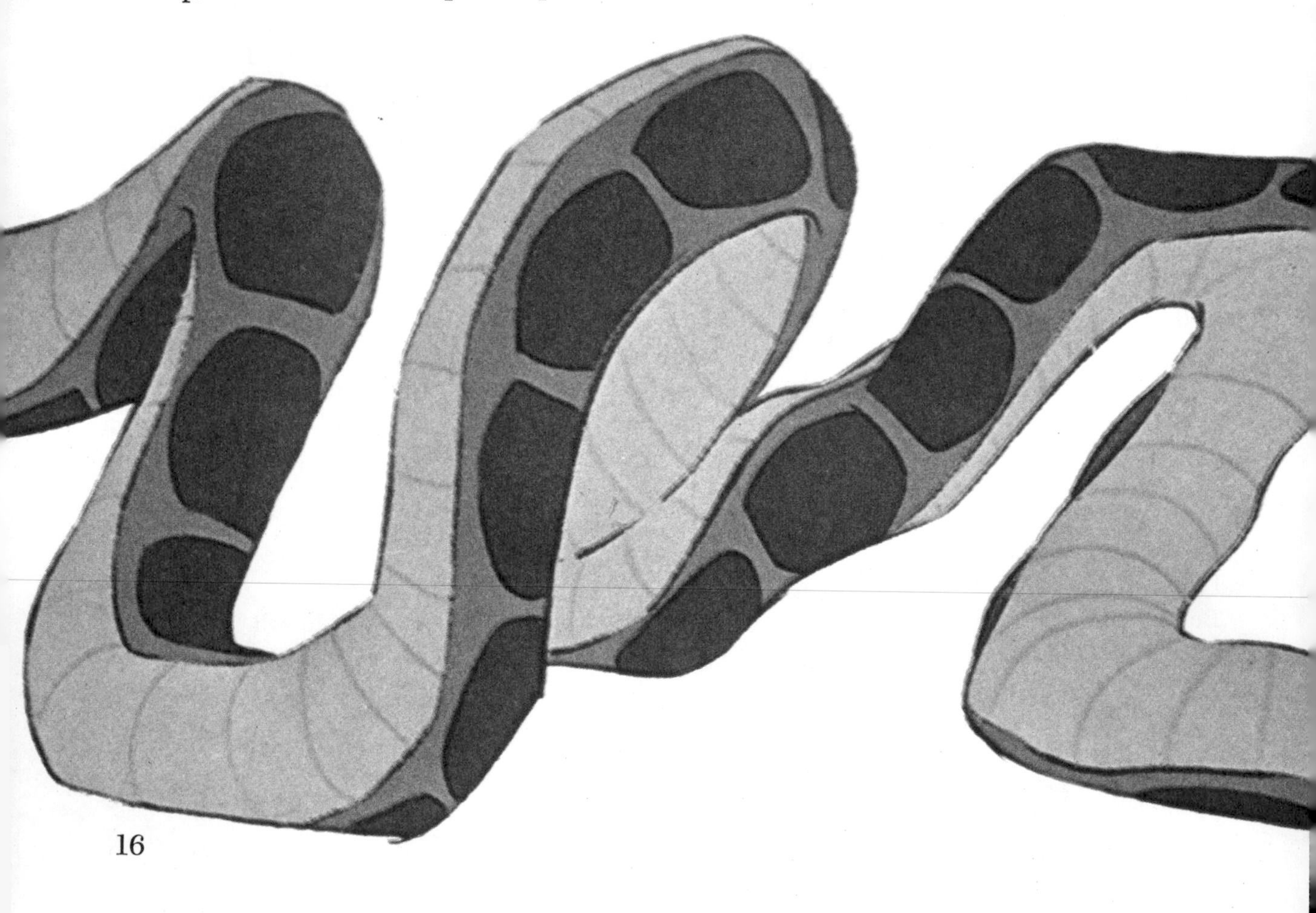

But Mowgli was now free of the prison of coils, and of the snake's paralyzing stare. He was up on his feet, pushing and heaving at the python. And, quite suddenly, there was a crashing of small branches and a horrid thud from below, and Kaa was gone. Mowgli slapped Bagheera on the jaws, begging the panther to wake up.

Bagheera came to himself and shuddered from head to tail. "What? What happened?" he demanded.

"Kaa was all curled up on the branch," Mowgli explained brightly. "I shoved him off. Look down there, Bagheera."

Bagheera looked down. On the jungle floor Kaa was hunching his coils uneasily along, moaning. When a knot in his tail caught in the fork of a bush, Mowgli doubled over with glee.

"It's not funny!" scolded Bagheera. He watched as the snake crawled slowly and painfully away. Kaa was threatening and groaning as he went.

"He won't be back tonight, at any rate." Bagheera was much relieved.

"Not with a knot in his tail," laughed Mowgli. Then the boy saw Bagheera's stern face and his laugh trailed away.

"You still want to stay in the jungle, do you?" said Bagheera. His voice was challenging. "You still think you can look out for yourself? Well, man-cub, what would have happened to you just now if you had been alone?"

Then the wise old panther settled his head on his paws once more and closed his eyes.

The Elephant Patrol

It seemed to Bagheera that he had barely dropped off to sleep when the branch on which he was resting began to vibrate to a strong, steady beat. Bagheera opened his eyes. Not only was the branch vibrating. The tree itself was swaying to and fro.

Indeed, the entire jungle shook.

"Hup, two, three, four,

"Keep it up, two three, four!"

The voice came from the jungle floor, almost directly under the tree.

"Oh, no!" moaned Bagheera. "The dawn patrol!"

Mowgli looked down. A herd of elephants was parading along in single file, trunk to tail.

In the lead was a gigantic old bull who kept time by swinging a bamboo twig back and forth.

The man-cub was instantly wide awake. He caught at a length of trailing vine and scrambled to the ground.

Mowgli hid himself behind a tree and watched the elephants march past. Bringing up the rear of the line was a young elephant calf. Compared to the others, he was very small indeed. He had to break step and run a bit every so often just to keep up with the company.

"What are you doing?" called Mowgli.

"Shhh!" The baby elephant seemed shocked that anyone would interrupt with a question at a time like this. "We're drilling," he told Mowgli.

It made no sense at all to the man-cub, but

it looked like a good game. "Can I drill, too?" asked Mowgli.

"Sure. Just do whatever I do. But don't talk in ranks," warned the baby. "It's against regulations."

Mowgli fell into line behind the elephant calf. He bent until his hands touched the ground and marched along. He tried to sway as he walked, the way the elephants swayed. For a glorious new idea had just come to Mowgli. The wolf pack had cast him out. He could not stay in the jungle as a wolf. Why not join the marchers and stay as an elephant?

Suddenly the old leader bellowed a command: "Companeee—halt!"

Every elephant in the line suddenly stood still. Mowgli bumped into the baby elephant.

"Halt means stop," said the little one.

The elephants swung around and stood in a straight line, facing the big bull. He began to pace up and down, swinging the bamboo twig from side to side.

"Dress up that line!" roared the bull.

Out of the corner of his eye, Mowgli saw the baby elephant line his trunk up with the trunk of the elephant next to him.

"Inspection!" announced the big bull.

The elephants extended their trunks stiffly in front of them. "Stick out your nose!" whispered the baby elephant.

Mowgli stuck out his nose. As an elephant looks at things, it wasn't much of a nose. Still, it was the best Mowgli could do.

It was not quite enough. The big bull elephant came down the line, inspecting his troops. When he reached Mowgli, his dim, red little eyes sparkled with interest. "A new recruit, eh?" he remarked. And then he saw that all was not well. "I say, what happened to your trunk?" he asked.

Mowgli wondered what an elephant would reply if he was asked this question. But before the boy could think of an answer, it dawned on the old bull that this strange, skinny, snub-nosed little creature was not an elephant at all.

"A man-cub!" roared the big elephant. "Sabotage! I'll have no man-cub in my jungle!"

He snatched Mowgli up, lifting the man-cub in his trunk until Mowgli could look directly into his eyes. "This is treason!" bellowed the elephant. He gave Mowgli a good, strong shake, then put the boy firmly on the ground.

It took Mowgli a second or two to get his breath after that. The instant he could speak, however, he did. "This is not your jungle!" he pointed out.

Bagheera had watched the entire thing from his tree limb. Now he groaned to himself. Why couldn't Raksha have taught the man-cub better manners? It was dreadfully rude to speak in such a way to an elder. And it was idiotic to speak so to a bull elephant—especially Hathi, who called himself a colonel and pretended that his herd was a man-thing called an army. Hathi was a bit mad. Everyone in the jungle knew it. It could be dangerous to make him angry.

And angry he was. "Silence!" he cried to Mowgli. "You are under arrest!"

Bagheera did not know what this meant, but he could tell it boded no good for the man-cub. Like a black streak, Bagheera was down out of the tree and racing toward the elephant herd.

"Just a minute, Hathi!" he called.

Hathi barely glanced at him. "*Colonel* Hathi, if you please!" he said.

Bagheera quickly admitted his breach of manners. "Ah, yes. *Colonel* Hathi. Of course, Colonel Hathi." Bagheera had not lived to be a wise old panther by picking fights with his fellow creatures. "Perhaps I can explain, Colonel," he said to Hathi. "The man-cub is with me. I am taking him to the man-village, where he belongs."

"But I don't want to go to the man-village," protested Mowgli. "I want to stay in the jungle!"

Neither Hathi nor Bagheera paid any attention at all.

"Will he *stay* in the man-village?" Hathi wanted to know.

"You have the word of Bagheera," the panther assured the elephant.

That was good enough for Hathi. He lost all interest in Mowgli and turned back to his herd. "Let's get on with it!" he snapped. "Right face! Forward march!"

The dawn patrol tramped away, and Bagheera drew a deep breath of relief. "Man-cub," he said, "what you have done this morning is to show once again that you do not belong in the jungle. You were extremely rude to Hathi. You are lucky he didn't simply step on you, the way you might step on a bug. Now let's get away from here before something else happens."

Mowgli would not admit it to Bagheera, but he was willing enough to leave the place where he had been so roundly scolded by Hathi. It was clear even to Mowgli that he would never make an elephant. He did not have the size for it. He did not have the hide for it. He did not have the nose for it. He followed, quietly enough, while Bagheera led the way down a jungle trail to a place where a tree trunk had fallen across a swiftly running stream.

Mowgli stopped and listened. The sounds of the elephants marching had faded away completely. "Bagheera, where are we going now?" asked Mowgli, in his most innocent voice.

Bagheera did not even break his stride. He leaped up onto the tree trunk and was half way across the stream before he spoke. "We are going to the man-village, of course."

Mowgli backed away from the log that bridged the water. "No," he declared. "I'm not going."

"You are!"

"I'm not!"

"You are!"

Bagheera turned about on the log. "You are going if I have to drag you every step of the way," he declared.

Mowgli wrapped his arms around the trunk of a tree. "I'm staying right here."

"Why . . . why this is outrageous!" sputtered Bagheera. "You let go of that tree!"

The panther's teeth closed on the loincloth around Mowgli's waist. "Let go!" he snarled, tugging mightily.

"I won't!" Mowgli planted his hard little heels against Bagheera's muzzle and pushed as hard as he could. There was a sudden ripping sound.

The panther clawed for a footing on the muddy riverbank. Then he tumbled backward and the stream closed over him.

Bagheera came to the surface gasping with shock and outrage. He blew the water from his nose and blinked it out of his eyes. Then he padded out of the stream.

"That does it!" he raged. "I've had it! So you want to be on your own? Well, from now on you're on your own—alone!"

And with that Bagheera leaped up onto a tree limb and disappeared into the jungle.

The Lesson of Baloo

Mowgli was feeling quite pleased with himself when he strutted away through the jungle. He had outsmarted Kaa the python. He had not exactly outsmarted Hathi the elephant, but he had survived the encounter. Now he had left old Bagheera behind. What nonsense to think that he belonged in a man-village! He was Raksha's cub. He was a child of the jungle. He belonged here. Even if he had to stay alone, he would remain in the jungle.

Mowgli went at a brisk clip down the trail which was marked with the prints of many paws. He felt very happy and very brave—at first. Raksha had never allowed him to wander so far alone. Always she had spoken of the time when he would be grown, and a man-cub no longer. Mowgli was no bigger than he had been the day before. Yet he felt that perhaps the time was at hand.

Then Mowgli noticed how very quiet it was in the jungle. No birds sang in the trees above him. No small animals scuttled through the grass as he passed. Even the wind seemed to have died away.

Mowgli stopped walking. He sat down with his back against the security of a big rock and he listened.

At first there was nothing—nothing but the silence. Then Mowgli heard a crashing of underbrush off to his left. Something was coming—something very large. Mowgli felt a lump of unhappiness growing in his middle. He felt a shiver of fright chase itself down his spine. He felt very much alone.

The steady crashing, smashing sound came nearer. "Dooby-dooby-dooby-do!" sang a big, soft, warm, grumbly, rumbly voice. "Dooby-do-do!"

Mowgli stared, letting his mouth open a little. The bushes beside the jungle trail parted and a stout, shaggy bear looked out. His bright black eyes fell upon Mowgli.

"Well now, what have we here?" said the bear.

Mowgli breathed a weak sigh of relief. The bear seemed friendly enough. Mowgli could see that he meant no harm.

To Mowgli's dismay, the bear put his huge head down next to Mowgli's small one and he sniffed a mighty sniff.

Mowgli drew back. "Go away!" he cried.

The bear wasn't a bit angry. Mowgli had the impression that it would take a great deal to make this bear angry. "Oh, boy!" he chuckled. "A man-cub. Now I've seen everything in these woods!"

Mowgli stood up. "Leave me alone!"

The bear tapped Mowgli on the shoulder, nearly knocking the man-cub down. "That's pretty big talk, Little Britches," he said.

Mowgli didn't know what little britches might mean, but he didn't like the sound of it. "I'm big enough!" he shouted. Then, very foolishly, he struck at the bear's midsection with his fist.

The bear shook his head. "Pitiful!" he said. "Kid, you need help! Why don't you let old Baloo teach you how to fight like a bear?"

Mowgli forgot to be angry. This was the nicest idea he had heard all day.

The bear stepped away from the man-cub, held his paws high and began to dance. He was amazingly nimble for his size. "First comes the footwork," he told Mowgli.

Mowgli put his fists up and began to dance, too.

"Keep moving!" warned Baloo. "Loosen up! Get real loose and then start to weave."

Baloo showed how, and Mowgli aped the bear, skipping back and forth. Suddenly he dodged in under Baloo's paw and landed a punch on the bear. Then he slipped away. It was like another game, he thought.

"That's it!" cried the bear. He stopped dancing and commanded, "Now give me a big growl. Scare me!"

Mowgli pulled back his lips, set his teeth and growled as terrible a growl as he could manage.

The bear began to laugh. "No, no!" he cried. "Kid, I'm talking about a *real* growl. Like a bear. A *big* bear!" Baloo's chest swelled. His head went back and his eyes closed. Then his mouth opened. Out came a truly magnificent growl. It echoed and rumbled through the forest, and at last it came to the ears of Bagheera the panther.

"Oh, good heavens!" said the panther to himself. "The man-cub! He's in trouble."

The panther turned and raced back the way he had come. "I shouldn't have left him alone!" he said.

Another growl sounded. It was louder and more terrifying than the first.

Bagheera sped across the log bridge that crossed the stream. He leaped up to race through the treetops. His eyes scanned the jungle floor below for a trace of the man-cub.

Suddenly Bagheera heard a laugh. "Like that!" said Baloo. "Growl a big one, right up from your toes."

Bagheera heard Mowgli give a feeble imitation of Baloo's huge growl. Baloo laughed again.

"Oh, no!" moaned Bagheera. "Baloo! Of all the creatures in the jungle, why did the man-cub have to meet that stupid, shiftless . . ." Bagheera stopped and groaned again. Then he settled down on a tree limb to see what Baloo and Mowgli were up to.

Baloo had finished the course in growling, at least for the time being. He had also grown tired of his demonstration of boxing, plain and fancy. He was now sitting on the ground. Mowgli was comfortably settled on his broad middle, and was telling the bear of his adventures. Bagheera listened with deep gloom as Mowgli told of overcoming Kaa and defying Hathi the elephant. And he told how he had run away from the panther.

"Bagheera wants me to go live in the man-village!" Mowgli finished his tale.

"The man-village?" Baloo was horrified "That's terrible! They'll ruin you! They'll make a man out of you."

"I want to stay here in the jungle," said Mowgli.

"Of course you do," Baloo agreed. "Say, you know something, kid?"

Mowgli shook his head.

"You're all right," said Baloo warmly. "What do they call you?"

"They call him Mowgli," Bagheera put in before the man-cub could answer. "He's a man-cub and he is on his way to the man-village!"

"Oh, no!" Mowgli felt that Baloo would support him. "Baloo, can't I stay here with you?"

"Certainly," said the bear. "And I'll teach you everything I know."

"That shouldn't take long," muttered Bagheera.

But Baloo wasn't listening. The bear's attention was on Mowgli.

"You've just got to learn to take things easy, Mowgli boy," he said. He began to dance, bouncing around the clearing, waving his stub of a tail. And he sang:

Look for the bare necessities,
The simple bare necessities,
Forget about your worries and your strife.
I mean the bare necessities
Are Mother Nature's recipes
That bring the bare necessities of life.

Baloo reached up and plucked a banana from a hanging bunch of ripe fruit. He peeled back the yellow skin and handed half of it, deliciously sweet, to Mowgli. Then he went on singing, only stopping now and then to take another banana, or to pick a mango or a cactus fruit.

Wherever I wander, wherever I roam,
I couldn't be fonder of my big home.
The bees are buzzing in the tree
To make some honey just for me.
When I look under the rocks and plants
I nibble up some fancy ants.

Baloo easily upended a big boulder and scooped a colony of ants into his mouth.

"You eat ants?" exclaimed Mowgli in wonder.

"You better believe it," said the bear.

Mowgli picked up one of the insects. It escaped by running up his arm and down his back.

"Don't worry," advised Baloo. "There'll be another one along in a second or two. The bare necessities of life will come to you."

"Oh, of all the silly nonsense!" growled Bagheera, who was still brooding in his tree.

Baloo turned his back on the panther. "Hey, Mowgli, how about scratching my old left shoulder for me, huh?" he invited.

The boy was only too happy to clamber up on his back and scratch vigorously.

"Just a hair lower!" directed Baloo. "Ah, beautiful!"

Mowgli went on scratching.

"This is living!" sighed Baloo. "Oh-hoo! Huh! Hah! Oh, yeah!"

Mowgli laughed. Wolves enjoyed a good scratch, of course. But none of them had ever seemed to enjoy it quite the way Baloo did. He made scratching sound like the major pleasure of life.

Now, limp with enjoyment, Baloo reeled away from Mowgli and staggered happily to the stream. He let himself slide lazily down the bank into the water.

"Just relax," rumbled the happy bear. "Yeah, cool it!" Floating on his back, he drifted slowly toward the middle of the river.

Mowgli had no intention of losing sight of this wonderful new friend. He tumbled after Baloo, down the riverbank and into the water. Then he paddled after the bear, using all fours, wolf-fashion.

"That's it, kid!" encouraged Baloo. He scooped Mowgli out of the water and set the man-cub high and dry on top of him. "Fall apart in my backyard," invited Baloo.

Mowgli was happy to stretch out and listen to Baloo's good advice. And Baloo had a great deal of good advice to offer. Mowgli mustn't work too hard. He mustn't worry. He mustn't hurry. He mustn't fuss.

Bagheera, on his tree limb, was completely forgotten. "Lazy shiftless bear!" he said to himself. "Well, I can't help it. I tried to get the man-cub back to his own people, and that's all anyone can ask."

Mowgli's high, thin laugh sounded as he and Baloo drifted out of sight around the bend in the stream. "Baloo, I like being a bear!" he said.

"That's my boy!" said Baloo. "And you're going to make one swell bear!"

"Swell bear, indeed!" snorted Bagheera. He turned and started away from the little river.

Then, quite without warning, there was a shrieking and a chattering in the tree-tops. Mowgli cried out, and then screamed a terrified scream.

Bagheera suddenly felt very cold. He knew instantly what had happened. It was the monkey people—the Bandar-log. No doubt of it. They had gotten Mowgli.

The Bandar-log

Mowgli knew about the Bandar-log, of course. His wolf parents had warned him of the monkey people. None of the jungle creatures would have anything to do with them. They were vain, idle, useless beings. They raced through the treetops on journeys that had no purpose. Or else they forgot where they were going before they got to their destination. They gossiped endlessly of the other jungle animals. And they did not know the law of the jungle.

The monkeys had been still enough when they swooped down to snatch Mowgli away from Baloo. But once the man-cub was in their hands they burst into a torrent of howls and shrieks.

"Baloo!" cried Mowgli. "Baloo! Help me!"

Baloo looked up and shook his fist. "Take your flea-picking hands off of my cub!" he cried.

A rain of fruit, some of it very ripe and some of it very hard, descended on Baloo. The bear came raging and crashing out of the stream. Bagheera arrived on the scene in time to see him bump into a tree, and roll down a small hill.

The monkeys shouted a few choice insults at the bear and sped off through the treetops, taking Mowgli with them. Bagheera had a horrifying glimpse of the man-cub being passed from one monkey to another as they fled. The imbeciles! They were holding Mowgli by the ankle.

"Bagheera!" bellowed Baloo. "Bagheera, help!"

The panther looked at the bear, who was just lumbering to his feet. "I see that it's happened," he said nastily.

"They ambushed me!" said Baloo. "There were thousands of them!"

"I'm sure there were," snapped the panther. "But what happened?"

"Those mangy monkeys carried him off," admitted Baloo miserably.

"I saw that!" roared Bagheera. "But how could you let them? How did they . . . ? Oh, never mind!"

The panther turned his eyes toward the treetops. Now that they had Mowgli, the monkeys would take him to the ancient ruins, there was no doubt of that. "We'd best get started," said Bagheera briskly. "It will be night before we can reach the old temple."

"The man-place?" said Baloo, wondering.

"That's where the monkeys are going with the man-cub," said Bagheera. "They'll take him to that lunatic king of theirs."

"But Bagheera," protested Baloo, "none of us ever goes to the ruined place."

"Well, we're going now. And we'd better hurry, or we'll be too late."

Without stopping for further discussion, Bagheera was off through the jungle. Baloo hesitated for only a moment. Then he started after the panther. The bear wasn't singing now. He was moving silently, and with amazing speed.

The Monkey King

The man-place was deep in the jungle. Raksha had told Mowgli of it once, long ago, when the man cub had snuggled close to the wolf mother in the safety of their den. It had been built at the command of a mighty one, a king among the men. On the crest of a hill, this king had ordered stones to be piled upon stones until there were walls and towers, courtyards and palaces. The men had roofed some of the walls over to shut out the jungle, and they had left others open to let in the sunlight. And they had lived for many seasons in the place. They had gone about their affairs with much bustle and importance.

Then one day the king who ruled in the place died. For some reason, the others who lived there were greatly afraid. They had all fled in a single day and a night, taking very little with them.

The jungle had waited patiently while the men dwelled in the city. Once they were gone, green vines crept in to tumble down the stones. Roofs had fallen in and trees had grown up to push the walls askew. Flowers now bloomed in the empty rooms, and the courtyard of the king's palace was a jumble of tree roots and fallen stones.

This lost and ruined place was the home of the Bandar-log. The foolish monkey people liked to play at being men. They scampered in and out of the roofless houses. They shook the trees in the old king's garden and caught the fruits and flowers when they fell. And in the courtyard the monkey king sat on a ruined throne and scratched himself.

The monkeys came to the place and scaled the wall easily, carrying Mowgli with them. "Here he is, O King!" they shouted. "We have him! We have him!"

They held Mowgli by his heels and dangled him in front of their king.

Even though he was upside down, Mowgli saw that the monkey king was much larger than any of his subjects. He was also much uglier, with his face creased in a thousand folds and his red-brown pelt. When Mowgli first set eyes on him he was happily eating a banana. He had gotten rid of the peel by putting it on top of his head.

The king chuckled when he saw Mowgli. "So this is the man-cub," said he.

Mowgli felt uncomfortable, to say the least. The longer he stayed, dangling before the ape, the more flushed and swollen his face became and the harder the blood pounded in his ears. "Put me down!" he shouted.

The monkeys who were holding him let go, and he thudded down onto the mossy stones that paved the courtyard.

The monkey king's hairy hand seized Mowgli's breechcloth. The man-cub felt himself lifted into the air again. "Come on, cousin," coaxed the ape.

"I am not your cousin," protested Mowgli.

"Of course you're my cousin," said the king. "You're a man-cub, aren't you? You walk on your hind legs, don't you? Well, so do I, cousin." The king took a short stroll around his throne to demonstrate. Then he offered Mowgli a banana. Mowgli did not especially want a banana at that moment. However, the monkey king popped the fruit right out of its peel and into Mowgli's mouth, and there was nothing for the man-cub to do but eat it.

"You have a thumb that turns in, man-cub," said the monkey king. "Well, so do I." He waggled his hands in front of Mowgli's face.

The monkey king leaned close to Mowgli. "I am the king of the Bandar-log," he said. "We are the wisest and the cleverest people of the jungle. We are just like men, man-cub."

Mowgli shuddered. Could it be true? He tried to keep his voice from trembling as he asked, "What do you want me for?"

The king grinned. Mowgli noticed a strange glint in his eye and realized that Raksha had spoken the truth. The monkey people were quite insane.

"Word has reached my royal ear that you want to stay in the jungle," said the king. "Well, your good old cousin can fix it for you—in exchange for a small favor, of course."

Mowgli gulped down the last of his banana. "I do want to stay in the jungle," he admitted.

"Fine!" said the monkey king. "Now you may have noticed, cousin, that we monkeys live here just like men. Except for one small detail. We don't have the red flower."

"The red flower?" echoed Mowgli.

"Right, cousin. Now you just lay the secret on me of man's red flower, and you can stay as long as you like."

"But I don't know how to make fire!" cried Mowgli.

"Don't try to fool me, man-cub! Any monkey knows that the red flower blooms in all the man-villages. You must know the secret. Tell it to me!"

The monkey king's smile had vanished. His long fingers tangled in Mowgli's hair and pulled tight. Mowgli felt his heart leap up to his throat. What would the monkey king do to him? How could he convince him that he did not have the secret of the red flower?

Mowgli tried to think of the right words to say to the king. But then the king's attention strayed from the man-cub. Lost in some twisted dream, the monkey king began to croon softly of being a man, of having the secret that every jungle creature shunned—the secret of fire.

On and on went the monkey king's chant, and

all around Mowgli there was a stirring and a shifting. The monkeys began to weave and sway. Their little hands clapped to keep time to the king's song. Their feet began to beat on the stones that paved the courtyard.

Almost against his will, Mowgli found himself swaying, too. Then one of the monkeys took his hand and he began to dance along with the Bandar-log.

It was growing dark in the courtyard. None of the monkey people noticed the big figure that came dancing from a gateway. Was it a monkey? It couldn't be. It was too big. Why, it was as big as old Baloo the bear.

"Bee-da-beedle, ho-ba-dong-day!" sang the newcomer.

The monkey folk danced faster. They fell into line and whirled around the courtyard. They danced into the empty rooms and out again. The king danced along with them. And so did Mowgli. And so did the strange, large monkey person. They stamped and sang and whined through their noses. They beat on the few great stone columns that still stood to hold the palace roof toward the sky. Even when the huge, shaggy newcomer whirled very close to the monkey king, no one raised an outcry.

But then the newcomer went too far. He uttered a deep, joyful "Doo-be-doo-be-do!" and almost stepped on the monkey king.

"What?" cried the monarch. "Who?"

The king stopped dancing long enough to see that this was a very large monkey indeed. He was too big for an ape. He was more like—more like a bear.

"Baloo!" shouted the king.

"Uh-oh!" said Baloo the bear. He did not pause for an instant. He seized his man-cub, tucked him firmly under one arm and ran.

He ran in the wrong direction, of course. There hadn't been time to plot a course. Baloo's first frantic rush took him into one of the dark corridors of the old palace.

"Stop him!" cried the king. "Don't let him get away!"

Dozens of little feet scurried around Baloo. Small hands clutched at his head and his ears and covered his eyes. Still he ran on, holding fast to the man-cub.

Suddenly Bagheera was beside him in the darkness, and the monkey folk shrank away. The bear and the panther sped along the corridors and out again into the dusky courtyard.

In a frenzy, the monkey folk raced after them. They pushed one another. They collided with the teetering columns. The masses of carved stone above the ancient gateway began to shift and sway. Then, with a rumble and a roar, they collapsed in front of the monkeys.

Baloo stopped, gasping, and Mowgli quickly leaped onto Bagheera's back. Then the three friends were racing down the hill. There was another roar behind them as one of the tottering pillars that held up the palace roof gave way. When they paused to look back, a cloud of dust was rising above the tumbled ruins on the hill. From the dust cloud sounded chattering cries.

"Man!" exclaimed Baloo. "That was a real swinging party."

Baloo's Sacrifice

Night came to the jungle. Mowgli slept beneath a banyan tree far from the shattered city of the monkey king. Beside the man-cub, the panther rested. Bagheera's nose twitched at the scent of small animals passing upwind. On any other night Bagheera would have hunted, but tonight he had other business. He and Baloo were standing guard over the man-cub.

Baloo was serenely content. He would have liked to drop off to sleep, but Bagheera would not let him.

"Mowgli seems to have man's ability to get into trouble," the wise old panther observed. "And I must say, Baloo, that you have been no help at all."

Baloo scratched his ear and frowned. "Let's keep our voices down," he growled, in what passes for a whisper among bears. "You'll wake the man-cub, and he's had a big day. If you're going to talk some more, Baggy, let's move over to that pond where he can't hear us."

Bagheera did not feel like arguing that point. He got up and followed Baloo to the edge of the pool. The bear bent and took a drink of water.

Bagheera got briskly to the point. "Now about the man-cub . . ." he said.

Baloo nodded. "A real smart kid," was his only comment.

This was not exactly what Bagheera had been thinking. "I only hope that he has learned something from his experience," said the panther. "What a disgraceful performance! Raksha has spoiled him. Imagine associating with those undesirable, scatterbrained monkeys!"

Baloo had heard all this before. It did not interest him. A cold, thin light was showing in the east. Soon it would be morning. Baloo began to think about breakfast.

"The man-cub must go back to his own people," insisted Bagheera. "The jungle is not the place for him."

Baloo spotted some berries hanging from a bramble nearby and began to eat them slowly, one at a time. "I grew up in the jungle," said the bear, "and look at me."

"Yes indeed," snapped Bagheera. "Just look at yourself."

Baloo leaned over and peered at his reflection in the pool. He grinned. His left eye was swollen almost shut. No doubt it had been the clutching hands of the monkeys that had done that. Baloo didn't care. It was a marvelous shiner, a real mark of courage. "Beautiful, isn't it?" the bear gurgled.

Bagheera hastily abandoned that subject. "Baloo, you cannot adopt Mowgli," he said firmly.

"Why not?"

The panther hesitated. How could he convince this silly bear that the very idea was idiotic?

"Birds of a feather should flock together," said Bagheera at last.

Baloo nodded. This made sense.

"Like seeks like," said Bagheera.

Baloo nodded again, still eating, and Bagheera knew that he had not reached the bear at all.

"The man-cub is not a bear," Bagheera pointed out. "He is a man-cub and someday he will be a man."

Baloo sighed. Bagheera was tiresome. He was always worrying about what might happen someday. "Now, Baggy," he pleaded, "I'll take care of Little Britches, and . . ."

"Of course you'll take care of him," said Bagheera coldly. "Just the way you took care of him when the monkeys stole him away, eh?"

Baloo began to scratch himself on a tree trunk. "Can't a guy make one mistake?" he mumbled.

"Not in the jungle!" said Bagheera. "And another thing—sooner or later the man-cub will meet Shere Khan!"

Baloo quickly stopped scratching.

"Shere Khan?" he asked.

Bagheera nodded.

"The tiger?"

Bagheera nodded again.

"But what's Shere Khan got against the kid?" asked Baloo. "I know he's pretty mean, even for a tiger. But why should Mowgli be his dish of cat food?"

"Shere Khan hates man with a vengeance," explained Bagheera. "You know that. He fears man's gun and man's fire."

"But Mowgli doesn't have any gun," protested Baloo. "He can't make fire."

"Shere Khan won't wait until he learns how," countered the panther. "He'll get Mowgli while he's still young and helpless. Just one swipe of his paw and . . ." Bagheera shrugged his satiny black shoulders.

"Oh, no!" moaned Baloo. But he did not argue. He knew Shere Khan. "What are we going to do?" he asked.

"We'll do what's best for the man-cub," said Bagheera.

"You'd better believe it!" cried Baloo. "You just name it and I'll do it!"

"Good!" said the panther. "Then you'll make Mowgli go to the man-village where he'll be safe."

"But I promised him he could stay in the jungle with me," wailed the bear.

"And as long as he does remain here with you, he's in danger. It's up to you."

"You mean . . . you mean I've got to tell him?"

Bagheera nodded.

"But why me?"

"Because he won't listen to me," said the panther simply.

"But I love that kid like he was my own cub!"

"Do you love him enough to do what's best for him?" asked Bagheera. "Do you love him enough to make the sacrifice and take him to the man-village?"

Baloo was utterly defeated. "Can't it wait until morning?" he asked.

Bagheera stretched and looked at the sky. "It's morning now, old friend," he said.

The bear gulped. Then he went very slowly back to the banyan tree. "Mowgli," he said, "it's time to get up."

The boy opened his eyes. Then he sat up and stretched.

"Rub that old sleep out of your eyes," said Baloo. "We have a long walk ahead of us."

Mowgli was up in a flash. "Great!" he cried. "We'll have lots of fun, Baloo."

"Yeah," replied Baloo glumly. To Bagheera who sat, stern as a statue, he said, "See you around, Baggy."

"Good-by, Bagheera." Mowgli dismissed his old friend with a wave. "Baloo and I have things to do."

"Good-by, man-cub," said Bagheera, "and good luck."

A butterfly fluttered past and Mowgli, light-headed as any monkey, scampered after it. "Come on, Baloo," he called. "We have to find ourselves some bare necessities." And he began to sing.

Baloo trudged after the man-cub. Mowgli watched the butterfly flit away. Then he danced up to a banana tree and shook down some fruit. Very politely, Mowgli handed a banana to Baloo. The bear took it, but he didn't eat it. He just looked at the banana. For once in his life, he wasn't a bit hungry.

"Where are we going, Baloo?" Mowgli asked happily. When Baloo didn't answer, he went on, "I don't really care as long as I'm with you. I like being a bear!"

Baloo found this very upsetting. "Look, Mowgli, there's something I've got to tell you."

"Okay, Baloo."

"Birds of a feather flock together," said Baloo.

Mowgli laughed. What a silly thing to say! "I don't know what you're talking about," he told Baloo.

Baloo tried again. "Mowgli, don't you realize that you're a human?"

"Not anymore, Baloo. I'm a bear now, like you."

Baloo took a deep breath and caught both of Mowgli's hands in one big paw. "Look, Mowgli, I've been trying to tell you . . . I've been trying since you woke up. I've got to take you back to the man-village!"

Mowgli stared at him in horror.

"I can explain," said Baloo hastily. "Like Bagheera says . . ."

"You told me we were partners!" shouted Mowgli.

"Now wait!" pleaded the bear.

"You're just like Bagheera!"

"Just a paw-picking minute!" cried Baloo. "That's going too far!"

Mowgli turned and ran.

"Mowgli!" Baloo shouted. "Stop! Come back here!"

Mowgli didn't even look around. He plunged into a bank of undergrowth and disappeared.

"Wait!" The bear crashed into the bushes. "Wait, Mowgli! Listen to old Baloo!"

The man-cub was gone.

"Mowgli!" called Baloo.

There was no sound.

"Mowgli?" Now the bear's shout echoed through the jungle. "Answer me!"

The only answer was Bagheera, who appeared suddenly at Baloo's side. "Now what's happened?" said the panther.

"You're not going to believe this," mumbled the bear, "but I told him just what you told me to tell him."

"Yes?" said Bagheera.

"He ran away," said Baloo.

Bagheera closed his eyes for a moment as if his head hurt. "I believe it."

"I goofed, huh?" asked Baloo.

The panther nodded. Then he turned away. "Don't just stand there," he said over his shoulder. "We have to find the man-cub. I just saw Shere Khan's paw-print down at the waterhole!"

To the Rescue

During the night many animals had stopped at the waterhole to drink their fill. Now most of them were hidden in the sheltering thickets. There they would sleep away the day. Only one small deer remained at the waterhole. Its nose was deep in the muddy water when Shere Khan the tiger came slinking through the brush.

Shere Khan saw the deer and he sank low to the ground. The deer was small, but it was young.

Shere Khan crept forward. He set his great paws down one by one while his cruel yellow eyes measured the distance between himself and the deer. He was almost close enough for a spring. Three more steps. Then two more. One . . .

The deer's head went up. The slender neck quivered and drops of water fell from the black nose. It sniffed the air. Then with a bound the animal was off into the brush.

"Blast!" The tiger uprooted a small plant with one swipe of his paw. He had been so careful. What had alerted the deer?

Then the tiger heard it. It came to him very faintly at first. Then, in the sunrise, the earth began to tremble.

"Those blundering pachyderms!" snarled Shere Khan. The tiger melted away into the brush on the far side of the pond.

"Hup, two, three, four,

"Keep it up, two, three, four!"

Colonel Hathi chanted as he led the dawn patrol toward the watering place. His trunk swung, keeping time as the troops marched. Somewhere along the way Colonel Hathi had lost his bamboo twig.

The sound of the marching herd carried through the jungle. Not far away, Baloo and Bagheera had followed Mowgli's trail to the place where Mowgli had started to cross a log which spanned a river. The man-cub's scent went along the tree trunk to the middle of the river. Then it vanished.

"He fell off here," said Bagheera.

Baloo looked down at the swift water. "You don't suppose he . . . he . . .

"Drowned?" Bagheera finished the question for him. "I hardly think so. None of Raksha's cubs would ever drown. He must have come to one bank or another, farther downstream. We can pick up his trail again. You take the left bank, and I'll take the right. If you find the place where he came out of the water, call me."

Baloo didn't need to be told twice. He was down off the fallen log in an instant and shuffling his way along the riverbank. Bagheera, for his part, took to the trees. He felt there was just a chance that he could catch sight of the boy if he had a higher vantage point.

"Hup, two, three, four,

"Keep it up, two, three, four."

Bagheera heard the chant. And he saw the elephant herd. They were marching toward him. In a few moments they would pass directly under the tree in which he was standing. "Perhaps they'll help," breathed the panther to himself. And he leaped down to a branch that overhung the trail.

"Colonel Hathi!" called Bagheera.

The elephants continued to thunder on their way.

"Stop, please!" cried the panther.

Not a head turned.

"HALT!" roared Bagheera. It was the closest he could come to Hathi's bellow. At once the line of elephants came to a skidding, bumping, thudding halt.

Colonel Hathi looked around with rage burning in his small eyes. "Who said that?" he thundered. "Who said *halt*? I give the commands around here! Who was it?"

Bagheera stepped forward on his branch. "It was I, Colonel Hathi," he admitted in his smoothest tones. "I'm sorry to interrupt your drill. I know it's very important. But I desperately need your help."

"Help?" snorted the colonel. "Absolutely impossible. We are on important cross-country maneuvers!"

"But it's an emergency, Colonel," said Bagheera. "The man-cub is lost in the jungle. He ran away, and we must find him."

"Ran away?" Hathi was horrified. "That's frightful! Terrible! Deserters everywhere. Don't know what the army's coming to these days!"

"No, no!" Bagheera protested. "He didn't run

away from the army. He ran away from Baloo. Have you seen him?"

Hathi frowned. He disliked all this talk about runaways. It made for unrest in the ranks. He wished that Bagheera would go away and let him get on with his maneuvers. "Certainly I saw him," said Hathi. "It was yesterday. Or was it the day before? He was trying to enlist in my troop, and I told him then . . ."

"No, no!" howled Bagheera. "Today! Today! Have you seen the man-cub today? He ran away this morning!"

"Disgraceful!" bellowed Hathi. "I told that man-cub to get out of the jungle, and when I give an order, I expect to be obeyed."

"What's the trouble?" muttered one of the elephants behind Hathi.

"Someone's lost," answered another of the troops.

"We're all lost," groaned a third.

"Of course you expect to be obeyed," said Bagheera, "but the point is that I must find the man-cub. He's alone and helpless and in great danger. Shere Khan may be near and he hates the man-cub."

"Oh, I am sorry," said Hathi. The old elephant meant it. He was truly sorry for anyone who was hunted by Shere Khan.

"Think how you would feel if it were your own son," said Bagheera.

Hathi's eye fell upon the baby elephant at the end of the marching line.

"It *is* highly irregular," he told Bagheera.

"I know," said the panther.

Hathi turned to face his troops. "Troopers!" bellowed Hathi. "I need volunteers for a special assignment. All of you will help find a lost man-cub."

Bagheera thought that this was an interesting way to get volunteers, but he said nothing.

"We will keep three trunk-lengths apart," said Hathi. "That way there's no chance of his slipping past us. Remember, I expect everyone to do his duty."

The troops moved out, a careful three trunk-lengths apart. Bagheera sighed as he watched them go. They might be of some help. But Bagheera feared that the blundering Hathi would accomplish nothing. The panther patiently returned to the riverbank.

Bagheera did not see Shere Khan hidden in the reeds. The tiger licked his whiskers and smiled a delighted smile. So there was a man-cub lost in the jungle! Now that was good news indeed.

And Shere Khan joined the search for the man-cub. Unlike Hathi and his troops, Shere Khan did his searching very quietly.

The Python's Coils

Mowgli ran and ran until he could run no more. When at last his breath was gone and his knees were shaking, he stopped and threw himself down in the shade of a tree. He stared at the ground and waited for his breathing to quiet.

"Well now!" exclaimed a soft voice in Mowgli's ear. "I do believe that it's-s the man-cub!"

Mowgli turned, and his heart gave a nasty little lurch. The huge, flat head of Kaa the python was just inches from Mowgli's shoulder. Kaa's wicked eyes glittered with a cold glee.

"Kaa!" cried Mowgli. Then he quickly looked away.

"Yes-s-s, man-cub," hissed the snake. "S-so nice to s-see you again."

Mowgli didn't answer. "Won't you look at me?" said the serpent, after a moment.

"No, I won't," Mowgli told him. "I know you, Kaa. I know what you want to do."

"Oh dear!" exclaimed Kaa. "I *am* sorry, man-cub. You don't trust me!"

Mowgli just laughed at the very idea.

"Well then," Kaa went on, "there's nothing I can do to help."

Mowgli laughed again. It seemed that everyone he met wanted to help. Bagheera wanted to help; he wanted to bring Mowgli to the man-village. The monkey king had offered to help, but what he really wanted was the secret of the red flower. Baloo the bear had promised to help, but in the end he had betrayed Mowgli, too.

At the thought of that betrayal, the man-cub

lowered his head quickly. But Kaa had seen tears glitter in his eyes.

"I can s-s-see to it that you never leave the jungle," promised Kaa.

Mowgli looked at the snake. Then he quickly looked away again. "How can you do that?" he asked. It was more of a challenge than a question.

"Oh," said Kaa, "I have my own s-subtle little ways," said Kaa. "I can do it, if you'll just trus-s-st in me."

The thought came to Mowgli that he had better leave. He would just get up and walk away. Then he hesitated. Kaa's head swayed back and forth in front of him. Kaa's eyes were very wide open. Kaa never blinked.

"Trust in you?" Mowgli asked.

"Trus-st in me!" pleaded the python. "Res-st little man-cub. S-sleep! S-sleep!"

Sleep. Of course. That was the thing to do. Mowgli wouldn't get up and walk away. He would stay here and sleep, safe with Kaa. Mowgli's eyes began to close.

"Trust in me," whispered the python. Softly his coils wrapped around Mowgli.

The man-cub did not stir or struggle. He just smiled a sleepy smile.

"That's my good man-cub," murmured the python, and he crept off the trail into the underbrush with Mowgli in his coils. He hummed happily as he went.

Of course Kaa did not hear Shere Khan come down the trail. No one heard Shere Khan when the tiger chose to go silently. But Shere Khan heard Kaa humming. And Shere Khan's eyes fell upon the tip of the python's tail, which showed at the edge of the brush.

Shere Khan's first thought was that it was very careless of the python to leave a part of himself lying about like that. Mischief glittering in his eyes, Shere Khan swiped at Kaa's tail.

"Now what?" Kaa released the sleeping man-cub and turned part of his length back toward the trail. "Who is it?" he said, rather crossly.

Something in his tone made Shere Khan smile. The tiger dearly loved to annoy his fellow creatures. He had a strong suspicion that Kaa would provide him with an amusing few minutes.

"Shere Khan!" exclaimed Kaa. "What a surprise!"

"Yes, isn't it?" said the tiger. He was one of the few who did not fear the huge snake. Now he noticed that Kaa seemed just a trifle nervous. Shere Khan sniffed at the air. Of course Kaa was nervous! There was the scent of man-cub on the breeze. Was it possible that Kaa had the man-cub? If not, what was Kaa hiding? For, the tiger decided, Kaa had to be concealing something to be so on edge.

"I just dropped by," said Shere Khan. He stretched out comfortably and crossed his fore-paws, as if he were prepared for a long visit. "I do hope I'm not interrupting anything," said he.

"Oh, no. Nothing at all," said Kaa.

Shere Khan unsheathed his claws and inspected them, one by one. "I thought that perhaps you were entertaining someone."

"Entertaining someone? Oh, no."

"Hm!" said Shere Khan.

"I . . . er . . . I was just curling up for my siesta," said Kaa weakly.

"Oh? But you were singing." Shere Khan's paw flashed out and pinned Kaa's neck to the ground. "Who's here?" he demanded.

"No one!" gasped Kaa. "I was just singing to myself."

"Indeed?"

"Yes. Yes, you see, I have trouble with . . . with headaches. Yes, that's it. Headaches."

"What a pity!" Shere Khan's paw rested still more heavily on Kaa's neck.

"Oh, you have no idea," Kaa assured the tiger. "It's simply terrible. I can't eat. I can't sleep. So I sing to myself. It's called self-hypnosis, you know. Here, let me show you how it works."

The python tried to pull himself up and fix the tiger with his powerful gaze. But Shere Khan's paw shifted and came crashing down on top of Kaa's head.

"I can't be bothered with that," said Shere Khan loftily. "I have no time for that sort of nonsense. At the moment, I'm searching for a man-cub."

"Man-cub?" Kaa tried to sound like a python who didn't even know what manner of thing a man-cub might be. "What man-cub?" he asked.

Shere Khan's claw scratched quite lightly at Kaa's nose. "The man-cub who is lost," purred the tiger. "Now where do you suppose he could be?"

"Search me," said Kaa.

"Search you? That's an excellent idea." Shere Khan grinned in a way that sent a shiver down Kaa's long spine. "I'm sure you won't mind showing me your coils."

The python did mind, but he felt it wouldn't do a bit of good to say so. Hoping against hope that the man-cub would remain where he was, and wouldn't awaken, Kaa withdrew his gigantic length from the bushes. And Shere Khan inspected the serpent's coils from nose to tail.

"Baa!" muttered the tiger. "Absolutely nothing!"

"I told you there was no one here," said Kaa. "I was just singing to myself. You see, when I can't sleep . . ."

"I know, I know!" snapped Shere Khan. He felt sure that he was being tricked somehow. But how? It was plain to see that Kaa had nothing hidden in his coils. "Well, if you do happen to see the man-cub, you will inform me first, won't you, Kaa?"

The tiger's sharp talon scratched just under the python's chin. "Understand?" asked Shere Khan.

Kaa gulped. "I understand."

"Good," said the tiger. "Now you will excuse me. I must continue my search for the helpless little lad."

The tiger released the python and got up to go.

"Helpless little lad indeed," thought Kaa, as the tiger disappeared into the jungle. "Who does he think he's fooling?"

The snake started to wriggle back into the underbrush. But he was brought up short at the sight of Mowgli. The man-cub was awake and on his feet. Once released from the python's coils, he had come to his senses.

"You lied to me, Kaa!" shouted Mowgli. "You said I should trust you!"

Kaa shook his head sadly. "It's a wicked world," he told the man-cub. "You can't trust anybody."

But Mowgli wasn't waiting to discuss the point. He had turned and fled from the python.

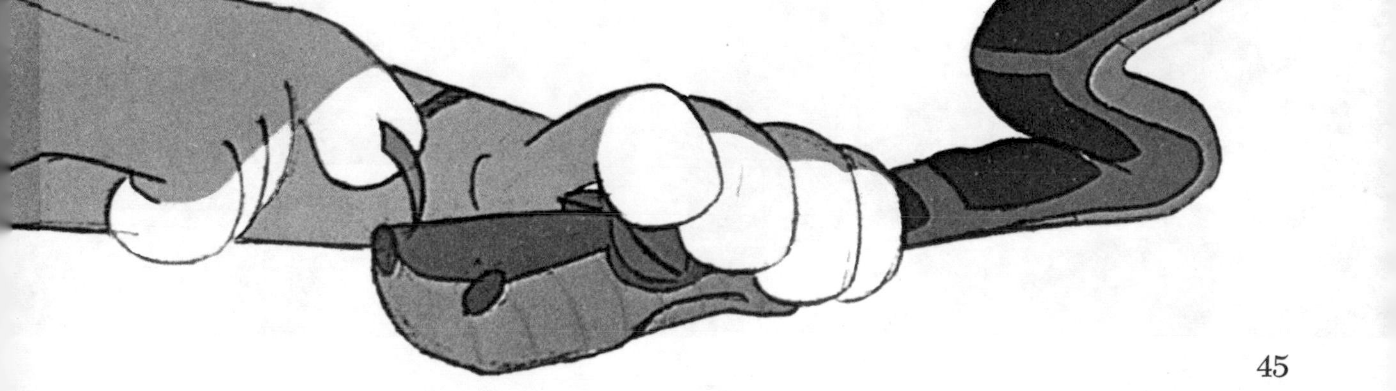

Friends in Need

There was a pool at the place where the jungle ended and the treeless, desert plain began. Mowgli was exhausted when he came to it, and he bent to drink. But he drew back quickly when he saw that the water was black. Beside the pool, on a blasted and leafless tree, sat a company of huge birds. Mowgli looked at them and shuddered. He had seen their like before. They were vultures—carrion eaters. They rode on the high winds and scanned the jungle below. When they saw a dead animal they cleared away his remains. They did needed work. Yet none of the other jungle creatures would have anything to do with them. Theirs was a lonely existence.

Mowgli sat down beside the pool and stared out across the plain. It seemed to him that he could not go that way. There was no shelter there. At the same time, he really did not want to go back into the jungle, where Kaa lurked.

"I say," said a voice behind Mowgli, "what a crazy-looking bunch of bones!"

Mowgli turned around. It was one of the vultures who had spoken.

"Yeah! And sitting about by themselves," said a second big bird.

Mowgli turned his back on the vultures and began to poke at the water with a stick.

"Come on, lad," whispered one of the vultures. "Let's have some fun with this little fellow!"

Mowgli heard it, and he quickly decided that he had better get up and move along. But before he could stir there was a flapping of wings, and the man-cub found himself surrounded by the ugly birds.

"He's got legs like a stork, he has," said one, peering at Mowgli's skinny knees.

"Can't be a stork," decided a second vulture. "He ain't got no feathers."

The birds seemed to think this was terribly funny. They laughed and beat their wings against the ground until the air was filled with black feathers.

"Go ahead and laugh," said Mowgli. A big tear spilled out of one eye and ran down beside his nose. "What do I care?"

He got up and began to walk away, out across the barren, wind-swept plain.

"Now what's wrong with him?" whispered one of the vultures.

"We were only joking," said a second bird.

"I think we overdid it," suggested a third.

Mowgli put his head down and walked a little faster.

"Just look at him," said a fourth vulture. "Aw, the poor little fellow. You know, he must be down on his luck, or he wouldn't be in our neighborhood."

The birds thought about this. It was true that no other jungle animals or birds ever came to the dead tree by the black pool. If the man-cub were there, he must be an outcast of some kind. Or perhaps he was lost.

"Hey, kid!" called one of the vultures. "Wait a minute."

Mowgli walked on, so the vulture flapped up into the air, then flew past the boy and landed right in his path.

"Just leave me alone!" demanded Mowgli.

"Oh come on," coaxed the bird. "You look like you haven't got a friend in the world."

"I haven't," Mowgli declared.

A second vulture hurried up to join the conversation. "Haven't you got a mother or a father?" he asked.

Mowgli thought of Raksha and Rama, and of his wolf brothers. But they had sent him away. "Nobody wants me around," said the man-cub.

"We know just how you feel," one of the vultures told him. "Nobody wants us around, either."

"It isn't fair, you know," said another vulture. "We may look a bit shabby, but we've got heart—and feelings, too."

The largest of the birds sidled close to Mowgli. "We *do* have feelings," he repeated. "Kid, would you like to join our little group?"

A second bird straightened up. The red skin on his naked neck absolutely glowed with pleasure. "Great idea!" he croaked. "Kid, we'll make you an honorary vulture!"

There was no doubt of it. The birds were completely sincere. And they meant the offer very kindly. Still, Mowgli had been raised as Raksha's cub. To join the vultures was unthinkable!

"Thanks," he told them, "but I'd rather be on my own, alone."

The biggest vulture disagreed. "Now look, kid, everybody's got to have friends."

"We'll be your friends," said another bird.

"We *are* your friends," insisted a third vulture.

Mowgli didn't know *what* to say. The birds were so serious about it. They seemed so pleased at the idea of being friends—of helping someone. But it would never do. If he couldn't be a bear or an elephant, there was no way on earth that he could ever be a vulture.

Suddenly, "How extraordinary!" said a voice at the edge of the jungle.

Mowgli spun around. There was a tremendous flapping of wings all around him as the vultures fled frantically to the safety of their dead tree.

"Thank you for detaining my victim!" said Shere Khan the tiger.

Mowgli knew it was Shere Khan. It could be no one else.

"Run, friend," squawked a vulture. "Run!"

Mowgli felt a strange surge of anger. Was he to run from every creature on earth? He was Raksha's cub. What's more, he was a man-cub. He was done with running.

Shere Khan padded forward. Then he stopped. He was puzzled by this man-cub who stood so quietly. "Is it possible that you don't know who I am?" he asked.

"I know you, all right," said Mowgli. "You're Shere Khan."

"Precisely," said the tiger. "Then you must also know that everyone runs from Shere Khan."

"I don't," said Mowgli.

"Ah, you have spirit for one so small," observed the tiger. "That spirit deserves a sporting chance. Besides, I like a chase. It makes things more interesting for me. I will close my eyes and count to ten before I come after you."

Mowgli did not answer. The tiger sat down on his haunches and began to count. "One, two, three, four . . ." said Shere Khan.

Mowgli bent and picked up a stick which he could use for a club.

"Five, six, seven, eight," the tiger went on.

The branches at the edge of the jungle parted. A gray, shaggy shape hurtled into view.

"Nine, ten!" counted Shere Khan.

"Run, Mowgli!" cried Baloo. And the bear flung himself onto Shere Khan just in time to spoil the tiger's leap.

Shere Khan whirled on Baloo with a snarl.

The bear backed away then, but Mowgli did not. He leaped at the huge tiger and swung with his stick. It caught Shere Khan on the nose.

Shere Khan roared, and the vultures nearly fell out of their tree in their excitement. Who ever heard of hitting a tiger in the nose? It was madness! But it was magnificent madness.

Shere Khan started a slow, menacing advance on Mowgli, and Baloo caught the tiger by the tail.

It saved Mowgli for the moment. But even Baloo, with his great weight and his shambling strength, was no match for Shere Khan. The tiger whirled upon him with his fangs bared. Poor Baloo! All he could do was hang on for dear life to the lashing, twitching tail.

It was no wonder that no one near the pool noticed the changing sky. The sun had vanished behind a bank of dark clouds. As Shere Khan circled, pursuing Baloo, and the bear held tight to the tiger's tail and dodged away from his teeth, there was a rumble of thunder. The gray sky became darker and darker until it was almost black. Then, with a mighty crash, a streak of lightning split the clouds. Vultures exploded out in every direction as a bolt struck their tree and it burst into flame.

"The red flower!" cried one bird. He was staring at the burning tree. "Fire! It's the only thing Shere Khan is afraid of!"

"Get the red flower!" the vulture said to Mowgli. "Get the fire, man-cub."

Then Mowgli understood. The red flower was man's weapon, and he was a man. If he had the red flower, even Shere Khan would fear him.

Mogli raced to the burning tree and snatched at a branch where the red flower bloomed.

There was no time to think twice. Shere Khan had reached Baloo at last. The bear was down on the ground, and the tiger stood over him. One huge paw was raised, the talons extended.

The man-cub ran with the blazing branch. Shere Khan saw him coming. The tiger stepped back away from the bear. "Put that down, man-cub!" he ordered.

The flame that licked at the wood was mirrored in the big cat's eyes. Mowgli laughed.

"I said put it down," snarled Shere Khan.

Again Mowgli laughed, and he thrust the fire forward, almost into the face of the tiger. For an instant the boy thought that Shere Khan would leap, fire or no fire. But Shere Khan did not leap. Instead he remembered a long-ago night. He saw the villagers again, and heard the thunder of guns. The old wound in his shoulder throbbed. The tiger turned away his head.

"Coward!" taunted Mowgli.

"You'll burn yourself, little one," whined the tiger. "Put down the red flower before it's too late."

"No," said Mowgli proudly. "I am a man, and men do not fear the red flower. Only cowards like you fear it. Run away, coward!"

Shere Khan went without looking back. In a twinkling the jungle had swallowed him up.

Mowgli dropped the blazing branch. It had begun to burn his fingers.

The Man-Village

Bagheera the panther was the last to come to the pool. He padded from the edge of the jungle and came to stand quietly beside Mowgli.

"I saw what you did," said Bagheera.

Mowgli said nothing. He just put his hand on the panther's head.

Bagheera looked down at Baloo. The bear lay motionless, his eyes closed. "You have won, man-cub," said Bagheera.

Mowgli went down on his knees beside Baloo. He touched the bear's head with his hand. "Baloo, get up," he whispered.

The bear didn't move, and Mowgli scratched at his ears. "Please get up," he begged.

"Mowgli, don't," said Bagheera. "Now you must be brave—as brave as Baloo was."

"Was?" repeated Mowgli. "You don't mean that he's dead?"

"Now, now," said Bagheera gently. "You must remember that there is no greater expression of love than to give one's life for a friend. Baloo loved you, Mowgli. And when great deeds are remembered in the jungle, his name will stand above all the others."

Baloo stirred and opened one eye. "Beautiful!" he murmured.

Bagheera gasped. "Why . . . why, you old fraud!" he roared.

"Baloo, you're alive!" Mowgli threw himself upon the bear.

"You'd better believe it." Baloo sat up, the better to give Mowgli a bear hug.

"Good old papa bear!" laughed Mowgli. "I'm never going to leave you again!"

"That's my boy!" Baloo ruffled Mowgli's hair with his paw.

Wise old Bagheera shook his head. It was wrong. It was all wrong. Shere Khan was lord of the jungle. All the animals fled when he approached. Yet the puny man-cub had managed to drive the tiger away. When word of this spread through the jungle even Kaa would fear the man-cub. There was no doubt about it. Mowgli had earned the right to stay in the jungle. But Mowgli was a man. He had said it himself when he faced Shere Khan. He belonged in the man-village, among his own people.

But Bagheera could argue no more. And there was nothing to be gained by argument. Perhaps there was another way.

"It's rather a shame to come so far and not see it," said Bagheera suddenly.

Mowgli stopped hugging Baloo. He looked around at Bagheera. "See what?" he asked.

"Why, the man-village," answered Bagheera. "It's really an interesting place."

"But I'm not going to the man-village."

"Naturally you're not. But I thought we might just look at it. It's not far from here."

Both Baloo and Mowgli looked very doubtful.

"We couldn't possibly go into the village, of course," said Bagheera. "That would be madness. We'll just peek at it from the edge of the jungle."

"Well," said Mowgli, "I guess it wouldn't hurt if we just looked."

"Of course we'll just look," said Bagheera cheerfully.

So Mowgli and Baloo waved good-by to the vultures and followed Bagheera down the jungle trail. After a while they came to a place where the trees thinned and they could see the sky. Beyond the trees a stream ran down, and beyond the stream were the patches of cleared land which men call fields.

Mowgli moved a huge fern leaf to one side and looked across the fields to a cluster of thatched huts surrounded by a stake fence. Drifts of fragrant smoke rose from some of the huts. Mowgli could hear the laughter of the children playing on the village street.

"Are all the men in their village now?" asked Mowgli.

"Perhaps," said Bagheera. "Night is coming, and at night men stay inside their walls."

"Oh," said Mowgli. "There's one!" He pointed to the gate in the stake fence. A little girl came out and started across the fields toward the stream. She carried an earthen water jar on her head.

"That's a girl-cub," said Bagheera.

Mowgli stared. He had never seen anything like this child. She was about Mowgli's age, or perhaps a bit younger. Her long hair was caught back from her face with ribbons on either side. She wore a loose, flowing garment that was the color of dawn, and of sunset.

"You didn't tell me about girl-cubs," said Mowgli. "I'm going to have a better look." He slipped away and climbed up into the tree that overhung the water.

The little girl had reached the edge of the stream. She knelt and began to fill her jar. She was singing to herself, and after a moment she put the water jar aside and began to smooth her dark hair with her fingers.

Mowgli edged his way out along a slim branch. It gave a warning creak. The little girl looked up, saw Mowgli, and looked away again.

When her hair was properly arranged and her water jar was full, the child stood up and lifted the jar to the top of her head. Without looking at Mowgli again, she turned and started back toward the village.

The branch to which Mowgli clung snapped suddenly and broke. Mowgli fell, splashing into the river. The little girl turned and looked at him. Then she giggled. Then she tilted her head suddenly, and the water jar fell and rolled down the path toward Mowgli.

Mowgli jumped to his feet and ran to catch the jar. He picked it up in both his hands, marveling at its smooth roundness. There was nothing like this in the jungle.

The boy dipped the jar full of water again and held it out to the girl. But she did not take it. Instead she just smiled and started along the path toward the village.

Mowgli was puzzled. What was he to do? At last he lifted the jar to his head as the girl had done. He steadied the thing with both hands and hurried after the girl.

Just before he reached the gate into the man-village, Mowgli stopped and looked back toward the jungle. He waved once. Then he went through the gate.

"He's gone!" groaned Baloo.

"That's right, Baloo," Bagheera agreed. "It had to happen. He's with his own people now."

Then the bear and the panther turned back toward the jungle. And for Mowgli, the man-cub, a new life began.

The Seven Dwarfs Find a House

Once upon a time, in a secret place in the middle of a deep, dark forest, there was a wonderful diamond mine. It belonged to seven little men. They were the seven dwarfs, and they liked their marvelous mine very much.

Now a diamond mine is a delightful thing to own. But perhaps the seven dwarfs overdid their mining a bit. Every morning they woke up before sunrise and marched to the mine. They worked in the mine all day long.

First they dug diamonds out of the earth.

Then they washed the diamonds carefully in running water and piled them into a cart.

Then they hauled the cart to a big vault so that they could lock up their diamonds.

When night came, the seven dwarfs were tired after all that hard work. They marched out of their diamond mine and had their supper. Since they were too tired to cook, it wasn't much of a supper—just some bread and a bit of cheese.

After supper, the dwarfs didn't bother to wash their faces or brush their teeth. They were so tired that they curled up and went to sleep.

Some of them slept in hollow trees.

Some of them slept in rocky caves.

Some of them simply nestled down on beds of leaves.

The seven dwarfs were very, very rich. They had a great vault filled with diamonds. But they had no place they could call home. And they were always busy digging more diamonds out of the earth and locking more diamonds up in their vault. They had no time to look for a home.

In spite of the fact that they were not at all comfortable, the seven dwarfs were the best of friends.

The leader of the group was Doc. He was the oldest and wisest of the dwarfs. He was the one who thought clever thoughts. Sometimes he thought such clever thoughts that he stuttered when he tried to talk about them. The other dwarfs didn't mind Doc's stutter. They all paid attention whenever Doc said anything.

Grumpy, the second dwarf, was almost as old as Doc. He didn't think wise thoughts. Not at all. He thought grumpy thoughts. He pretended that he didn't like people. He even pretended that he didn't like Doc. But this was all make-believe. Grumpy didn't fool anyone.

After Grumpy came Happy. He woke up smiling and he chuckled all day and he went to bed laughing. Happy loved everyone and everything.

Bashful was the dwarf who blushed a lot. He was very, very shy.

Sneezy had a dreadful case of hay fever. He was allergic to dust, feathers, ragweed pollen and

numbers of other things. He sneezed and he sneezed and he SNEEZED!

Sleepy was a pleasant enough dwarf, when he could manage to stay awake.

The youngest of all the dwarfs was Dopey. He was so young that he didn't even have a beard.

And for all anyone knew, he had no voice, either. Dopey never talked. He didn't know whether he could or not. He had never tried.

One morning, Doc was sitting in his office in the diamond mine adding up the monthly bills.

There was a bill from the hardware store for new picks and shovels.

There was a bill from the candle shop for candles to light the mine.

There was a bill from the grocer for the bread and cheese that the dwarfs ate every day.

Doc was not worried about the bills. The dwarfs had plenty of diamonds, and diamonds are as good as money. Some people think that diamonds are even better than money.

What worried Doc was that there were no bills for soap or toothpaste or laundry detergent.

There were no bills for roast beef or corn flakes or carrots.

There were no bills for cream puffs or potato chips.

There wasn't a single bill for milk or butter or eggs or ice cream or chocolate frosted cake.

"Oh, dear!" said Doc. "This isn't right! It isn't right at all!"

The squirrel who was running across the rafters above Doc wondered what wasn't right. He chattered at Doc in a questioning way.

"We ought to have a home," said Doc.

The squirrel had a very nice home high up in a hollow tree. He decided that Doc was right. The seven dwarfs needed a home, too.

Doc quickly called all the little men together. His idea was so wonderful that he stuttered and stammered when he told them about it. And when they heard him out, they thought a home would be fine. All except Grumpy, of course. He wasn't sure he'd like living in a house.

But Grumpy was out-voted. The dwarfs sent the squirrel scampering through the forest with a message. All the animals were to be told that the dwarfs were looking for a house.

The squirrels let the rabbits know, and the rabbits told the chipmunks.

The chipmunks told the deer family that lived in the pine grove.

When they went to the river to drink, the deer told the turtles.

The turtles passed the word to the wild heron who lived on the lake, and the heron called to the owl. The owl was up and about early that day.

It was the owl who came hurrying to the dwarfs. He was so excited that he could hardly

hoot, for he knew of just the house for them. It was a lonely house. No one had lived in it for a long, long time. The owl was sure that the seven little men needed the house—and the house needed the seven little men.

The dwarfs were delighted to learn about the house—all except Grumpy. He had forgotten how to be delighted about anything.

Doc led the way, and the little men marched off through the woods singing a merry, "Hi, hi-ho!" They hadn't far to go—just down the path and across the brook and over the hill—and there it was!

All the dwarfs had to agree that the house looked quite comfortable. It was exactly big enough, but not too big.

Friend owl looked in through the window. "How nice!" he cried. "There's a table there, and seven little chairs!"

Doc opened the door and led the way inside. The other dwarfs followed.

There was no doubt about it. The house was just right for the seven little men. Not only were there seven little chairs and a table, there was a nice little cupboard with stacks of plates and cups and saucers and pots and pans. And there was a teapot that was just big enough for seven cups of tea.

There was a fine big fireplace with an iron hook to hold kettles over the fire.

There was an oven at one side of the fireplace.

And there was a heap of wood all ready and waiting for someone to light the fire.

Of course, everything was very dusty. The house had been empty for such a long time. All of the little men began to sweep and mop and scrub and polish.

Except for Grumpy—who wasn't sure he wanted to be so clean.

Sneezy worked especially hard. But then the dust got into his eyes and up his nose and he began to sneeze.

"Katchoo! Katchoo!"

He sneezed so hard that the friendly chipmunk who was helping him sneezed, too, just to keep him company.

Sleepy didn't care for all this work. He crept away and tip-toed up the stairs. At the top of the stairs he saw something that made him blink.

There in a row stood seven little beds. Each bed had a name carved on it.

Sleepy blinked again when he read the names. There was a bed for Doc and one for Sneezy and one for Dopey. Happy had a bed and so did Grumpy and so did Bashful.

"This house *was* meant for us," thought Sleepy. But he was too tired to wonder about it very long. He yawned and yawned and crept into the bed marked "Sleepy." When Doc came hunting for him, he was deep in dreams.

Doc just laughed and let Sleepy sleep for a while. Then he called "Wash time!"

The dwarfs were surprised. They had never bothered much with soap and water when they lived in the open, under the trees. But they didn't live under the trees any more.

"We can't have supper until our hands and faces are clean," Doc told them.

So the seven dwarfs scrubbed and scrubbed until they were nice and clean.

Grumpy didn't want to wash. He said he didn't believe in it. But the other dwarfs threw him into the water, so he was clean in spite of himself.

And Dopey turned it all into a game by blowing soap bubbles with a bubble pipe.

When they had finished washing, the seven dwarfs dried themselves on seven little towels which Doc had hung on the fence. Then they went into the house.

Happy began to get supper. He popped a big roast of beef into the oven next to the fireplace. Then he set the table. He put out knives and forks and spoons and plates and cups from the cupboard.

Bashful wanted to help with the supper. He stirred up a nice big kettle of soup.

Soon there was a delicious meal ready for the seven bright, clean, happy little men.

They had soup and roast beef and baked potatoes and carrot curls and celery sticks and peas.

They had bread and butter and cheese and corn on the cob.

And for dessert they had cream puffs *and* ice cream *and* chocolate frosted cake.

After supper, the dwarfs washed and dried every plate and cup and put everything away. They swept up every crumb. Then they wanted to celebrate.

Happy pointed to the old pipe organ that stood in the corner. "Play for us, Grumpy," he begged.

Grumpy sat by the fire and scowled. He wasn't sure he wanted to play the organ. But all the other dwarfs asked him several times, and at last he gave in and began to play.

Sneezy and Sleepy joined in on the flute and the concertina. Happy strummed the guitar and Doc clapped his hands.

Soon every one of the seven dwarfs was playing or singing or dancing. Some of the dwarfs were doing all three at the same time. The party went on and on and on until long past bedtime.

It was Sleepy who became sleepy at last. When he mentioned bed, the other dwarfs were willing to listen to him. They all went up the stairs to their very own little beds in their very own house in the middle of the deep, dark forest.

And as they put out the light, even grumpy old Grumpy said that he liked having a home. He liked it just fine!

Mickey Mouse's Picnic

MICKEY MOUSE sang.

"What a beautiful day for a picnic,
What a picnical day for a lark!
We will frolic all day
In the happiest way,
And we won't get back home until dark!"

Mickey was feeling very happy as he skipped up the walk to Minnie Mouse's house.

"Ready, Minnie?" he called.

Pluto and Goofy and Daisy Duck and Clarabelle Cow were waiting in Mickey's car.

"All ready," Minnie smiled. "I've packed us a nice big basket of lunch."

She let Mickey peek inside.

"Whee!" cried Mickey.

For Minnie had packed
peanut butter and jelly sandwiches and
cold meat sandwiches and
deviled eggs and potato salad,
radishes and onions and
pink lemonade and
a great big chocolate cake!

"Let's go!" said Mickey. And he picked up the basket and led Minnie out to the car.

"Let's go!" cried Goofy and Daisy and Clarabelle Cow.

"It seems strange to start off on a picnic without Donald Duck," said Mickey. "Don't you think maybe we should ask him anyway?"

"No!" said everyone.

"You remember last time, Mickey," Minnie Mouse reminded him. "We all decided not to take Donald on the next picnic. Because there always is trouble when Donald is along."

"Well, all right," Mickey said. "I guess we do have a carful anyway."

So Mickey hopped into the driver's seat. And away they went.

None of them saw a figure watching from behind the bushes. And when they were far down the road, none of them saw that figure come out from hiding and jump up and down in rage!

"What a beautiful day for a picnic,
What a picnical day for a lark!"

Everyone sang as Mickey Mouse drove merrily down the road to the picnic grounds.

And it did start out to be a perfect day. First they went for a walk along the river bank. They found a grassy spot beneath a tall shade tree. And they left Minnie's lunch basket there.

Then everyone went swimming in the old swimming hole. And how good that fresh, cool water felt! They swam and floated and played around, and had a wonderful time.

"I'm hungry enough to eat that whole basketful of lunch myself," Mickey Mouse said after a while.

"We'll see that you don't, Mickey Mouse!" Minnie laughed. "But it is time to eat, I guess."

So they all scrambled out of the water and hurried off to dress.

"Say!" Goofy cried. "Look at this, will you!" Goofy was holding up his pants. The legs were all tied into knots. So were his shirt sleeves. And Mickey's were, too.

"Some mischief maker must be around," Mickey said, with a shake of his head.

But Minnie had a worse thought than that.

"The lunch!" she cried. And she ran up the bank to the shade of that big old tree.

The lunch basket was gone!

"Oh!" groaned everyone. "Not the lunch!"

"Hurry into your clothes, everybody!" Mickey cried. "We'll soon find out about this."

They struggled to undo the knots in their clothes. Then they dressed in a flash and were off on the hunt.

All through the woods they hunted, under every bush and trailing vine. But not a sign of that lunch basket did they see.

At last they came out on the road again, near where they had left Mickey's car. They were hot and tired and hungry and cross.

And it was then that they met Donald Duck, walking along the road all by himself. He had a fishing pole over one shoulder. And a bundle hung from the end of the fishing pole.

Donald was whistling as he walked along, and he looked very pleased with himself.

"Well, hello!" he cried. "Imagine meeting you folks out here. I just came for some fishing myself. Got tired of spending a lonely day at home."

"Oh—er—yes," said Mickey. He felt bad because they had left Donald behind.

"Where are you folks going?" Donald asked.

"We are hunting for our lunch," Mickey said.

"For lunch?" said Donald. "Why, I have enough for us all in my bundle here. I will be glad to share it with my friends."

Now everyone felt guilty. But they were hungry, so they said thank you, they would like to eat with Donald.

Under the same big shady tree Donald opened his bundle and spread out his lunch.

It was delicious. There were
peanut butter and jelly sandwiches and
cold meat sandwiches and
deviled eggs and potato salad,
radishes and onions and
pink lemonade and
a great big chocolate cake!

A strange look came into Mickey and Minnie Mouse's eyes as they saw that picnic lunch. But they did not say a word.

So they all sat down and ate and ate.

"This is delicious, Donald," said Clarabelle Cow.

"And it is nice of you, too, Donald," Daisy Duck added, "to share it with us."

"Sure is," said Goofy.

"Yes," Mickey admitted. "I guess we misjudged you, Donald, old boy."

"Humph!" said Minnie Mouse. Then she turned to Donald with her sweetest smile.

"Did you bring a knife for cutting the chocolate cake, Donald?" she asked.

"Er—ah, I had one somewhere," Donald said. He looked all around. But he could not find it.

"I fastened a knife to the bottom of the cake pan with paper tape," Minnie said, "when I packed my picnic lunch today."

Mickey turned the cake pan upside down. And there, sure enough, was a knife, fastened to the bottom of the pan with paper tape. And on the knife handle were the letters M. M.

"Well!" said Mickey.

"Why, Donald!" cried Daisy Duck.

"So that's where our lunch disappeared to," cried Clarabelle Cow.

Donald dropped his eyes before their stony frowns. "I'm sorry, honest I am," he said. "I won't ever do it again."

"And where is my lunch basket?" Minnie asked.

"In the back of Mickey's car," Donald admitted.

Everyone looked so solemn that Mickey had to laugh.

"Well," he said, as he cut the cake, and handed big slices around. "It was a good lunch anyway. And we've all learned a lesson, I think. Donald won't snatch any lunch baskets soon. And we know it's better luck for a picnic to bring Donald."

Everyone had to laugh then. And they all piled back into Mickey's car. They made room for Donald to sit in the empty lunch basket.

Then away they went toward town, singing merrily:

"We will frolic all day
In the happiest way,
And we won't get back home until dark!"

Uncle Scrooge, Lemonade King

"Now, Uncle Scrooge!" Donald Duck said soothingly. "Calm down!"

Uncle Scrooge stamped his foot. His glasses trembled. He scowled fiercely and smacked his fist on the counter of Scrooge's Scrumptious Lemonade Parlor.

"Lemonade Leo is stealing all my customers!" he roared. "I was making a bankful of money every day until he put up that stand over there!"

Donald Duck looked down the beach. There *was* a crowd in front of the other stand. Over the roof loomed a huge sign.

Donald scratched his head.

"Well—maybe you could buy bigger glasses than Leo's," he suggested. "And put up a bigger tent!"

Uncle Scrooge thought. After a moment his glasses stopped trembling, his scowl faded, and he began to smile.

"Hmmm," he murmured. "Perhaps—perhaps you've got something there. I wonder!"

The next day when Donald came down to the beach, he was delighted to see a long line of customers in front of Scrooge's Scrumptious Lemonade Parlor attracted by the new sign.

"Come on, Uncle Scrooge," Donald said happily. "Let Huey, Louie, and Dewey serve the customers while we go for a swim. We ought to celebrate!"

Soon Donald was sailing along on his rubber horse and Uncle Scrooge was floating on his rubber goldpiece. Everything was as peaceful as peaches, when suddenly there was a roar from the beach.

"Look at that!" bellowed Uncle Scrooge, and he slipped right off the goldpiece. "Everyone's running to Lemonade Leo's!"

The two bathers hurried back to shore and stared in horror at Leo's new sign.

The next morning Donald came to the beach bright and early. There had been a strange gleam in Uncle Scrooge's eyes last night, and Donald was eager to find out what it meant.

He didn't have long to wait. His uncle was just hoisting a new sign into place.

The news spread fast. Soon a funny kind of parade came filing down the road from town. Everyone was carrying, pulling, or pushing a

bathtub. There were white tubs and pink ones, blue ones and black-and-white marble ones. There was even one shaped like a big swan.

"How's that for beating Leo at his very own game?" demanded Uncle Scrooge. He tumbled another gallon of lemonade into a purple tub.

Donald swallowed. "Good, Uncle Scrooge! Fine! Only—look!"

He pointed. Lemonade Leo was up on his roof painting a new notice over the old ones. The new sign said:

T A K E H O M E
A T R U C K F U L
O F
L E M O N A D E

And once again the crowd was moving. Everyone who owned a truck or could borrow one was on his way. Uncle Scrooge and Donald could only watch unhappily as Lemonade Leo used a hose to fill one truck after another.

"Well," Donald said finally, "I guess you're licked, Uncle Scrooge."

But Uncle Scrooge was scowling fiercely once again. His glasses trembled and his hand shook as he scribbled some words on a sheet of paper and handed it to Donald.

"Take this shopping list and get everything on it," he roared. "I don't care if it takes every penny in my money bin. I want those things here by dawn tomorrow."

Donald stared at the list. It looked like this:

10 airplanes (with pilots)
10 cement mixers
1 million lemons
100 tons of sugar
100,000 straws (extra long)

"Do as I say!" roared Uncle Scrooge. "And hurry!"

Donald hurried. Nobody ever disobeyed Uncle Scrooge—at least not when he looked like that.

Filling the order was a hard job, but at last Donald had arranged for everything to be delivered to the beach at dawn the next morning. He meant to be there himself, to see what Uncle Scrooge was going to do, but when his alarm went off, he was sleeping so soundly that he never heard it.

When he finally awoke, people were running past his house, all of them laughing and talking as they hurried to the beach. It looked as if everyone in Duckburg were going.

Donald jumped up and followed.

And it wasn't long before he knew. He knew what the planes were for and what the cement mixers were for. He knew why Uncle Scrooge had needed a million lemons and tons of sugar and thousands of straws. He even knew why Lemonade Leo was trudging away from the beach, the only unhappy face in all that happy throng.

For around the shores of the lake waited thousands of people with straws in their hands. Behind them, cement mixers ground up thousands of juicy lemons, and overhead the airplanes dumped the ground-up lemons and tons of sugar down into the lake.

"You've done it, Uncle Scrooge!" Donald shouted. "You've won!"

But Uncle Scrooge was too busy to answer. He was rushing up and down the beach, collecting handfuls of money from everyone who wanted to try to drink a whole lakeful of lemonade.

Perri

ONCE upon a springtime, deep in a forest, a little squirrel was born. Her name was Perri.

Perri's home was in the hollow of an oak tree whose top had long ago been torn away in a storm. The nest was softly lined with grass and it was warm and dark.

The baby squirrel enjoyed the warmth, as she lay cuddled beside her brothers. At first, Perri did not even know that it was dark. Like many other new-born creatures, she could not see. Then one day, when her mother had gone from the nest for food, Perri opened her eyes. She could see!

Through a small window in back of the nest, sunlight appeared. Perri crawled over to the window and looked out for the first time on a bright world. She saw the earth and trees and a blue sky. She saw her mother picking brown seeds from a pine cone. She saw her father watching, sharp-eyed, from his nest in a pine.

Then suddenly, across the earth, a shadow fell—the long, slinky shadow of the marten. The marten was not so large and fierce as other enemies, but he was more dangerous, because he could climb a tree as well as any squirrel.

"Save the babies! Quick!" warned Perri's father, as the mother leaped for the hollow tree. "I'll head the fellow off!"

The father squirrel was quick, but he was not quick enough. The marten pounced. . . .

"How brave your father was!" Perri's mother mourned. "He saved us this time, but the marten will be back. We must leave."

One by one, she carried her children to the nest the father had left in the high branch of the pine tree.

Perri was the last to be moved.

"Let me climb to the nest by myself," she begged.

"Nonsense!" her mother scolded gently. "A little thing like you! Don't think you are grown up because you've opened your eyes on the world!"

"It's a lovely world," Perri said.

"It is," the mother sighed. "Yes, it's a lovely world, but not an easy one. We will never see your father again."

Perri had many neighbors in the pine-tree nest. At the tip of the branch, a hummingbird's family raised hungry beaks for the seeds their mother brought. In a nearby oak, a raccoon was coaxing her brood down to the ground. And nearby, some young skunks were taking their first wobbly steps.

"It's time you children learned to get about," Perri's mother announced.

How far away the ground looked when Perri made her first journey to the tip of the limb! But in a week she could run along the branch from her home to the hummingbird's nest. She could hang by her tail, too. Still, her mother said she was not old enough or strong enough to venture down to the ground.

One evening, the frisky little adventurer pranced out to the hummingbird's nest and peered inside. She meant no harm, but the mother bird darted forward on whirring wings.

Perri felt herself falling. Down, down, down she fell to the soft spongy earth.

"So this is what falling feels like," Perri said, not at all alarmed. "I'll just explore a bit before I climb back to the nest."

She frisked and danced along the warm earth, until she came to the bank of a swift stream. Perri had heard of this creek, where all the grown-ups came to drink.

"I'll have a sip of cool water myself," she said.

Just then a woodpecker called a sharp warning: "The marten!"

Perri started for a tree, but the marten was close on her trail. What should she do?

"Jump in the creek, you silly little squirrel," cawed a bluejay. "You can swim if you try. Martens can't!"

Perri plunged boldly into the swift water. The marten stood on the bank and watched her swim. How furious he was when he saw her reach the opposite bank!

Perri was safe, but wet and forlorn. She longed to go home, but not for anything would she risk the journey alone. She was wondering what to do when a warning squirrel bark came to her ears.

Close by, his great paw lifted to pounce, was a giant creature, more terrible than a marten. Perri leaped up a tree and sat trembling on a slippery branch.

"I'll give that wildcat a chase," a voice said, as a young boy squirrel swung down by his tail. "Watch me. I'm Porro!"

Perri was too frightened to watch. She closed her eyes, shivering, until she heard the hungry wildcat slink off.

"He's gone," Porro called. "Come down and we'll have a feast."

Proudly, he led the way to a hollow log half buried in pine needles. He showed Perri his store of pine cones and seeds.

"Is this where you and your family live?" Perri asked in surprise. After all, the proper place for a home was in a tree.

"Don't have a family. Can't be bothered with a nest," Porro answered. "At night I just sleep on the branch of my pine tree."

"Everybody has to have a home," Perri said. "I intend to build one at once."

But finding a place for a home was not easy. Perri discovered a hole in a nearby tree, but when she looked, an old bearded flying squirrel drove her away with a flick of his tail. She found a lovely rotted stump, but a family of woodpeckers lived inside.

At last she found a hole in an aspen tree. She lined it neatly with grass and leaves, then popped her head out and looked around. Darkness was creeping over the forest. But Perri was safe. She curled up inside her new nest and went to sleep.

The heat of summer covered the forest before Porro decided to build a nest for himself. He threw a few twigs and bits of bark together and invited Perri and their bird neighbors to see his fine new home. The jay looked at it and screeched:

"Haw, haw! Even the magpie builds a better nest than that!"

Porro paid no attention. Up the tree he went,

and into the nest. Then he fell right through the bottom and tumbled back down to the ground.

Even after the nest was mended, Porro was too venturesome to stay in it. On a midsummer's eve, when the moon was high, Perri looked out from her nest to see an owl perched on a limb. He was eyeing Porro, who had decided just then to get a drink of water.

"Danger!" Perri called.

The owl swooped down, and Porro barely had time to escape into his hollow log. There he stayed, until the owl flew away.

Perri and Porro frolicked and played together through the long summer days. They stored acorns and fresh pine cones in the hollow log, without exactly knowing why. They faintly remembered that their mothers had told them this was the thing to do.

The flying squirrel was hoarding, too; and grumpy old Scarface, the black squirrel.

The birds began to talk of making journeys. Perri and Porro hardly listened. They danced about in the red and gold leaves, their little jaws bulging with nuts to store in the hollow log.

Suddenly, one evening, Perri was startled by a loud noise she had never heard before. Porro was leaning against an oak, just as surprised and frightened as she was.

Then they heard the noise again. The jays and crows—the only birds left in the forest—fluttered and screamed. A light flashed, followed by a louder noise than before.

Porro dashed for his hollow log and Perri scrambled after him. There was another peal of thunder, and Perri saw her tree house bright with flame.

The fire spread, and all the animals began running from the smoke and flame. Smoke tickled Perri's nose, and she and Porro followed the other animals to the creek. They plunged into the water and swam to a floating log.

A weasel and a raccoon were clinging to the log. The wildcat floated by. They paid no attention to the squirrels. Enemies and friends huddled together against the enemy of them all—fire.

At last it began to rain. The fire died away. But, all night, Perri clung to the log in the creek. At dawn she crept to the land and to her burnt-out nest. Porro's nest was gone, too, and he refused to make another. The hollow log was good enough.

But Perri was a neat housekeeper. With twigs and brown, rustling autumn leaves, she bravely began to build again.

The days grew short, the nights long and cold. One morning Perri was wakened by Porro.

"Come, look!" he called. "The beaver is making a dam! He's got his whole family working with him. They're building a bridge over the Big Water, from one bank to the other!"

All day the two squirrels watched the beavers at their work. But as the short day ended and the shadows of night came, Perri saw a frightening thing. The marten stood on the opposite bank, eyeing her hungrily.

"Danger! Danger!" Porro called.

Perri was too terrified to move.

The marten began to cross the bridge the beavers had built. Carefully he moved, putting down first one paw and then another. Soon he would reach the bank.

Suddenly the beaver dived underneath the dam. The twigs and branches heaved and swayed, and the marten tumbled into the swift current of the stream.

Perri found her voice again.

"He can't swim! Martens can't swim!" she cried, and she leaped into the tree beside Porro.

The squirrels raced from treetop to treetop, feeling the joy of being safe. But their delight lasted only a few days. One morning, Perri woke to see fat, white flakes falling softly in front of her door. The whole forest was white, piled high with snow. The only creatures she could see stirring were the rabbits and the deer.

"Will the world stay like this?" Perri wondered, shivering.

She called Porro, but he did not answer. She was too sleepy to find him. "Later," she said to herself. "Now I'll just take a little nap."

And she rolled up in her tail and slept. Through the long winter, Perri slept, or woke drowsily to eat and sleep again. Sometimes she dreamed that she was frisking in the trees with Porro.

Porro was asleep, too, in his hollow log—and so were the raccoons and skunks and badgers. All winter they slept, while the rabbits and the deer ran swiftly over the silent snow.

There came a day when the sound of bird song filled the forest. Perri opened her eyes, yawned, and looked out. The snow was almost gone, and here and there little green things were sprouting. The sun was warm. It was spring.

She heard a call. Porro's voice! There he was, hanging by his tail from the limb of his pine tree. Perri scurried to the treetop. Porro raced after her as she darted to the edge of the creek.

Across the water, all green and gold in the spring sunlight, was the home of her childhood. She danced across the beaver's bridge, running straight to the tree where she was born. Her family was no longer there, but it did not seem to matter. Perri was grown up now, and Porro was with her.

They found a store of nuts which Perri's mother had left behind, and they both ate hungrily.

"We must get busy at once and build a nest," Perri said.

"Whatever for?" Porro asked.

"Whatever for?" Perri scolded happily. "For babies, of course! I shall take this hollow tree. I'll line it with grass and leaves to keep the children warm."

Porro folded his paws across his chest. "Build away, Perri," he said. "I'll keep intruders away."

He looked around at the greening earth as if he owned it. "It's a lovely world," he said.

"Yes, it's a lovely world, but not an easy one," Perri answered, just as her mother had, a whole long year ago.

Davy Crockett & Mike Fink

THERE'S A STORY told about Davy Crockett, and how he went after the river pirates with Mike Fink.

Now, Davy was king of the wild frontier, as everybody knows. But Mike Fink was king of the river. And when two kings get together, there's bound to be a rumpus. And there was.

The place where the rumpus started was old Kentucky, many a year ago. Davy was tramping down the road above the Ohio River, with his friend, George Russel. Each of them was leading a horse. The rifles in their hands, the packs on their backs, and their dusty buckskins showed that they had been on a long hunt in the woods.

And the heavy load of furs on their horses showed that the hunting had been good.

As they walked along, Davy and Russel heard the blast of a horn from a keelboat on the river. The boat was the *Gullywhumper,* heading for the nearby town of Maysville.

"There's our boat ride!" said Davy. "We'll jest set back in the sun an' ride down to Natchez. Our furs will fetch a better price there."

" 'Tain't the price o' furs you're thinkin' of," Russel said. "It's all that new country we're goin' to see."

The two men grinned at each other, and went on. Soon they reached Maysville. After leaving their horses, packs, and rifles at the livery stable, they started toward the river. Then they stopped, puzzled.

People were running through the streets, trying to get out of sight. Mothers were calling their children. Doors slammed. Storekeepers were boarding up their windows.

"What do you figger is goin' on, Davy?" asked Russel.

Before Davy could answer, there was a commotion at the river. The *Gullywhumper* was coming in. One of the boatmen jumped to shore. He was a big, burly man, wearing a leather hat with a red turkey feather in it. Heaving the mooring line over his shoulder, he pulled the boat halfway up on shore.

"Ya-hoo!" he bellowed. And he roared with laughter as most of the boat's crew tumbled to the deck.

Davy and Russel hurried over to him.

"Say, mister," Davy said, "which o' them fellers is the captain o' this boat?"

The big man stared at Davy.

"Why, you ol' bushwhacker!" he said. "Everybody knows the captain o' the *Gullywhumper!* It's me, Mike Fink—the king o' the river! I'm the original ring-tailed roarer from the thunder-an'-lightnin' country! I'm a snorter an' a head-buster! I can out-run, out-jump, out-swim, out-sing, out-dance, out-shoot, out-eat, out-drink, out-talk, an' out-fight any man on the Ohio an' the ol' Mississip'!"

"King o' the river, eh?" said Russel. "Well, this here is Davy Crockett, king o' the wild frontier. He's a bit o' a ring-tailed roarer himself."

Mike Fink looked Davy up and down.

"So you're Davy Crockett," he said.

"That's what they tell me," Davy said, smiling. "Think you could take us down to Natchez with a load o' furs?"

"Why, sure!" Mike said. "An' seein' as how you're Davy Crockett, I'll only charge you a thousand dollars. Now gangway, because I'm fresh off the river an' jest a-spilin' fer fun an' frolic!"

As Mike walked away, Russel shook his head.

"We're not payin' any thousand dollars fer a trip to Natchez," he said.

"Not while there's more boats on the river," Davy said. "Come on!"

Tied up at the landing was another keelboat, the *Bertha Mae.* But her owner, Captain Cobb, wasn't taking any passengers.

"Not that I wouldn't like to," he said, "but my boat's not goin' anywhere. My crew's run off, an' I can't git another. It's because o' the Injun trouble below Shawneetown. The redskins are attackin' every kind o' boat that comes along—wreckin' an' lootin' an' massacreein' the crews."

Then Captain Cobb had an idea.

He said, "I hear you two fellers are good at Injun fightin'. Maybe if folks knew Davy Crockett was comin' with me, we could git a crew. I wouldn't need more than four men, if you two would lend a hand."

"Sure thing," said Davy. "And burn my boots if Russel an' me don't round up the men fer you." Davy turned to Russel. "We might do better if we split up."

Russel nodded. "Meet you later, back at the landin'."

And so, while Russel followed a likely-looking fellow around the corner, Davy searched the streets of the town. By nightfall, he had rounded up some men. None of them had ever poled a keelboat, but they were willing to try.

At the landing, Russel was nowhere in sight. Davy started off to look for him. Passing the tavern, he heard a yell.

He went inside—and his mouth fell open. Hanging by a chain from the ceiling was a crossbar with two oil lanterns on it. And hanging from the crossbar was Russel. He was swinging around and around, pushing himself with a keelboat pole. And cheering him on were Mike Fink and his men.

"Georgie!" called Davy. "What's got into you?"

"Jest a couple o' Mike Fink specials," said Mike Fink. "Have one with me."

Mike motioned to the bartender, who emptied jugs and bottles into two huge mugs. When the mixture was ready, smoke rose from it.

"Don't think I care fer any," said Davy.

"Then I'll drink 'em both!" roared Mike. And after he did, he said to Davy, "That would'a done you good. Specially seein' as how you got a race on your hands."

"Race? What kind o' race?"

"A keelboat race, o' course," Mike said. "All the way to New Orleans. You an' Russel an' your crew in the *Bertha Mae*, against me an' my crew in the *Gullywhumper*. Russel's bet all your furs that you'll win."

"We will, too! Yippee!" said Russel, still going around and around.

"You tarnal idiot!" Davy said to him. "You really got us into trouble this time! Now git down from there!"

Russel wanted to keep whirling around. But the next minute the chain broke loose from the ceiling. Down came Russel, crossbar, lanterns and all. Before he could crash to the floor, though, Mike caught him in his arms.

"Here," said Mike, pushing Russel toward Davy. "Take good care o' him, Crockett. I wouldn't want him to miss our keelboat race."

While the men in the tavern howled with laughter, Davy took Russel outside. He ducked Russel's head in a watering trough, until Russel began to feel a little better.

"Davy," Russel said, "I—I'm awful sorry I got us into that race. Couldn't you tell Mike I was only foolin'?"

"You think he's the kind to let you off that easy?"

Russel shook his head. "No. Guess he ain't."

"All right, then," Davy said. "You git yourself some sleep. We're racin' Mike Fink tomorrow, an' you'll need your strength. There's not much chance o' us winnin'—but by thunder, we can try!"

The next morning, Davy got his crew aboard the *Bertha Mae*. He and Russel picked up their long boat poles. So did the rest of the crew, except for Captain Cobb, who was at the tiller.

Near the *Bertha Mae* floated the *Gullywhumper*. Mike Fink took the tiller, while his crew picked up their boat poles.

A crowd had gathered on shore to see the great race. The town magistrate was on hand, too, with a small cannon, to give the signal for the start.

"Citizens of Maysville!" he said. "You are about to see the start of a keelboat race to New Orleans, between Davy Crockett, king of the wild frontier, and Mike Fink, king of the river!"

Mike flapped his arms, clicked his heels together, and crowed like a rooster.

"Hey, Crockett," he said, "you might as well gimme them furs o' yours right now."

"You ain't won 'em yet," Davy said.

"If I don't," roared Mike, "I'll eat my hat, red feather an' all! An' that's a promise! Ya—hoo!"

The magistrate held up his hand. "Are the captains ready? Then take your starting places!"

The magistrate brought down his hand. The cannon boomed. The crowd raised a mighty cheer, and the great race between Davy Crockett and Mike Fink began.

Mike's men poled their boat smoothly down the river, singing:

Some row up, but some row down,
All the way to Shawneetown,
All the way to Shawneetown,
Long time ago!

Davy's men leaned on their poles, pushing hard. They pushed so hard that some of them fell into the water. Davy and Russel fished them out, and they tried again. At first they had a hard time keeping the boat straight. After a while, though, they began to get the hang of it.

Looking back at them, Mike said, "Them clod-hoppers ain't doin' so bad! If we're not careful, they'll catch up with us!"

Then Mike smiled. "But there's no need to worry, boys. We'll fix 'em!"

As the *Gullywhumper* floated past a camp of friendly Indians, Mike picked up his rifle. He squeezed the trigger, shooting the feathers off the chief's head. Shouting and jabbering, the Indians scrambled for their bows and arrows. Mike's boat was out of sight by now, but Davy's boat was just passing the camp. Naturally, the Indians thought that Davy's men had shot at them.

The chief shouted out an order—and the next minute a regular shower of arrows fell on the *Bertha Mae*.

"Look out!" warned Captain Cobb.

Davy and his men had never poled a boat, and at first they had a hard time.

Up in the tree, Davy waited for Mike's boat.

Tricks and Traps

As THE arrows hummed around him, Captain Cobb jumped away from the tiller. He crouched behind the deckhouse, with the rest of the crew. Then the boat swung around, and the arrows came at their backs. One stuck in Russel's powder pouch.

"Help!" yelled Russel. "They got us surrounded!"

"Not yet, Georgie," Davy said. "It only *seems* that way."

Running to the tiller, Davy straightened out the boat. It floated around a bend, leaving the Indians behind.

"That's the dirtiest trick I ever saw!" Captain Cobb said. "Mike could'a got us kilt!"

Davy rubbed his chin thoughtfully. "Any place ahead he'll come in close to the bank?"

"Sure. He'll be roundin' Mulehead Point some time tonight."

Davy grinned. "That's jest fine! It'll give us a chance to pay Mike back!"

That night, Davy jumped ashore. He went down the path that followed the river, carrying a big coil of rope around his shoulder. Davy hurried along in the darkness, until he got a little ahead of the *Gullywhumper*. Then he climbed a tree that hung over the river, and tied a noose in one end of the rope.

It wasn't long before the *Gullywhumper* came floating by. Davy dropped the noose over a cleat on the back end of Mike's boat, and pulled it tight. He did it so fast, nobody on the boat saw what was happening. As the *Gullywhumper* went on, Davy kept one end of the rope in his hand.

In a little while, the *Bertha Mae* passed under the tree. Davy dropped down to the deck. Grinning at Russel, he tied the end of the rope to the front end of the boat.

"Mike doesn't know it, but he's givin' us a free ride," Davy said.

All through the night, everybody on the *Bertha Mae* had a good rest. The boat glided down the river, pulled by the *Gullywhumper*. Mike's men worked twice as hard, poling two boats instead of one. When morning came, they were worn out. Luckily for them, Mike noticed the rope. Roaring with anger, he ripped it off.

"So Crockett thinks he can trick the king o' the river, does he?" Mike said. "I'll show that backwoods bushwhacker a thing or two about trickin'!"

While he steered the boat, Mike tried to think of ways of tricking Davy. He didn't hit on anything, though, until he reached a place where the river split into two channels. One channel was known as Dead Man's Chute. In it floated a marker with these words:

DANGER! TAKE OTHER CHANNEL!

Mike picked up the marker and dropped it in the *other* channel.

"We'll go polin' down here nice an' easy," he said. "Meanwhile, the marker will trap Crockett into takin' Dead Man's Chute. Jest wait till he hits that rough water—an' them big rocks! That boat o' his won't last long!"

"Mike," said one of his crew, "I'm right proud o' you. You're gettin' worse every day!"

Later, when Captain Cobb saw the marker, he steered the *Bertha Mae* right into Dead Man's

Chute. Soon the boat began to pick up speed. Carried by the swift rush of the water, it tossed and bobbed and rolled.

"Jumpin' Jehoshaphat!" Captain Cobb said. "We're in the wrong channel! Somebody must'a moved that marker!"

"Look out! We're gonna hit a rock!" yelled Russel.

Captain Cobb heaved on the tiller, and the boat narrowly missed the rock. But the tiller swung out so far it carried Captain Cobb out over the churning water. Davy pulled him back, taking over the tiller himself.

The boat tilted and shook, and creaked in every timber. Water crashed over the deck, almost sweeping some of the crew overboard. With Russel's help, Davy managed to get the boat under control. The men hung on while the *Bertha Mae* raced through the rapids. Time and again it scraped against the great rocks. Time and again water broke over the deck. Somehow, Davy kept the boat from going down. At last it shot out of Dead Man's Chute, passing the *Gullywhumper*.

Russel waved to the amazed Mike Fink. "Yahoo! Who do you think's gonna win now?"

At evening, Davy was still in the lead. But Captain Cobb pointed to the lights of Shawneetown, shining out in the darkness.

"We'll have to put in at the town for fresh supplies," he said. "Everything on the boat is soakin' wet. An' we better be sure to git some dry powder, jest in case we have to fight off the Injuns."

"Makes sense to me," said Davy, and the *Bertha Mae* headed for shore.

Aboard the *Gullywhumper*, one of the crew spoke to Mike. "Listen! Sounds like Crockett an' his boys are puttin' in at Shawneetown!"

Picking up a big wrench, Mike jumped overboard. He swam to the *Bertha Mae*, keeping out of sight in the water. With the wrench he took out two bolts from the hinge of the rudder, so that it hung by just a single bolt.

When he was back on his own boat, he said, "No tellin' when that rudder'll fall off!"

And his men laughed at his trick as the *Gullywhumper* went on.

The pirates hid on shore, watching the boat.

The River Pirates

Down the river, past the Illinois shore, went the *Gullywhumper*. Mike kept one big hand on the tiller, and cupped the other around his ear.

"Burn my boots if I don't hear music!" he said.

Looking at the shore, he saw the opening of a cave in the rocky cliff. Above was a sign:

WILSON'S CAVE-INN

Good Drinks and Entertainment

"So that's where the music is comin' from!" Mike said. "They've made that ol' cave into a tavern."

He ordered his crew to set poles and stop the boat. Two of his men helped him spruce up to go ashore. One smoothed the red feather in Mike's hat, while the second shined Mike's boots.

As Mike was wriggling into a fresh shirt, he caught a glimpse of Davy's boat. It was still some distance from the *Gullywhumper*, but it was coming on fast.

"Thunderation!" roared Mike. "Ain't Crockett's rudder busted yet? Guess I'll have to fergit about them drinks an' entertainment fer now. We better git movin' again, afore that bunch o' landlubbers catches up. Down on them poles, boys! Ho!"

On shore, hidden by trees and brush, three rough, cruel-looking men watched the *Gullywhumper*. They were Sam Mason and the Harpe brothers, Little Harpe and Big Harpe. They were the leaders of the river pirates who had been making raids on boats and stealing their cargo.

It had been Mason's idea to put up the tavern sign on the cave, just to get boatmen to come ashore. Inside the cave there were tables and chairs, to make the place look like a tavern. But this time the scheme was not working.

"Don't worry," Mason said. "Mike's boat won't get far. You know what to do."

The Harpe brothers nodded. They turned and slipped off toward the gang of river pirates hidden a little deeper in the brush. They were white men, but they were dressed and painted to look like Indians. Mounting horses, they rode on until they were ahead of the *Gullywhumper*. In a few minutes they had uncovered three canoes that were hidden on the bank.

When the *Gullywhumper* came along, all the canoes shot out on the water. Yelling and whooping, the pirates in the canoes fired their rifles at Mike and his men.

Mike had no way of knowing that the pirates weren't really Indians.

"Wa-hoo!" he bellowed. "Injuns! Here's where we have some fun, boys!"

It turned out, though, not to be so much fun. Bullets sang through the air from all sides. The pirates came closer and closer to the boat, until some of Mike's men were battling them with poles. The pirates were about to swarm over the deck when Davy's boat came into sight.

"Injuns!" said Davy. "This is what we been waitin' fer! Let's git our rifles workin', Georgie!"

Davy and Russel fired at almost the same time. Two of the pirates fell, overturning their canoe. A moment later a second canoe turned over as one of Mike's shots hit the mark. The third canoe made for shore, with the pirates in the water swimming after it.

The two Harpe brothers were still watching.

"Where did that other boat come from?" Big Harpe said.

"I don't know," Little Harpe said. "An' I ain't waitin' to find out. Let's git!"

They rode off, while the other pirates scrambled up the bank and ran into the woods.

"Head fer shore, Cap!" Davy called to Captain Cobb. "We'll round up the rest o' them varmints!"

Captain Cobb nodded and shoved at the tiller. He almost fell over the side as the rudder broke off and quickly floated away.

"Now what made that rudder bust loose?" he said, scratching his head.

"Can't say fer sure," Davy said. "But I got a pretty good idea."

He and Russel glared at Mike Fink, who smiled sweetly at them.

"You fellas is sure havin' bad luck, ain't you?" said Mike, shaking his head sadly. "Sorry we can't help you none."

Turning to his crew, Mike shouted, "Shove off, boys! We got a race to win!"

And while the *Bertha Mae* drifted helplessly in the current, the *Gullywhumper* went on. Working as fast as he could, Captain Cobb rigged up a sweep oar to use in place of a rudder.

Then the *Bertha Mae,* too, went on, down the Ohio and into the broad Mississippi. Late one night Davy and his crew put in at the town of New Madrid, to buy a new rudder. The first thing they saw was the *Gullywhumper.*

"Guess Mike didn't expect us to catch up so soon. There's nobody aboard," Russel said. "It sure would be easy to take his rudder!"

"Sure would," Davy said. "But we better not. We gotta win this race fair an' square."

"I guess so," said Russel, sighing.

"Well, I'll go an' git us a new rudder," Captain Cobb said. "Won't take too much time if they've got one already made up. I hope they have. 'Cause Mike Fink ain't gonna wait, once he finds out we're here."

Just then there was a burst of laughter, coming from the Devil's Elbow Tavern nearby.

"Sounds like Mike an' his boys are havin' a good time," Davy said. "Maybe me an' Russel can keep 'em entertained fer a while." He took two rifles from the gun rack and handed one to Russel. Davy and Russel walked over to the tavern. Looking in at the window, they could see Mike Fink. He was standing next to the owner of the tavern, a rifle in one hand, a mug in the other.

He put his mug on the tavern owner's head. The man shook so hard that the mug jiggled and almost fell right off.

"Y-you ain't aimin' t-to shoot this off'n my h-head, Mr. Fink!" said the owner. "Supposin' you m-miss?"

"They's nothin' to it. Jest hold steady—like this." Mike took off his cap and put the mug on his own head.

The next minute there was the crack of a rifle shot. The mug on Mike's head broke into bits, drenching his head and face. Slowly Mike looked around. His eyes grew round with surprise as he saw Davy and Russel in the doorway.

"How's that fer shootin'?" said Davy, lowering his smoking rifle.

Mike ripped a piece off the shirt of one of his crew. After wiping his face, he put on his cap.

"Crockett," he said, "it's mighty lucky fer you I can take a joke. To tell the truth, I feel sorry fer you. Why, I'll be halfway to New Orleans afore you git that rudder fixed." Turning to his men, Mike shouted, "Come on, boys! Let's shove off!"

Russel whispered to Davy, "We gotta keep him here till our rudder's fixed. Let me handle him."

Then Russel started talking to Mike. And he didn't stop talking until he'd talked Mike into doing some fancy shooting.

Putting a mug on his head, Mike faced the mirror on the wall. He pointed his rifle over his shoulder, sighted in the mirror, and fired at a copper pan hanging over the fireplace. The bullet hit the pan, bounced back, and drilled a hole in the mug on his head.

"Tolerable good shootin', fer a river man," Davy said. "Now watch this."

Winking at Russel, Davy stood facing the mirror. He pointed his rifle back over his shoulder and pulled the trigger. The bullet hit the copper pan, bounced off, and hit a ship's bell hanging on the wall. It bounced from the bell, hit the re-

Mike let Russel talk him into doing some fancy shooting against Davy.

flector of a lantern, and bounced again. Davy jumped around, catching the bullet in his teeth.

At least, that's the way it looked. Davy had really held a bullet in his mouth all the time. The bullet he fired had hit a keg standing near him. Russel had plugged up the hole in the keg with a cork. But Mike Fink hadn't seen any of this, nor had his men. They were sure that Davy had caught the bullet.

"I . . . I don't believe it," said Mike. "I know I saw it with my own eyes, but it can't be so."

Just then Captain Cobb stuck his head in at the door. He signaled to Davy that their boat's rudder was fixed.

Russel frowned.

"We still gotta keep Mike here a while, if we want to get ahead," he whispered to Davy. "What'll we do now?"

Mike Eats His Hat

It didn't take Davy long to figure out what to do.

"Maybe we could git 'em to fightin' amongst themselves," he whispered.

Russel nodded and looked around. Standing closest to him were two of Mike's crew—a big fellow named Moose, and a little fellow named Jocko. Passing behind Moose, Russel cut Moose's suspenders with his hunting knife. While Moose grabbed for his pants, Davy picked up Jocko's drink and poured it over Moose's head.

Moose blamed Jocko for what had happened, and swung a big fist at him. Jocko swung back, and the two started fighting. By the time Davy and Russel reached the door, every man in the room had joined the fight. Mugs and bottles flew through the air. Tables and chairs crashed to the floor. Roaring at his men, Mike tried to pull them apart. But his men roared right back and went on fighting.

Davy and Russel smiled at each other.

"That'll do nicely," Davy said.

They hurried down to the landing, where the *Bertha Mae* had been fitted with a new rudder. Captain Cobb and the crew were all on board, ready to go.

"Git your poles, boys," Davy said. "Here's our chance to git ahead o' Mike—an' maybe win the race."

For a week Davy and his men poled down the mighty Mississippi, until it wound its way through the fields of Louisiana. Davy kept a sharp lookout for Mike, but there was no sign of the *Gullywhumper*. It looked as though Davy couldn't help winning the race.

Then, as the boat was passing a little island, Davy heard a shout. An old man, his clothes all in rags, was calling for help.

When the boat drew closer, the old man said, "You're the first folks I've seen since my flatboat went to pieces an' marooned me here!"

"Well, we'll fix that. Come aboard," Davy said.

"Thankee kindly, son," the old man said. "Mind waitin' till I fetch my livestock?"

And he went into the underbrush and began driving out a cow, a goat, a sheep, a mule, and some pigs and chickens.

"We ain't got time to load all them critters!" said Russel.

"We sure ain't!" shouted Captain Cobb, pointing upriver. "Here comes the *Gullywhumper!*"

"Cap's right!" Russel said. "It's Mike an' his boys, sure enough, an' they're polin' like fury!"

Captain Cobb nodded. "Even if we did git them animals aboard, it'd be too crowded fer us to pole. Davy, tell the old man to fergit his livestock an' come on!"

"No," Davy said. "That wouldn't be right. Let's give the old feller a hand, an' take him an' his critters home."

Davy and his crew rounded up the livestock.

Led by Davy, the crew jumped ashore and helped round up the old man's livestock. They were still at it when the *Gullywhumper* came by.

"Well, well!" Mike said. "If it ain't my old friend Davy Crockett! Mighty obligin' o' you to wait fer us like this!"

Mike let out a big laugh, while his crew worked the poles even faster. As the *Gullywhumper* left the *Bertha Mae* behind, Mike looked back over his shoulders.

He roared, "See you in New Orleans! I'll be waitin' fer your furs, Crockett! Wa-hoo!"

It took a long time to load the old man's livestock on the boat. And it took just as long to get him to his home on the bayou.

"I'm sure thankful to you fellers," he said. "Too bad, though, your boat's so big. If she was a mite smaller, you could save forty mile by takin' this here bayou."

"Eh? What's that?" Captain Cobb said. "I don't know of any other passage here."

"There is one, though. I been down it in my skiff plenty o' times. It runs right back into the Mississippi jest above New Orleans."

"What's the difference," grumbled Russel. "We lost the race already."

"Jest a minute! Think there's a chance o' us gittin' through?" Davy asked the old man.

"Well," the old man said, "it would be a tight

squeeze, all right. But if you'd cut a few trees out o' your way an' don't mind scrapin' the bottom o' your boat a little—well, you might make it, at that."

Davy shouted to the crew, excitement in his voice. "Boys, maybe we ain't lost this race yet! Let's git goin'—we got a lot o' time to make up!"

"Davy, you jest don't know when you're whupped," Russel said.

But he picked up his pole with the others, and the *Bertha Mae* started off.

It was hard work getting the boat through the overgrown bayou. Sometimes Davy and his men dragged the boat along with a line. At other times they pushed, standing waist-deep in the slimy water.

They had to cut down trailing vines and limbs of trees, and keep a sharp eye out for alligators and water snakes. Still they went on, while overhead the swamp birds cried out, darting through the Spanish moss that hung thickly from the huge trees everywhere around.

At last they reached a wider channel, and then the Mississippi itself. A cheer burst from the men as they saw the *Gullywhumper* just ahead.

"We been practicin' long enough, boys," Davy said. "Now let's show 'em somethin'!"

Aboard the *Gullywhumper,* Mike Fink let out a roar of rage and surprise.

"Down on them poles!" he shouted to his crew. "If you don't git me to that landin' ahead o' Crockett, I'll split your heads wide open an' toss you in the river for catfish bait!"

Downstream raced the two boats, getting closer and closer to the landing at New Orleans. Mike's men worked at their poles for all they were worth—but so did Davy's. The *Bertha Mae* overtook the *Gullywhumper,* then drew slightly ahead.

"By thunder," yelled Mike, "we still got a trick

One man after another fell off, as Mike's crew used the Pittsburgh punch.

or two to show 'em! Boys, give 'em the Pittsburgh punch!"

"The Pittsburgh punch it is!" Mike's crew shouted back. And they began jabbing at Davy and his men with their long poles.

Davy managed to duck, but one of his men staggered and fell overboard.

"So they want to play rough, do they?" said Davy, raising his pole.

"Let's give 'em what fer, Davy!" called Russel. "We're almost there!"

The next thing that happened, both crews were going for each other with their poles. *Splash! Splash! Splash!* One man after another fell into the river, until only Davy, Russel, and Captain Cobb were left aboard the *Bertha Mae*. Mike Fink wasn't doing any better. Besides himself, only two crewmen were still on their feet.

"Git to the landin'! Git to the landin'!" Mike roared.

Leaving the tiller, he picked up a pole and pushed with all his might. The trouble was he pushed too hard, and the pole snapped in two. Mike went flying through the air, hitting the water with a tremendous splash.

At the same time, the *Bertha Mae* shot forward. It plowed into the mud at the landing, just a few feet ahead of the *Gullywhumper*.

"Ya-hoo! Ee-yip-ee!" yelled Russel. "We win! We win!"

He gave Davy a bear hug, while Captain Cobb danced around the deck. Mike came splashing toward the boat, and Davy and Russel helped him aboard. He stood there, looking sheepish, and dripping water as though he'd been left out in the rain for three weeks.

Mike shook his head sadly. "What's the world gonna say? Mike Fink, king o' the river, losin' to the king o' the wild frontier an' a pack o' land-lubbers." And he heaved a great sigh.

"Well, now," Davy said. "I don't see no reason why the world ever has to know about this."

"What!" said Mike, astonished. "You mean—you'd keep somethin' as historical as this quiet?"

"Why not?" Davy said.

"We won fair. Ain't that enough?" Russel said. "Leastways, it is fer us."

A big smile spread all over Mike's face. "Where's my hat?" he asked.

Captain Cobb had fished it out of the water, and now he handed it to Mike.

"Crockett," Mike said, "I said I'd eat my hat if I lost, and a promise is a promise."

And, while Davy and Russel watched, grinning, Mike ate his hat, red feather and all.

"We won fair," Russel said.

"It's been a real pleasure knowin' you, ol' hoss," Davy said to Mike.

Trouble with the Chickasaws

AFTER WINNING the keelboat race, Davy and Russel sold their furs in New Orleans. Then they said good-by to Captain Cobb, and traveled back up the river on the *Gullywhumper*. For weeks they helped pole the boat up the Mississippi, until they reached Tennessee.

"You can put us ashore anywhere along here," Davy said to Mike.

Mike swung the tiller over.

"Don't see why you bristle-headed varmints can't land at a settlement, instead o' here in the wilderness," Mike said.

"Because this is the shortest way for us to git home," Davy answered. "We'll git us some horses from the Chickasaw Injuns. This is their country, an' they're real friendly."

As the boat pulled up at the river bank, Davy shook hands with Mike.

"It's been a real pleasure knowin' you, ol' hoss," Davy said.

"I ain't likely to forgit you two, neither," said Mike.

Picking up their rifles and bed-rolls, Davy and Russel jumped to shore.

"Hey, wait!" called Mike. "You forgot this!" And he held up a sack with something heavy in it.

"Oh, that's for you!" Davy said. "Jest a little somethin' to remember us by."

Opening up the sack, Mike lifted out a small brass cannon. On it were inscribed these words:

TO
MIKE FINK
KING OF THE RIVER
FROM HIS ADMIRERS
Davy Crockett and G. Russel

Russel winked at Davy. "Mike, we figgered you'd need somethin' to pertect you from them redskin pirates upriver. But that ain't all. There's somethin' else in the sack for you."

Reaching into the sack again, Mike found a new hat with an extra-long feather. Proudly he put it on his head.

"Aw, you shouldn't 'a done it!" he said. But anybody could see that he was pleased with his gifts.

"That's all right, Mike," Davy said. "Georgie an' me didn't want anybody thinkin' you wasn't still king o' the river."

"Huh!" Mike roared. "No danger o' that! An' if you bushwhackers ever git a hankerin' to be river men again, look me up!"

"We will, Mike," Davy said.

Mike shouted an order to his crew, and the *Gullywhumper* began to move upstream.

Grinning, Davy and Russel waved good-by, then turned into the woods. They soon came to a trail that wound through the trees and brush.

"Sure is good to be back," Davy said, as they walked happily along.

Russel nodded. And he sang:

Davy, Davy Crockett—
Back in the woods again!

But when they reached a small clearing, Davy held up his hand.

"What's the matter?" Russel asked.

"If you'd listen, you'd know. Ain't nothin' singin' but you."

Russel listened. "Hey, you're right! Ain't a sound. Birds, squirrels—nothin'. Somethin's scared 'em. Must be a Chickasaw huntin' party around. Let's find 'em!"

"Reckon they'll find *us,* if we stick to the trail," Davy said.

They walked on again, until Russel stooped to take a twig out of his moccasin. Suddenly there was a loud twang and the clatter of a rifle falling to the ground. Russel looked up quickly. Davy had stepped into the loop of a snare tied to the top of a sapling. Now he hung in the air, head down.

"Ain't nothin' singin' but you!" said Davy.

Russel started toward him, laughing. "Stepped in an ol' Injun deer snare, did you? Good thing Mike Fink can't see the king o' the wild frontier now!"

Davy waved his arms. "Stop laughin', you tarnal idiot, an' cut me loose!"

"No need to fuss," said Russel, still laughing.

But before he could get out his knife, there was another loud twang. A bent sapling near him snapped upright, and the snare tied to it pulled Russel into the air. He, too, had stepped into the loop of a trap—just as Davy had done a minute before.

"Hey!" cried Russel, dangling helplessly by one leg.

Then, whooping and shrieking, a band of Indian warriors burst out of the woods. They cut down Davy and Russel, threw them to the ground, and tied their hands behind their backs.

"What's got into you crazy Chickasaws!" Davy said. "We're friends!"

And Russel added, "You Injuns are makin' a terrible mistake. That's Davy Crockett you're hog-tyin'. Understand? He's Davy Crockett!"

The Indians seemed to understand, for they stared at Davy for a moment. But they did not release their prisoners. Instead, they pulled Davy and Russel to their feet, stuffed gags in their

Rushing out of the woods, the Indians threw Davy down and tied his hands.

mouths, and forced them to mount horses that had been hidden in the woods. The Indians mounted horses themselves, and they all rode off. After many weary miles of travel, they reached the Chickasaw village.

The warriors took the gags away from Davy and Russel and pushed them, still bound, into a little log hut. Several of the Indians stood guard outside.

Russel took a deep breath and sat down.

"So we was gonna git horses from the friendly Chickasaws!" he said bitterly. "Friendly!"

Davy sat down beside him. "I don't understand it. Somethin's mighty wrong to put these Injuns on the warpath. Never had a bit o' trouble with 'em before."

"What do you think they're gonna do to us?"

"Shouldn't be too hard to guess," Davy said.

They stopped talking and stood up as two Indians entered the hut. One was Black Eagle, the Chickasaw chief. The other was a warrior of another tribe. His body was painted a bright red.

"My braves say you are Davy Crockett," Black Eagle said. "They say you are friend of red man."

"We both are!" Russel said. "An' look how you're treating us!"

"We will not hurt you," Black Eagle said. "But we cannot let you go."

"But why? An' what are you all doin' in war paint?" asked Davy.

"We go to avenge murder of our brothers," Black Eagle answered. Pointing to the warrior beside him, he went on. "This messenger come from chief of the Kaskaskias. White men are killing his people—hunting them like animals!"

Davy looked thoughtful. "Kaskaskias. . . . Their country is up on the Ohio River, around Cave-In Rock, ain't it?"

"Sure!" Russel said. "An' no wonder folks is shootin' at 'em! They're the ones who've been attackin' the boats on the river!"

The warrior spat on the ground at Russel's feet. "Lies! White man's lies!" he shouted, his voice filling the hut.

"No," Davy said. "We saw 'em ourselves. We helped bust up a raid on Mike Fink's boat not more'n three months ago. I tell you, we saw 'em!"

"More lies!" the warrior said. "Three months ago my people were far from the river! They were hiding from white men."

All four men were silent, as Davy and the warrior stared at each other.

At last Davy said slowly, "I believe you. Them river pirates must've been white men dressin' as Injuns, so you'd git the blame. You turn me an' Russel loose, an' we'll run them varmints out in the open. We'll see that folks hear the truth an' stop puttin' the blame on you."

"It is too late," Black Eagle said. "Already other war messengers have gone to the Shawnee, the Miami, the Kickapoo, and the Chippewa."

"You got to stop 'em! Send out runners o' your own! Tell the chiefs they must keep the peace!"

"Peace!" repeated Black Eagle. "Know this, Davy Crockett. We have always wanted peace with white man. But he does not want peace with us. He makes treaties, but he believes any evil he hears of us."

Davy nodded. "That's right. But it works two ways. Why start a war jest because of a few no-good, murderin' whites? It ain't worth it, chief."

Again there was silence. Then Black Eagle spoke. "I will send the runners. I will try to stop the war. But we will wait only until the full of the moon."

Calling in two of the guards, Black Eagle ordered them to untie Davy and Russel.

The two frontiersmen were free. But unless they could run down the river pirates, there would be war between red man and white.

Yaller, Yaller Gold

Using horses that the Chickasaws had given them, Davy and Russel rode to the river. They reached it at night.

"The ol' *Gullywhumper* ought'a be passin' by soon," Davy said. "We got a long way ahead, thanks to them Injuns."

"You sure Mike will want to throw in with us?" Russel asked.

"It's his river we aim to clean up, ain't it?" said Davy.

They didn't have long to wait until the *Gullywhumper* came floating by. Mike was glad to see them. They all had a good rest that night, and the next day they tried to figure out the best thing to do about the river pirates.

"You know, Davy," Mike said, "you showed good sense, comin' to me fer help. Makes no difference if them pirates is white or red. Me an' my skullbusters will make mincemeat out o' 'em."

"Sure," said Davy. "But we gotta find 'em first."

Mike grunted. "That ain't gonna be so easy. I ain't sartin they'll show themselves after the whoppin' I give 'em comin' downriver. They'll recognize the ol' *Gullywhumper* an' keep out o' sight."

He broke off as one of the crew called out, "Hey, Mike, look what's comin'!"

Another keelboat, with nobody on board, was drifting toward them.

"Why, it's the *Monongahela Belle!*" said Mike.

Ordering his crew to hold the *Gullywhumper* alongside, Mike jumped to the deck of the *Monongahela Belle*. Davy followed him, and the two looked around. Broken boxes, barrels, and empty sacks were strewn everywhere. Arrows were stuck in the wood of the cabin, and a tomahawk was stuck in the planking of the deck.

Mike shook his head slowly. "More o' them pirates' work. Looks like the crew put up a real fight afore they was wiped out."

Mike picked up one of the arrows.

"Don't tell me the pirates ain't Injuns!" he said.

Davy looked closely at the arrow. Russel had been watching from the *Gullywhumper*, and now he jumped across and stood at Davy's side.

"No Injun ever made this arrow," Davy said.

"You're right, Davy," agreed Russel. "There's no tribal markin's, an' it ain't feathered right." Looking thoughtfully up the river, he said, "Wonder how far this boat drifted since the massacree."

"No way o' tellin'," Mike said. "But I know one thing. When I meet up with them pirates, they better look out, because they're gonna git what's comin' to 'em."

And, with a fierce look on his face, he made a fist of one huge hand and drove it hard into the palm of the other.

After his boat was disguised, Mike helped Davy search for the pirates.

A few hours later, the *Gullywhumper* was drawn up at the bank of the river. But it no longer looked like the *Gullywhumper*. On its cabin was some fancy scrollwork that had been taken from the *Monongahela Belle*. The little cannon had been hidden in the cabin and covered with a blanket.

Even the boat's name was different. The word *Gullywhumper* on the side had been painted out. Over it had been painted the boat's new name—*Bonanza*.

But it wasn't only the boat that had been disguised. Mike no longer wore his red shirt and his boatman's hat with a red feather in it. He was wearing a tight cutaway coat and gaiter pants. Besides, he had on a dickey, a tie, and a plug hat. He was dressed exactly like a banker—and that's just what he was supposed to be.

Pushing out his chest, Mike turned around, while Davy carefully looked him over.

"Not bad," Davy said. "Pretty lucky for us, findin' these duds on the *Monongahela Belle*. They fit kinda tight, but they'll do."

Mike pointed toward a few of his men. They were carrying heavily loaded sacks up the gangplank and into the cabin.

"Hey!" he said. "What're they doin'?"

"Carryin' sacks."

"I can see that, you ornery bushwhacker! What's in them sacks?"

"Rocks," answered Davy.

Mike's mouth fell open. "What in thunderation you up to?"

"Well, it's like this," Davy said. "You're pretendin' to be a banker, ain't you?"

"Yes, sir!" Mike said. "King o' the bankers—

that's me! On my way to Shawneetown to open a new bank! But what's these here rocks got to do with it?"

"You sure are thickheaded. You can't open a bank without money—an' that's what's supposed to be in the sacks. Gold—real Spanish gold."

"Now I un'erstan'!" roared Mike, smiling. "That's so folks will think we're rich."

Davy nodded. "I figger that if we stop at a couple o' towns so's folks will hear about our gold, word will git upriver to the pirates faster'n we can."

"Then when we come along, the pirates will pop up an' try to nab our gold," Mike said. "But instead, we'll nab *them*."

"Yeah," said Davy. "At least, that's the way I'm hopin' it will work out."

And so Davy and Mike and the rest continued their journey up the river, stopping at a few towns along the way. Wherever they stopped, Mike let folks know that he was a banker and had sacks of gold aboard the boat. But not until the last town before Cave-In Rock was there any word of the pirates.

There, in the tavern, a well-dressed man said to Mike, "You're taking a big risk, sir—carrying your gold on the river. Things aren't safe up this way any more."

"Guess you mean them Injun pirates," Mike said. "Know what I think? That's jest talk! I'll believe in them Injuns when I see 'em!"

"You've got to believe it, sir! Wrecks of boats drift by here all the time. As for what happens to the crews—well, dead men don't talk much. But plenty have been fished from the river."

Mike laughed. "No use tryin' to scare me off, mister. I'm takin' that gold to Shawneetown to start a new bank, Injuns or no Injuns."

A jolly little man in a plug hat walked over to Mike. He had been sitting in a corner, playing a banjo.

"Let me introduce myself, sir," he said. "I am Colonel Plug, a peddler from down East. I carry a full line of medicines—pills and potions, salves and lotions, good for man or beast. I play the banjo and sing a bit to drum up trade."

Mike was dressed like a banker.

"I know," Mike said. "I was listenin' to you before. If there's anythin' I like it's good banjo music, an' I sure admire the way you play."

Colonel Plug smiled. "Thank you, sir. I couldn't help overhearing what you were just saying. Do you really intend to go on upriver?"

"I aim to, an' I'm goin' to," Mike answered.

"Well," Colonel Plug said, "it happens that I myself am most anxious to get up to Shawneetown. Do you suppose you'd have room for me on your boat?"

Mike glanced quickly at Davy and Russel, who were standing near by.

"We're mighty crowded already," Davy said.

Colonel Plug said smoothly, "I don't take up much room. All I have is my sample cases and my banjo."

"Now look here," Mike said to Davy. "A little music never hurt nobody. I'm the boss banker o' this here outfit, an' I say Plug goes!"

"Guess he does, then," said Davy, shrugging his shoulders.

As Mike and Plug left the tavern and headed for the boat, Russel turned to Davy.

"There's somethin' mighty fishy about that peddler," he said quietly. "Why are you lettin' Mike bring him aboard?"

" 'Cause he's the first sucker that nibbled at our bait," Davy answered.

And he and Russel walked out of the tavern and followed Mike and Plug to the boat.

The next day the keelboat *Bonanza,* formerly the *Gullywhumper,* was moving up the river again. Davy handled the tiller. Mike sat on a molasses barrel and smoked a big cigar.

"Like to hear a little music?" asked Plug, sitting down on the cabin near Mike.

"Don't mind if I do," Mike said.

"You know, I've got a little song I've been saving for a time like this," Plug said. "Hope you like it." He played his banjo and sang:

Her lips was red as cherries,
And her hair was yaller,
yaller gold . . .

He sang it sweet and he sang it loud, especially the words *yaller, yaller gold.* His voice carried over the water and to the shore, where two of the river pirates were hiding. They were the Harpe brothers, Big Harpe and Little Harpe.

"Hear that?" said Big Harpe, smiling a horrible smile. "That's Plug. And that song means he's found gold."

Little Harpe raised a brass telescope.

"Yeah," he said. "I can see him now, aboard the *Bonanza.* Plug don't make mistakes. He must'a seen where they got gold stacked up in the cabin. Won't be long till it's ours."

The two men grinned at each other. Hurrying to their horses, they rode off through the woods. By evening they had reached the big cave with the sign over the entrance:

WILSON'S CAVE-INN
GOOD DRINKS AND ENTERTAINMENT

The Harpe brothers pushed past a couple of guards and went into the pirates' hide-out. The great cavern was lit by smoking torches that threw strange shadows on the walls. Around the tables sat pirates playing cards, singing, quarreling noisily, or just drinking from jugs and bottles. Other pirates were looking over their loot—guns and knives of all kinds, kegs of gunpowder, bolts of cloth, tools, gleaming silverware. Still others were repairing the clothes they wore when they disguised themselves as Indians.

At the back of the cave sat Sam Mason, the pirates' chief. He looked up at the Harpes.

Little Harpe said slowly, "Keelboat comin' upriver. A fat one, too. And Plug's aboard."

"Good for him! What's the cargo?"

"Gold," answered Big Harpe.

Big Harpe smiled. "Yeah," he said. "Gold . . . yaller, yaller gold."

"Rocks!" Plug whispered hoarsely. "I've been tricked good and proper!"

The Pirates Attack

As THE sun rose above the misty river, Mike's boat moved quietly upstream. The only sound was the slap and swish of the water, and the cries of birds in the woods.

Davy was at the tiller, carefully watching the shore. Near him sat Russel. He was getting their rifles ready for use.

"This waitin' makes me nervous," Russel said. "Time's gittin' short—that moon was half full last night. If we don't come across them pirates soon, the Injuns will be on the warpath."

"We still got a few days," Davy said.

"Gonna take a few days to git word back to the Chickasaws."

"Well," said Davy, "don't reckon we got too long to wait, now."

"Glad to hear you say that, Davy," Mike said, coming across the deck. "My boys is all ready. They're chock-full o' fight an' itchin' to go!"

"Sh! Not so loud!" warned Russel. "We don't want Plug to hear."

"Aw, he's still sleepin'," Mike said.

"I better make sure," Davy said.

Going to the cabin, Davy opened the hatch and peered in. Barrels of molasses were stacked about, and the sacks of rocks. Plug lay stretched out, wrapped up in a blanket, his eyes closed.

"He's sleepin', all right," muttered Davy. Closing the hatch, he went back to the tiller.

But inside the cabin, Plug warily opened his eyes. He waited a moment, then kicked off the blanket and picked up a large auger. With it he bored a hole in the side of the boat. As water spurted in, he hastily closed the hole with a wooden plug. Attached to the plug was a cord, which he threaded through two eyelets on the wall and the roof of the cabin. Next he tied a brass hook to the end of the cord. He pushed it through a crack in the cabin wall, so that it hung out and could be reached from the deck.

Plug smiled with satisfaction. "A neat job, if I do say so myself. When the time comes, I'll pull the cord. The plug will come out, water will come in, and the boat will start sinkin'. That'll give Mason and the boys a chance to get at the gold."

Then Plug noticed that the cord was caught on one of the sacks.

"Better fix this," he said.

As he moved the sack, it split open. Rocks spilled out at his feet. Plug stared at them, amazed. Whipping out his knife, he slashed open a few more sacks.

"Rocks!" he whispered hoarsely. "And more rocks! So that's their gold! I've been tricked!"

Plug's hands shook with fury. He reached for his banjo, and accidentally pulled off the blanket that covered Mike's cannon.

"Huh! What's this here?" Plug said.

He stooped to read the inscription:

TO
MIKE FINK
KING OF THE RIVER
FROM HIS ADMIRERS
Davy Crockett and G. Russel

"Mike Fink!" Plug said. "Davy Crockett! Oh, no! What've I got into? I've been tricked good and proper! I better warn Mason before it's too late."

He rushed out on deck with his banjo. He smiled nervously at Davy and Mike.

"Excuse me, gentlemen," he said. "Had a little trouble sleeping. Thought you might like a little music."

He plucked his banjo once and began to sing at the top of his voice. He hadn't sung more than one note before Davy and Mike clapped their hands on him.

"From now on," roared Mike, "we want nothin' from you but silence—an' all-fired little o' that!"

In a few minutes Plug was tied, gagged, and tossed back into the cabin. Davy propped him up so that he sat wedged in between two molasses barrels, right opposite the hole he had drilled.

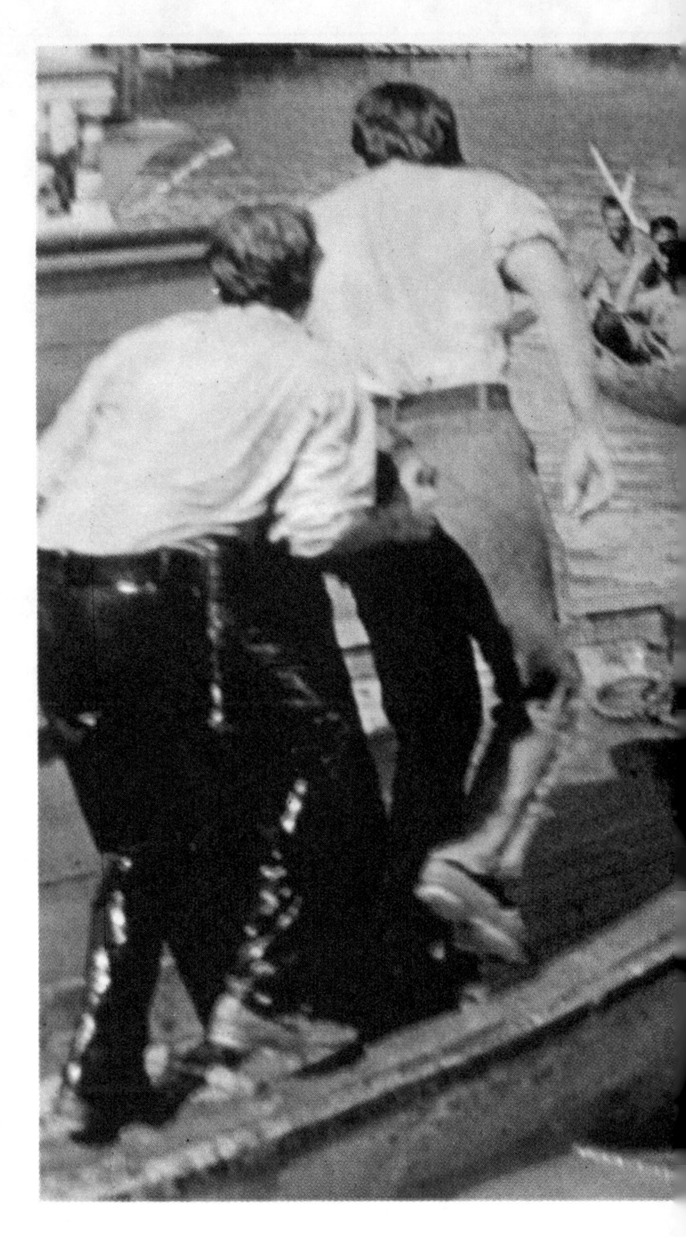

Russel came into the cabin, grumbling. "Mike wants his pop-gun."

Together, Russel and Davy picked up the cannon and carried it out on deck.

"If I'd'a knowed we was gonna have to tote this thing, I'd'a argued fer a pistol," Russel said.

But Mike paid no attention to him.

"Hey, Moose!" said Mike, calling to one of his crew. "Come back here an' be gunner!"

"Whatever you say, Mike," Moose said.

The river pirates came at the boat in their canoes, whooping like Indians.

Moose started toward the cannon, brushing against the cabin. The little brass hook sticking out through a crack caught on his coat.

Moose did not notice it—nor did he know that the hook was at the end of the cord Plug had rigged up. But as he walked back, the cord tightened, pulling out the plug from the hole in the boat's side.

Inside the cabin, a jet of water shot through the hole and splashed right in Plug's face. Frantically, he tried to move out of the way. But no matter how he tried, he could not budge, and the gag stopped him from calling out. His eyes bulging with terror, Plug could only make little squeaking sounds, while the water kept pouring in.

Standing on deck, Mike said to Davy and Russel, "We're almost to the place where they jumped us before. An' that reminds me—I've worn this monkey suit long enough!"

He ripped off his banker's clothes—the cutaway coat, the tie, and the dickey.

"That's better," he growled.

Davy and Russel crouched on deck, their rifles ready. Moose was bent over the cannon. Slowly the keelboat moved along the bluff.

Suddenly a shot rang out from the woods. There was a wild whooping and yelling, and the pirates, dressed as Indians, came paddling out from shore in their canoes.

"Here they come!" Davy said.

Mike bellowed to his men, "What you slowin' down for? Close in! Lay on them poles!"

"What you think we're doin'?" his crew shouted back. "We're draggin' bottom! Them blasted rocks are weighin' us down!"

"Moose! Git rid o' them rocks!" ordered Mike.

He gave Moose a kick to help him on his way. Moose went flying into the cabin, where he fell in the water with a great splash.

Sputtering and muttering, Moose got to his feet. He looked around in surprise and saw Plug, in water up to his chin. Moose picked up Plug, hung him by his coat collar from a hook in the ceiling, and rushed out.

"We're sinkin'!" yelled Moose.

The boat lurched, almost knocking the men on deck off their feet, but luckily the water was shallow. At the same time the pirates were coming closer and closer, shooting arrows from their canoes.

"Sinkin'?" roared Mike. "We're sunk! Drop your poles! Grab your guns an' let 'em have it!"

Then the crack of rifle fire echoed over the river, as Davy and Russel and the river men began to battle the pirates.

Playing Rough

TAKING COVER from the arrows behind a barrel, Davy and Russel fired their rifles. Their shots hit a pirate in each of the two lead canoes. The injured men fell back, overturning the canoes, and dumping the other pirates into the water.

More pirates were coming at the boat from the rear. Mike and Moose fired the cannon at them, but missed. While arrows hummed past his head, Mike picked up the cannon in his arms.

"Pour the powder in!" Mike said. "Don't be stingy! Fill 'er up!"

Moose did as he was told. Still holding the cannon in his arms, Mike aimed it at the pirates.

"Let 'er go!" he ordered, and Moose touched off the cannon with a piece of lighted punk.

With a tremendous blast, the cannon fired. It blew a large hole in a canoe—but the recoil sent Mike tumbling into the river. Splashing through the water, Mike saw pirates in another canoe showering Davy and Russel with arrows.

"Wa-hoo!" roared Mike.

Lifting one end of the canoe out of the water, he flung the pirates helter-skelter. One of them tried to sneak up on Mike from behind, but Mike caught a glimpse of him out of the corner of his eye. Mike turned quickly, bringing down his fist on the pirate's head like a sledge hammer.

Meanwhile, several canoes had reached the boat, and the pirates started to climb on deck. With no time to reload their rifles, Davy and Russel and the crew used their muskets as clubs. Davy leaped aside as a tomahawk came flying at him and buried itself in a barrel of molasses. Some of the molasses dripped down the side of the barrel—and that gave Davy an idea. He pulled out the tomahawk, knocked in the top of the barrel, and called to Russel.

"Give me a hand with this, Georgie!" he said.

Together they lifted the barrel and poured molasses over the deck.

"Now let 'em come!" said Davy. "Jest watch this!"

As the pirates stepped on the slippery stuff, their legs slid out from under them. Waving their arms and calling for help, they fell over the side into the water.

But there were more pirates swarming over the boat. Armed with tomahawks, knives, and meat cleavers, they came at Davy and Russel.

The two frontiersmen fought back with anything they could lay their hands on. Davy threw

Davy and Russel poured molasses over the deck.

the empty molasses barrel over the head of one ugly fellow waving a cutlass. Davy crowned another pirate with Plug's banjo. Then Davy pushed several pirates toward Russel, who hit them on the head with a big frying pan. And all over the boat, Mike's crew kept on battling, with rifles and clubs and their own big fists.

Watching the fighting from the shore was Sam Mason, the pirate chief.

"What's holdin' 'em up out there?" he said to the Harpe brothers.

"Them boatmen is puttin' up an awful good fight," answered Big Harpe.

"We'll fix that," Mason said. "Get the powder canoe into the water."

He pointed to a canoe hidden under a tree. In the canoe was a keg of powder, with a fuse attached to it.

Little Harpe looked up at Mason. "We can't use that now. It'll blow up our own men!"

"What of it?" said Mason. "It won't hurt *us* none. Now do what I tell you."

The Harpe brothers glanced at each other and shrugged.

"All right, Mason. We'll do it," Big Harpe said.

The Harpes got the canoe into the water, then Big Harpe went back into the woods.

"Hurry up!" Mason called after him.

In less than a minute, Big Harpe was back, carrying a flaming stick of wood. Mason took the stick from his hand and held the flame to the fuse. It sputtered and caught fire.

The three men waded into the water and began pushing the canoe. When the water was up to their chests, Mason said:

"Let 'er go!"

The three outlaws gave a mighty shove, and the canoe went skimming toward Mike's boat. The pirates who were still in canoes paddled frantically away and shouted out a warning. On

Davy and Russel fought with anything they could lay their hands on.

the deck of the boat, the pirates dropped their weapons, jumped into the river, and swam off in all directions.

"Yahoo!" yelled Russel. "We got 'em on the run!"

Davy pointed to the canoe with the powder keg. It was coming straight at the boat.

"No wonder!" Davy said. "Look what's comin'!"

"Wh-what'll we do?" said Russel.

Davy didn't bother to answer. He picked up a pole, and held off the canoe just as it was about to hit. Using all his strength, he gave the canoe a push toward shore.

Russel let out a long breath. "Whew! Somebody's playin' mighty rough! Where do you suppose that came from?"

"From them, out there," Davy said, pointing to Mason and the Harpes.

The three outlaws stood in the water, looking at the canoe in terror. On, on it came, while the flame crept along the fuse toward the powder.

"Help! It'll blow us to kingdom come!" cried Little Harpe.

"Duck!" shouted Mason.

They dived under the water, so that the canoe passed over their heads. There was a loud explosion as the canoe blew up near the shore, scattering wreckage everywhere.

Frightened but unhurt, Mason and the Harpes raised their dripping heads.

"Don't stand there like idiots! Come on!" Mason said. He scrambled to shore, and the Harpes followed.

Aboard the keelboat, Russel, Davy, and Mike had been watching the three pirates.

"Hey! They're gittin' away!" Russel said.

"Oh, no they ain't!" said Davy. He turned to Mike. "You an' your boys take the rest o' them. Me an' Georgie will run them three down."

He and Russel jumped into the water and swam for shore. Climbing up the river bank, they looked around.

"No sign o' them cutthroats," Russel said.

"Wait! Boot tracks! Under that tree over there," Davy said. "They're the ones we want."

Davy broke a branch off a tree to use as a club, and Russel did the same. Then, warily, they began to follow the tracks through the forest.

In the Cave

MASON AND the Harpe brothers hurried along the trail that led to the pirates' cave. At the entrance to the cave, Mason said to Big Harpe:

"You stay here and keep watch."

Big Harpe looked at Mason suspiciously. "What about my share?"

"You'll get what's comin' to you."

And so, while Big Harpe stood guard, Mason and Little Harpe walked into the cave. A few torches, set in brackets on the walls, were still burning. The flickering light fell on the tables, which had been covered with tablecloths to make the place look like a real tavern.

Picking up three saddlebags, Mason and Little Harpe went into a passage that opened off a side wall toward the back of the cave. In front of them was a heavy door with a huge iron lock. Mason unlocked the door, and the two pirates stepped into a small side-cavern. It was used as a storeroom for loot. Piled up in it were trunks, a big chest, kegs of powder, and all sorts of farm tools.

Mason opened the chest and began putting handfuls of gold coins into the saddlebags. Little Harpe reached for some silver candlesticks and a teapot.

"Gimme one o' them torches," Davy said. "This might lead to somethin'!"

Mason grabbed him by the wrist. "Leave that big stuff. We can't carry that on horseback."

Little Harpe grunted, and helped put gold coins into the saddlebags. When the bags were full, Mason slammed down the lid of the chest. "That's enough for now."

Little Harpe was amazed. "What're you doin'? We can't leave all this for somebody else."

"Nobody's going to find it till we can get back. Bring me one of those kegs of powder," Mason said.

Little Harpe grinned and nodded his head wisely. "Gonna blow it up an' block off this passage, eh?"

When he had brought the powder keg, the two men buried it in the passage, near the door. Then Mason broke open another keg. Holding it in his hands, he poured a trail of powder on the ground. It went from the buried keg, through the passage, and along the wall of the main cave.

Then, as Little Harpe brought the saddlebags from the storeroom, Big Harpe came running in.

"Somebody's comin' up the trail!" he shouted.

"Get out of sight!" ordered Mason.

The three outlaws scattered for cover. Big Harpe hid behind some packing cases, where he picked up a sickle and a hammer for weapons. Little Harpe dived under a table and was hidden by the long tablecloth.

Mason made for some barrels and boxes stacked along a wall. He still held the powder keg, and it left a trail of powder on the ground. He put down the keg and crouched behind the barrels and boxes.

By the time Davy and Russel walked up to the entrance, the cave was quiet. There was no sound. Nothing moved, except the flames of the torches and the shadows on the walls.

Peering in, Russel whispered, "Cave-Inn Tavern ain't doin' much business tonight."

"Don't reckon it ever was a tavern, Georgie," Davy said.

"You mean this is the pirates' hideout?"

Davy nodded. "Got to be."

Davy started forward, but Russel reached out a hand to stop him.

"Davy," Russel said, "you ain't goin' in!"

"Sure. Them varmints went someplace. This here's as likely as any."

Russel slowly shook his head. "This is wors'n crawlin' in a holler log after a b'ar!"

All the same, he followed Davy inside the cave. Holding their clubs in their hands, they looked around. Davy showed Russel a hollow in the wall, where boots and clothing were piled up.

"This must be the place them ornery skunks changed into Injun clothes," Davy said.

"Yeah," Russel said. He bent over and picked up an arrow from the ground. "An' look at this. Same kind o' arrow we found stickin' in that wrecked keelboat!"

"No two ways about it—this here is the pirates' headquarters. An' them three cutthroats we followed must be the ringleaders. We gotta git 'em. We jest got to, Georgie."

Moving carefully, Davy and Russel went into the passage that led to the storeroom.

"Plenty o' loot in there," Davy said.

"They wouldn't go off an' leave it," Russel said. "Reckon they're still around somewhere."

"Georgie! Look over there! That powder on the floor!"

Davy kicked the door away from the wall. He knelt, digging in the earth with his hands until he found the open keg of powder.

"Gimme one o' them torches," he said. "This is liable to lead to somethin' interestin'!"

First Davy cleared away the powder in front of the keg. Then he held the torch to the powder train. As the powder burned, Davy and Russel followed the flame. It went through the passage and out into the main cave.

From behind the boxes and barrels, Mason watched the flame creeping toward him. Terrified, he picked up the powder keg at his feet. He looked desperately around for a place to put it. But there was no place. He dropped the keg and leaped out from hiding.

At that moment, the powder exploded behind him. Boxes and barrels tumbled, while bits and pieces of wood flew through the air. Mason fell against a packing case. It dropped on its side, and Big Harpe, who had been hiding behind it, was in plain sight.

"There they are, Davy!" yelled Russel, and the two frontiersmen gripped their clubs tightly.

Quickly reaching out for an axe, Mason made for Davy.

"You get the other one!" Mason said to Big Harpe.

"I'll git 'im!" said Big Harpe, who was holding a sickle and a hammer.

He charged at Russel, made a swipe at him with the sickle, then threw the hammer. Russel jumped aside and the hammer went past his head.

Little Harpe was still under a table. He moved toward the hammer, table and all. He picked up the hammer and swung it at Russel's foot. But another swipe of Big Harpe's sickle sent Russel flying. Big Harpe took a step, and the hammer came down on his foot.

Yelling with pain, Big Harpe dropped the sickle. His hands found a pitchfork, and with it he chased Russel across the cave. Russel jumped again, and Big Harpe ran into some piled-up barrels. They came crashing down, knocking Big Harpe to the ground.

Meanwhile, Davy had been battling Mason. After a powerful blow from Davy's club made him drop the axe, Mason threw a big iron pot at Davy. Then the pirate went for Davy with an iron chain. Davy ripped the chain out of Mason's hand. Tossing it aside, Davy used his fists. He staggered Mason, who fell against the wall. But the fight was not over. Mason thrust a torch at Davy's face. Trying to keep away from the flame, Davy stumbled to the ground.

"Watch him!" cried Russel.

Davy's feet kicked out, sending Mason sprawling to the ground. The torch fell from his hand and landed on the powder keg in the passage.

"Davy!" shouted Russel. "Run!"

Davy jumped up and ran for safety, Russel at his side. They turned, eyes wide with horror, as the powder exploded. With a great booming sound that echoed through the cavern, the passage collapsed, burying Mason under tons of rock and earth.

Then, hearing footsteps behind them, Davy and Russel turned again. Little Harpe was running for the mouth of the cave. He rushed outside—only to run into the arms of Mike Fink.

"Got him!" roared Mike. "Hi, Davy! Georgie! Me an' my boys came as soon as we could, to give you a hand."

"You're a mite late," Davy said, grinning. "The fightin's over. But much obliged, jest the same."

Davy and Russel watched with horror as the powder exploded.

The chiefs sat around their campfires.

The Pipe of Peace

IT WAS a few days after the fight with the pirates. Davy and Russel had brought word of it to the Indians. Now the two frontiersmen sat in a circle with the Indian chiefs, smoking a pipe of peace.

The oldest of the chiefs puffed at the pipe, and slowly blew smoke from his mouth in the direction of the four winds. Then he passed the pipe to Davy. Davy took a puff, blew smoke to the winds, and passed the pipe to Russel.

Suddenly there was a loud blast of cannon fire from the river. Startled, Davy and the others got to their feet and stared. The *Gullywhumper,* its right name again painted on its side, was being poled upstream by its crew. Mike Fink was at the tiller, wearing his boatman's hat with a red feather in it.

Cupping his hands around his mouth, Davy called out, "Hello, the boat!"

Mike called back, "Hello, Davy! How's the king o' the wild frontier?"

"Tolerable!" Davy said. "How's the king o' the river?"

Mike leaped up in the air, flapping his arms like a rooster.

"Cock-a-doodle-doo!" he bellowed. "I'm a reg'lar ring-tailed roarer from the thunder-an'-lightnin' country! I'm a snorter an' a head-buster! I can out-run, out-jump, out-swim, out-sing, out-dance, out-shoot, out-eat, out-drink, out-talk, an' out-fight any man on the Ohio an' the ol' Mississip'! Ee—ya-hoo!"

Davy jumped into the air, neighing like a horse. "Wa-hoo!" he roared. "I'm half horse, half alligator, an' a mite touched with snappin' turtle! I can shoot further, run faster, jump higher, squat lower, dive deeper, an' come up drier than any man in this here neck o' the woods, bar none! I'm a ring-tailed roarer, an' this is my day to roar. Whoo-oop!"

Then Davy waved his coonskin cap and said, "So long, king o' the river!"

Mike waved his hat with the red feather in it. "So long, king o' the wild frontier!"

The boat went on, gliding through sunlight and shadow on the quiet water. Mike's men began to sing:

Hard upon the beach oar,
She moves too slow,
All the way to Shawneetown,
Long time ago!

Davy and Russel kept waving until the *Gullywhumper* was out of sight. The last echo of the boatmen's song died away, and Davy turned to the old Indian chief.

While Russel looked on, smiling, Davy and the oldest chief shook hands. Once again there was peace between red man and white man. And, with no pirates to raid the keelboats, there was peace again on the rolling river—thanks to Davy Crockett, king of the wild frontier.

Pigs is Pigs

In the Westcote Railway Station
In the year nineteen-o-five,
The agent there was Flannery,
The best there was alive.

Flannery ran his station
Exactly by the rule.
He tried to learn each one by heart,
Just like a kid in school.

Whenever a customer chanced to call,
Flannery let him wait
Until he could look up the rule
That would be appropriate.

One morning came McMorehouse,
A thrifty, crusty Scot,
To pick up a shipment of guinea pigs—
He wanted them on the dot!

"Good morning to you," says Section Two,
"And don't forget to smile."
"Morning it was," McMorehouse said.
"I've been standing here a while."

"I'm supposed to say, 'I'm sorry, sir,'"
Flannery read from Rule Three.
"Dry your tears," said McMorehouse.
"Have you got some pets for me?"

"Indeed I have—two guinea pigs—
See pigs, page forty-three—
According to the book of rules,
Your pets are pigs, you see."

"Pigs forty-eight cents, pets forty-four!"
McMorehouse read the rule.
"Guinea pigs is pets at forty-four!"
He cried. "You stubborn fool!"

"Pigs is pigs at forty-eight!"
Flannery insisted.
But paying freight at the higher rate
McMorehouse still resisted.

"Whenever an agent gets in a debate,"
Flannery read, "Concerning the rate,
The agent must wire for a ruling up high,
And hold onto the package awaiting reply."

"Hold them then," McMorehouse said,
"And when you find you're wrong,
Deliver them to my address."

Then Flannery sat down and sent
A telegram away,
Not dreaming he'd regret this move
Until his dying day.

"Big Town, on the Drive,
Flannery to Morgan,
May sixth, nineteen-o-five.

"Holding two animals in a crate;
Big dispute regarding rate.
Is a guinea pig a pig or pet?
Give ruling on the rate to set.
Flannery."

The supervisor's office was
The pride of the company.
It received old Flannery's telegram
With trained efficiency.

They examined the wire and immediately dated it,
Stamped the receipts, then communicated it

To the department that quadruplicated it.
Copies were sent out to all of the staff.

Each copy received was filed and related
To copies of copies, then checked and notated.
Nine copies of each were then validated
And contents were noted in ink on a graph.

Meanwhile Flannery tended the pigs.
"Now, I'll call one Pat and the other—
Mike!" But he changed it to Marie
When Mike became a mother!

Soon Flannery sent off a message:
"Regarding last wire of mine,
Instead of just two guinea pigs,
I now am holding nine!"

The legal department was next delegated
To study the problem now so complicated,
When all of the data was accumulated
To make a report and to tell what they knew.

The president wanted a full explanation
As well as an overall clarification
Of Flannery's wire that wanted to know
If a pig was a pig and to please tell him so.

The Board of Directors convened and debated
The question of pigs and were they related
To pigs or to rabbits as once indicated
By evidence found by the fact-finding staff.

A boy in the office first advocated it,
Then a professor formally stated it,
The office force triple- and quadruplicated it,
And this is the answer that Flannery got:

"The guinea pig makes a very nice pet,
But in family, shape, and size
It is certainly not a common pig,
So the forty-four cent rate applies."

With monotonous regularity,
Those pigs had produced more pigs,
While Flannery tried to stem the tide
By playing them Irish jigs.

Now each grandchild of the first two pigs
Had grandsons by the dozens,
And every time the clock would strike,
There were fifty brand-new cousins.

When Flannery got the telegram,
Straight down the road he tore
To take the news to McMorehouse, but—
McMorehouse didn't live there any more!

So Flannery wired the office,
"Tell me quick, what do I do?
There is no rule to cover this case
So now it's up to you."

It was a clever young clerk at last
Who made the recommendation
That the pigs should simply be crated up
And sent to the main-office station.

Flannery loaded the pigs in crates
In boxes, bags, and sacks.
He filled six hundred box cars up,
If you want to know the facts.

They unloaded the pigs at the main-office station,
And filled up the warehouse first;
Then they stored away pigs in the office,
Till the building almost burst.

Flannery heard, and he wired:
"It's not so bad," he said.
"What if all those guinea pigs
Had been elephants instead?"

Just as he finished, chuckling,
He glanced out the station door—
There stood a long circus train
With elephants galore!

When Flannery recovered, he swore:
"No more will I be a fool!
Whenever it comes to livestock,
Dang every single rule.

"If the animals come in singles,
Or if they come in sets,
If they've got four feet and they're alive,
They'll be classified as pets!"

Scamp

ONCE there was a small puppy. He was a Scamp of a puppy. He liked to sniff at things and taste things and poke his nose into things and chase things. He liked to find out why some things are the way they are, and other things aren't that way at all.

That Scamp of a puppy lived in a big house on a wide, quiet street. He lived with his mother and his father.

Lady was Scamp's mother. She was gentle and kind and good and beautiful. She was a cocker spaniel.

Tramp was Scamp's father. No one knew what kind of dog Tramp was. Even Tramp himself wasn't sure. But Scamp knew that his father was the smartest dog in all the world.

Scamp's three little sisters were as gentle and kind and pretty as their mother. They liked to nap in their basket in a corner of the kitchen.

When Scamp's sisters played, they played gentle little ladylike games.

When they barked, they barked gentle little ladylike barks.

But that other little puppy—that Scamp of a puppy! He wasn't a bit like his sisters.

Scamp liked to play rough games.

He liked to tumble and roll on the floor.

He liked to hide behind the cupboard.

"Where is that puppy?" his sisters would cry. "Where is that Scamp?"

And that Scamp of a puppy would jump out and bark at them.

At mealtime, the three gentle little puppies would sit in a row and wait nicely for their mistress to fill their bowl. They would smile their best puppy smiles and do their puppy tricks.

"What lovely puppies!" their mistress would say. "They're just like Lady!"

But the moment the puppy bowl was filled, that fourth little puppy, that Scamp of a puppy, would come running.

He did not wait nicely for his turn at the bowl.

He did not sit up or smile a puppy smile or do puppy tricks.

He just ate up all the dinner.

"What a Scamp of a puppy!" his mistress would say. "Whatever will we do with him?"

At playtime, the three gentle pretty little puppies would play quietly with their own puppy toys.

One had a rubber ball. She would throw it up into the air and then catch it again.

One had a toy mouse. She would push it with her nose until it made a whirring noise and ran across the floor.

One had a calico cat. She would touch it with her paw so that it rocked back and forth.

But that fourth little puppy, that Scamp of a puppy, wouldn't bother with toy mice or calico cats. He was not even very fond of rubber balls.

Scamp did not have time for the games that girl puppies play.

He had to see what shoes tasted like.

He had to nibble on the rug so he would know what rugs were made of.

He had to bite the umbrella and smell the potted plants and crawl under the sofa.

When bedtime came, the three gentle pretty little puppies would snuggle down to sleep in their basket in the corner of the kitchen.

They would close their eyes and go to sleep and dream puppy dreams. And all night long they never made a sound.

But that fourth little puppy, that Scamp of a puppy, wouldn't even get into the puppy basket.

He wouldn't stay in the dark corner of the kitchen.

He wouldn't be quiet.

He sat in the place where the moonbeams came in through the window and practiced howling, loud and long.

"Whatever shall we do about Scamp?" wondered his mistress.

"Whatever shall we do about Scamp?" said his mother.

Even his father sometimes wondered what to do about Scamp.

One day the four little puppies started off for a picnic. Each one carried a nice puppy biscuit for lunch.

The three gentle pretty little puppies trotted down the wide, quiet street until they came to the park. Then they hurried into the park to find a shady spot for their picnic.

But the fourth little puppy, that Scamp of a puppy, ran right past the park. He didn't want

to eat his puppy biscuit in a shady spot with his sisters. He wanted to have an adventure.

Scamp ate his puppy biscuit by himself. Then he found some new playmates. They were the Siamese cats.

The cats were strutting along a fence. They picked up their feet and set them down again without making a sound. They held their heads just so. They waved their tails just so.

Scamp thought that their game looked like fun. "Can I come up and play with you?" he called.

"Sss-ss-sst!" hissed one of the Siamese cats. His name was Si.

"Pss-ss-sst!" said the other Siamese cat. His name was Am.

Both of the cats glared at Scamp.

Both of the cats put out their long claws and swiped at Scamp.

"I don't like that game!" thought Scamp. And he got out of there.

Before long, Scamp found another playmate. It was a busy gopher. He was digging a tunnel. He worked so hard and so fast that the dirt flew.

"That looks like a good game," said Scamp. "Can I play, too?"

"Anyone can play," said the gopher.

"How do you learn to play that game?" asked Scamp.

"There's only one way to learn," said the gopher. "You learn by doing it."

So Scamp began to dig. He dug just the way the gopher dug.

Scamp dug and dug and dug and dug. Then he stopped. He had found something. What do you think it was? It was a nice, big, juicy bone.

It was a very large bone for such a very small dog. But that didn't worry Scamp a bit.

Scamp pulled at the bone.

He tugged it and hauled at it.

He wrestled it this way and rolled it that way.

He heaved and huffed and puffed and growled and shoved.

He didn't stop until he had that bone all the way down the street to the gate of the park.

Just as Scamp reached the park, a big bad dog found the three gentle pretty little puppies sitting in a shady place.

"Ha!" said the big bad dog. "I smell puppy biscuits!"

The three gentle little puppies would have been happy to share their puppy biscuits with the big dog. They were very kind, polite little puppies. But the big bad dog never gave them a chance to invite him to their picnic.

The big bad dog simply gobbled up their puppy biscuits—one, two, three!

The poor little puppies!

By now they were really very hungry. And there was nothing left of their nice picnic lunch but a few crumbs.

They felt very sad.

Two of the gentle little puppies began to cry big puppy tears. The third little puppy was just

about to cry. Then she saw the fourth little puppy, that Scamp of a puppy. He had come into the park tugging his fine big bone!

"Hi, girls!" said Scamp. "I was playing a wonderful new game, and look what I found!"

"A bone!" cried one of his sisters.

"A big bone!" said the second little puppy.

"A big beautiful bone!" added the third little puppy.

Scamp was very proud. "It's big enough for all of us," he said.

So all four of the puppies had the nice big bone for lunch. And they all had a fine time.

When picnic time was over, the three gentle pretty little puppies went happily home from the park.

And the fourth little puppy, that Scamp of a puppy, walked proudly in front of them. After all, if it hadn't been for Scamp, there wouldn't have been any picnic.

Scamp's mother and father were very pleased when they heard what Scamp had done. For two whole days, Scamp's mother never said, "Whatever shall we do with Scamp?" For two whole days, Scamp was a very good puppy.

But then the third day came. And what did that Scamp of a puppy do? He chewed up the master's new pipe!

The master spanked Scamp with a folded newspaper.

The mistress locked Scamp in the kitchen.

After a while, Scamp's mistress opened the kitchen door and let Scamp out. But Scamp still felt sorry for himself. He scooted up the stairs and into the best bedroom, and he jumped up on the bed.

That was strictly against the rules.

And he went sound asleep on the clean white

pillow. He dreamed that he wasn't a little puppy. He dreamed that he was a ferocious dog. He dreamed that he was chasing lions in Africa.

When Scamp woke up, he still felt very ferocious. He looked into the mirror and practiced barking.

"Now what's that Scamp of a puppy doing?" said his mistress.

And when she saw Scamp making faces in the mirror, she carried him downstairs and put him out of the house.

Soon two of Scamp's friends came to visit. They were Trusty and Jock.

Trusty was an old dog. He was a bloodhound. His keen nose could tell him if a squirrel ran across his path. It could tell him if a bird hopped in the grass. Trusty had had many adventures.

Jock was an old dog, too. He was a Scotch terrier. He could dig into the earth and find the tunnels where the moles lived. Jock had had many adventures.

But those adventures were long ago.

"I want an adventure of my own," said Scamp.

Scamp set out to find an adventure. On the way he passed his three gentle pretty little sisters. They had a beautiful new ball. They were rolling the ball back and forth near the flower bed.

"Stop, Scamp!" they called. "Come and play with us."

"No thank you," said that Scamp of a puppy. "I don't want to play that silly girl game. I'm going to find an adventure."

And Scamp ran away.

Out the gate went Scamp. He ran down the broad quiet street and around the corner. He ran across the empty lot. He wriggled through the hole in the fence.

Then Scamp saw something that made him stop and stare.

There was a horse and there was a driver. There was a wagon. And there were one, two, three, four turning wheels.

The wheels clattered on the cobblestones.

Scamp barked.

The horse trotted faster and the wheels clattered more loudly.

Scamp ran after the clattering wheels. They led him far, far away, to a place where Scamp had never been before.

At last the wagon turned off the road and drove in through a gate.

Still Scamp followed.

When the wagon stopped rolling, Scamp looked around him.

He was in a garden.

There were many children in the garden. Scamp counted one, two, three, four, five!

"Look at the puppy!" cried one little boy.

"We don't have a puppy!" shouted a little girl.

"Let's put him in our zoo!" said another child.

Scamp didn't know what a zoo might be. He looked across the garden and saw a row of cages. Could these be a zoo?

That Scamp of a puppy had to find out about those cages. He trotted up to the first cage and put his paws on top of it. He barked a small little bark.

Up popped a bunny.

It blinked its pink eyes at Scamp.

It wiggled its pink nose.

"Hello," said the bunny. "Are you going to be in the zoo, too?"

Then the bunny popped back into his cage.

Scamp sniffed at the second cage.

Inside the cage was a turtle.

The turtle nodded its head at Scamp in a friendly way.

Then it pulled its head inside its shell. It pulled its legs inside, too. And its tail.

In a moment, all that was left of the turtle was a shell on the floor of the cage.

The third cage was a beautiful cage. It shone like gold. Inside the cage was a canary with lovely golden feathers.

"Hello," chirped the canary. "Don't you think I'm the prettiest one in the whole zoo?"

Scamp thought she was very pretty. But he didn't think it was nice of her to mention it.

"You aren't very pretty," said the canary, "but you can be in the zoo, too."

Then the canary forgot about Scamp and began to nibble her lettuce leaf.

In the fourth cage was a white mouse.

It had pink ears and a pink nose and pink paws and bright black eyes.

It didn't look up at Scamp. It sat in the cage and washed its pink paws.

On the fifth cage was a big sign that said "Danger!"

And no wonder.

In the fifth cage were the two big Siamese cats, Si and Am.

The cats wouldn't talk to Scamp when he came near their cage.

They arched their backs at him.

They hissed and spit at him.

They would have scratched him with their long claws if they could. Luckily for Scamp, they couldn't get out of the cage.

Scamp hurried toward the sixth cage.

The sixth cage was empty. The door was open and Scamp could see a bone inside. It was a nice, fresh, juicy bone.

Scamp gave a happy little bark. He wagged his tail once. And he went into that cage.

Snap!

The door closed behind Scamp.

"Now we have him!" cried the children. "Now we have a puppy for our zoo!"

Scamp quickly decided that he did not like being in the zoo.

The cage was small. And right next to Scamp were the Siamese cats. They hissed and they spit and they yowled at Scamp.

Poor little puppy! Poor Scamp of a puppy. He was having an adventure, and he didn't like it a bit.

Scamp began to bark and bark.

A lady came out of the house into the garden. She was the children's mother.

"Where did you get that puppy?" she asked.

None of the children answered her.

"Why is the puppy barking?" she asked.

Again, none of the children said a word.

"That is not your puppy," said the lady. "Let that puppy out of the cage this instant!"

The children opened the door of the cage and Scamp ran out.

He raced across the garden and down the drive and through the gate.

He ran and he ran until he was very tired. But at last he came to his own gate. At last he was back home.

Scamp's three gentle pretty little sisters were having their supper when Scamp came in.

"Did you have an adventure?" they asked, looking up from their bowl.

"Whew!" said Scamp. "Did I ever have an adventure!"

Scamp didn't say another word after that.

He tumbled into his basket without even stopping for any supper.

In a moment he was fast asleep.

Scamp didn't go looking for adventures again. At least, he didn't go looking for adventures for another day or two!

The Flying Gauchito

It was early one morning in springtime, but already the small gauchito was out of his bed and scrambling into his clothes. And why was he up so early, this small gauchito, before the sun rose over the pampas? Because he was going hunting, all alone.

First he put on his *bombachas*—trousers, we would say—and tied his *cutipora,* or sash, around his waist. He slipped on his new *botas,* the high, shiny boots of which he was so proud. He had his *bolas,* his hunting lasso, handy, but still it seemed there was something he was forgetting. Ah, yes, his knife!

Now the little hunter was prepared for anything—even for the huge condor birds which live high in the mountains. That was what the gauchito planned to hunt this day—condors. So out he started, patting the knife at his belt.

From the little hut on the pampas to the high mountains was a long, long way. It was well that the little gauchito had an early start. For by the time he reached the first slopes of the mountains the sun was showing over the horizon.

Up, up, up went the gauchito till he reached the high peaks. While he rested, his eyes peered this way and that. Somewhere here there must be a condor's nest, he thought. Somewhere—ah! From behind a tall rock, a wing tip waved. The gauchito stood as still as stone. Almost he stopped breathing.

Now another wing tip appeared, and the wings began to spread—wider and wider. Caramba! thought the gauchito. This must be the biggest condor bird in the whole wide world! Should he go after him with the hunting knife, or should he lasso this fine fellow?

His eyes remained fixed on the rocks above. Now something moved up there, and the gauchito's eyes popped out in surprise. For he was face to face with—not a condor, but a flying donkey!

"A flying burrito!" gasped the gauchito, pulling out his *bolas*, the lasso. So rare a creature must not escape!

But he need not have worried. The flying burrito flapped his wings and flew down, straight to the gauchito. He sniffed at the gauchito's face. He snatched off his hat and chewed at it.

The gauchito twirled his *bolas*. Zip! the coils of rope twined themselves around the burrito's legs. Ha, he was well caught, thought the gauchito. But wait! Zap! the burrito flipped himself about; the ropes fell loose at his feet!

The little donkey bared his teeth in a friendly grin. He threw back his head and brayed—"Hee haw!" Then he lowered his head and butted the gauchito—right over the edge of the cliff!

"Help! Help!" cried the gauchito, plunging down through empty air.

But the burrito meant no harm. He dived through the air, came up below the falling hunter, opened his wings, and swish! the gauchito landed on his back!

Away streaked the donkey, with the gauchito clinging to him like a jockey. Through the clouds they dipped and soared—and bucked. For the burrito wanted to make it clear that no man or boy was to be his master.

At last they came to earth, far out on the pampas. There the gauchito built a campfire, and they fell asleep beside it, the tired little boy and the wondrous little donkey with wings.

Now the gauchito had a wonderful plan for himself and the flying burrito. What a future they would have! They would be rich and famous and would live like kings. The gauchito could picture his hands full of diamond rings.

It would all start at the fiesta, tomorrow, in town. Until then no one must know of this wonderful flying burrito!

So that night they slept out under the stars. But the next morning found them in the town, mingling with the fiesta crowd. That was a happy day for all the gauchitos. They danced the *samba* and the *gatos*, and gambled their *pesos* away.

The air was full of the twang of guitars, the beat of drums, the merry sound of concertinas, the singing of gauchos. There was dancing in the plaza, and games of chance on every corner.

But the little gauchito stood aside, his donkey

close to him. Their minds were set on something bigger. For soon the *caballo,* the horse race, was to begin. And the prize was one thousand *pesos!*

The gauchito made his way to the starting gate with his burrito stepping beside him. The donkey's wonderful wings were hidden away under a blanket as the gauchito climbed upon his back and guided him between two of the horses.

How those gauchos roared with laughter when the little boy and his donkey took their place in line! How everyone howled when, at the flash of the white flag, the horses leaped away from their posts! For the burrito was still standing. He did not understand the race.

"Burrito!" pleaded the small gauchito. "After them, little one! This way!"

At last the burrito started out, but the horses were far ahead, in a great cloud of dust, rounding the curve of the track. Pepito, the pride of Mendoza, was setting a furious pace. And Fuego, Gordito, and Pingo! What a race!

The crowd was shouting its heart out as the horses came pounding down the stretch. Now it was Pepito and Fuego. No, Fuego and Pepito, and here came Gordito like a bolt from the blue!

Far behind, lost to sight in the dust, the gauchito was whispering in his donkey's ear, and tugging at the blanket.

"Burrito! Now the wings, the wings!"

Down the home stretch came Fuego. Next Pepito, hugging the rail. Then Pingo, Gordito, Gato. Dorado was right on his tail. But where was Burrito?

A cloud of dust hurtled down the track. The horses seemed to stand still as the flying burrito whizzed past them. Down the home stretch he flew, faster and faster, and across the finish line! Burrito was the winner!

Now the crowd went wild with cheers. And the little gauchito was happy as he sat proudly astride the little burro. Then came the proudest moment of all. The mayor was coming toward them, holding out the grand prize, a big bag of coins.

"Ah, Burrito!" the gauchito whispered. "One thousand pesos! We are rich, and this is only the beginning!"

The burrito flicked his ears knowingly. Then, baring his teeth in a happy grin, he spread his wings and—

"Wait, wait!" cried the gauchito, and he hammered his heels into the little donkey's sides. "Down, Burrito, down! The prize! We must collect the prize!"

But the burrito was not interested in prizes. He only knew that now he was free, free to fly again. And the noise of the crowd beat harshly upon his ears, used to the silences of the high mountains and the open pampas. So away he flew!

Down below the mayor stood, looking much amazed, holding out the sack of pesos. High above, the poor gauchito leaned down, stretching out empty hands. But the burrito was happy. He dipped and wheeled and soared until, to the crowd below, he was only a tiny spot against the sun—then nothing at all.

And the gauchito? Of the gauchito and his flying burrito nothing more was heard, and they never were seen again.

This is my
only Authorized
Biography
(signed) d. duck

The Life of Donald Duck

THERE have always been ducks, but very seldom Great Ducks. No duck came over to this country on the *Mayflower*. No ducks fought in the Battle of Bunker Hill. Hardly ever, in all history, is a famous duck mentioned. Ducks have just been ducks.

Who were Donald's parents? No one even knows their names. Who were his grandparents, his great-great-grandparents? Did anyone in his family ever do anything at all? The author of this *Life of Donald Duck* determined to find out.

This was a discouraging search and long. He asked questions in duck farms all over the United States. He searched all over Europe and almost all of Asia.

Then one day, in Egypt, he found what he was after! In some crumbled ruins near the big pyramids, he unearthed an amazing picture carved on a stone. It was Donald's forgotten ancestor . . . the great Tut en Ka'duck, at one time Pharaoh of all the ducks in Egypt!

That Great Duck lived more than 5,000 years ago. Between then and now, Donald Duck's family evidently did nothing of importance. But, already, Donald has done enough to make up for them all.

The Days within the Egg

MOST baby ducks like to hatch out of their eggs just as quickly as possible. But Donald Duck was different.

When the time came for him to quack his first quack and burst the shell of his egg, he just wouldn't do it. It was the first place he'd ever been to and he liked it. There was nobody in there but he, and he was boss. He liked being boss and was in no hurry to be hatched.

This, of course, was very annoying to his mother. Day after day after day she walked nervously round and round the egg, scolding him through the shell: "What's the matter with you, anyhow! *Hatch yourself, Donald!* That shell's getting harder every minute. If you don't break out now, you'll *never* be able to crack it!"

But Donald never answered. He just kept on laughing "Heh-heh" to himself and kept right on sitting. Nothing outside, he thought, could be as much fun as sitting here inside his own egg.

After thirteen weeks of this, Donald's mother gave up. "I'm through!" she shouted. "You're obstinate. You're disobedient. You'll never amount to a thing. GOOD-BY!"

And she turned her back and stalked away.

"Pooh-pooh!" thought Donald. "She's only fooling. She'll come back."

But she wasn't fooling and she didn't come back. Gradually Donald began to grow worried. He felt cramped and stuffy. The air was giving

out. And his feathers began to itch. Not only that, but he was suddenly mighty hungry. Thirteen weeks and not a bite to eat. . . .

The fun was all over. Now he'd *have* to come out.

Donald stood up. *"Gangway!"* he shouted. *"Here I come!"* He swung back his foot and gave the egg a kick.

But the egg didn't crack.

"Oh-oh!" thought Donald. "This egg *is* tough."

He doubled up his fists. SOCK!

But the egg didn't crack.

"Look here!" muttered Donald. *"This egg can't do this to me!"*

He threw his fists at the shell again and again. He jabbed with his elbows. He butted with his head. He banged with his beak.

But the egg didn't crack.

Donald sank down, panting, on the floor of the egg. His head began to swim. The air inside the egg was almost all used up.

"This is a pretty fix," he gasped. "Feet can't break it. Fists can't. Head can't. . . . *This calls for brains!"*

He thought hard for an answer. Then he sprang to his feet. He drew in a deep breath. Deeper and deeper he breathed. Wider and wider his chest swelled out, till he'd breathed inside of him every bit of air that was left in the egg.

Then Donald Duck let go a QUACK!

It was the loudest quack, the mightiest quack, the most ear-splitting quack that had ever been quacked!

The egg shell was quacked and blasted into a hundred million flying pieces!

Donald Duck stepped out of the wreckage and into the world.

But *what* a world!

It was Friday the thirteenth. It was night. It was raining. Donald shivered. Icy-cold raindrops drizzled down inside his collar.

Donald looked around. There was no one in sight. No mother . . . no friends.

"What a terrible birthday," growled Donald. He was all alone. And, worst of all, he was hungry.

A Duck Must Eat

DONALD could think of nothing but food. And the more he thought, the hungrier he felt. He looked all around him and sniffed the air with hope. But there was no food to sniff. There was nothing but night, and the night was full of rain. It was running off the end of his nose. He was soaked with it, and his clothes clung soggily to his cold and empty stomach. A fine How-Do-You-Do!—especially for someone who had just been hatched.

Donald began stumbling around in the blackness, splashing through the puddles and smashing through the mud. Suddenly he bumped into something hard and rough.

"A-ha!" chuckled Donald. "A tree! Apples!" And he shook the tree as hard as he could. But no apples fell off.

So he shook it again, this time for bananas. No bananas fell off. Then he shook it for tangerines, hickory nuts, gooseberries, figs, and kumquats. But nothing whatsoever fell off the tree.

Donald was disgusted. He was now seven minutes old, seven times as hungry as when he was hatched, and in his seven minutes of life he had had no fun at all. It was unfair.

Donald was about to lose his temper, when suddenly he had an idea.

"Why, it's perfectly simple," he laughed. "I'll *buy* myself some food!"

Donald started whistling. Far in the distance he could see the little lights of a town. He walked straight toward them with big determined strides.

What an appetite he had! He could eat some pork chops . . . some lamb chops, too . . . some honey buns and reindeer chops . . . doughnuts, clams, and pickled pigs' feet . . . fishcakes, cheesecakes, frogs' legs, noodles . . . oysters on the half shell and caramel custard pie. . . .

The lights were getting closer. Soon he would be sitting in some fine fancy restaurant, tossing the waiter an enormous tip. He felt rich. He wondered just *how* rich?

Donald reached for his pocket. He reached on his left side. He reached on his right. He reached front and back.

A cold sweat broke out on his forehead. The clothes he was hatched in didn't have any pockets at all!

"Can you imagine that!" gasped Donald. Not a penny to his name! What to do now?

There was only one answer. He'd have to go to work!

But what of it? Other great people worked. Thomas Edison worked. When he was hungry, he invented the phonograph and didn't eat till afterwards.

That settled it. It was a crazy way to run a world, but if people *had* to work to eat, then so would Donald Duck.

He clenched his fists. He'd show 'em!

With nothing in his stomach, but high ambitions in his heart, Donald hurried on once more, sloshing down the highway toward the city.

A Young Duck in an Old City

It was miles. Night passed and at last the sun rose, just as the job-hunting Donald was marching bravely into town. The sunlight warmed his wetness and made him feel gay, hungry though he was.

"Getting a job will be easy," thought Donald, "for a handsome, good-looking fellow like me."

Just *how* handsome was he, anyhow? He felt good-looking, but, as yet, he hadn't seen himself. Just ahead was a store window. He walked up close and took a look at his reflection.

Donald stared in amazement.

"That's not *me!*" he gasped.

He shook his fist at the reflection, but the reflection shook its fist right back.

"Well, I'll be . . . !" gulped Donald. "It *is* me! Me . . . *in baby clothes!* I'll never get a job dressed in nonsense stuff like this!"

Donald boiled over. He lost his temper completely. He snatched at the silly bow that tied his baby bonnet under his chin. He yanked off the bonnet and tossed it into an ashcan. With a wild mighty rip, he tore off his baby dress.

"That's that!" snapped Donald. "*Now* I can get a job."

He turned on his heel and strode straight ahead.

After three or four steps, he began to feel strange. It seemed suddenly colder. And people were staring.

"What's wrong?" wondered Donald. And then he remembered. Say, this was worse than ever! Now he had no clothes on at all!

"Oh-oh!" thought Donald. "You can't go around on the main street like *this!*"

Out of the corner of his eye he caught a glimpse of a policeman. The policeman was watching him very suspiciously.

Donald ran!

It was his first day on earth. And he didn't want to spend it locked behind bars in some dark jail!

SALE

Duck Meets Bathtub

DONALD didn't go to jail. When the policeman caught him, he took him to a place that was fifty times worse.

Donald tried to argue . . . but the policeman wouldn't listen. He dragged Donald up the steps of a big dark building.

Just inside the front door, sitting behind a desk, was a very large woman, dressed all in white. The policeman shoved Donald toward her.

"Here's a foundling I found," was all he said. Then he left.

"A *foundling!* ME?" Donald was furious. "Let me out of here! I'm plenty grown up and I'm looking for a job. You can't do this to me! Let me out!"

The large woman in white smiled down at him. "Tut-tut, poor child." She patted his head. "Now don't get excited. Here . . . play with this rattle."

This was too much! Donald snatched the rattle out of her hands. He broke it, and hurled the pieces right back.

"Oh, so you have a temper, have you?" said the woman in white. She was no longer smiling.

She pushed a button on her desk, and into the room came two tall nurses in black. They rushed at Donald and each one grabbed an arm.

"A foundling . . . with a temper, too," said the woman in white. "Maybe a good cold bath will calm him down a bit."

A bath! This was more than too much. In his whole life, Donald had never been so mad. He kicked and fought. But it was no use. They dragged him off to a little room and dumped him in a little wooden bathtub.

"*Wash!*" they commanded, handling him a slippery hunk of soap.

"NEVER!" shouted Donald. He squeezed the soap in his fist. *Skow-oosh!* It squilched through the air and out the open window. He'd show them!

"He doesn't know how to wash," whispered one nurse. "It'll have to be done for him," whispered the other. "This is definitely a case for the Mechanical Bathtub!"

Donald never saw the thing . . . it all happened too fast. They hurled him right into it. Donald sank like a stone. He tried to crawl out. Then a boxing glove hit him and pushed him back under. There was a sudden chugging and grinding of machinery. Wheels whirred. Wild whistles blew and soapsuds filled the air. Bristle brushes swung and slapped and swozzled him around.

Faintly, at last, through the din and the clatter, Donald heard a faraway voice, "That's enough of the bathtub. *Now* for the barber!"

The bath machinery stopped, but the barber machinery started. And Donald was tossed into the middle of *that!*

When the ghastly nightmare ended, Donald found himself standing, woozy, dazed, and dizzy, in the center of the room, all washed and brushed and powdered and smelling like a pot of geraniums.

Worst of all, he was dressed again in baby clothes!

Looking down at him stood the large woman in white.

"There!" she smiled. "You're all calmed down. Now I'll let you go for a nice little buggy ride."

Donald was so weak he couldn't even snarl. She picked him up just as though he were an ordinary baby and tucked him into a baby's go-cart.

"Don't you try to escape," warned the woman in white. "Miss Baumgrass knows how to deal with runaway children."

"Miss *Who* . . . ?" asked Donald, looking around in back. There, right behind the carriage, stood a great black Mechanical Nursemaid!

Miss Baumgrass, the iron nursemaid, suddenly began to clank. Her tin hands squeaked and grasped the handle of the carriage. She pushed Donald ahead of her through the long hallways. They bumped down the steps and out onto the main street. At the corner, Miss Baumgrass stopped for a moment. Reaching into a tin pocket, she pulled something out and tossed it to Donald. It was a baby's milk bottle with a little rubber hose.

"Milk!" snorted Donald. "*What* a world!"

He gulped the warm liquid. It was the first food he'd ever tasted, and it tasted positively awful.

Oh, a Life on the Salty Sea!

THERE WAS something about that milk, even bad as it tasted, that made Donald feel stronger. It was like putting coal in a brand-new furnace. As he sipped it, Donald got his steam up.

He'd get out of that baby wagon . . . *somehow!*

Out of the corner of his eye he squinted at Miss Baumgrass. *What a woman!* Not the kind of a nursemaid you'd dare to take a slap at.

"And I'll bet she can run, too," figured Donald. "This getting away is going to take brains."

They had left the main street now. Miss Baumgrass had chosen to stroll on the waterfront and was pushing him along a walk by the very edge of the sea. Just ahead, at a dock, a tugboat was puffing . . . just about to sail away.

Donald shot another quick look at Miss Baumgrass. "Perhaps she can *run,*" he suddenly thought. "But I'll bet she can't *swim!* Madame Ironsides must weigh a ton."

They were passing the dock. The captain of the tugboat was casting off the rope. Slowly the ship was pushing out into the waves.

With one wild and mighty leap Donald dived out of the carriage, over the embankment, and . . . *splat!* . . . into the sea!

Free!

Miss Baumgrass didn't dare dive in after him. Helpless, she raced around in little circles on shore, waving her foolish arms like windmills.

Catching the tugboat was easy. Donald could swim like a duck and caught up to it in no time. When no one was looking, he swung himself aboard. He slipped into a cabin and found himself some clothes. Sailor clothes! Just what he'd always wanted! Then he snatched up a boat hook and rushed out on deck to take charge.

"Yo-ho!" he shouted. *"Ahoy and avast! Scuttle the scuppers, and jibber the jib!"*

It was the wrong thing to shout. The crew was bewildered, and the captain let go the wheel. The ship ran wild. It crashed head on into a rock! The boilers blew up! The ship's bottom fell out and the sea came pouring in.

Donald sank with the ship. That was the last thing that he remembered for a long, long time.

When he came to, he was hanging on a clothesline. He had been rescued and hung up to dry by a dog.

School Days

It was there on the clothesline that Miss Baumgrass found him. She unpinned him, wrung him out, and put him back in the go-cart. His life as a sailor was over. She rolled him back to the City Nursery.

There, the large woman in white gave him a terrible talking-to. "Running away to sea! At your age!" she scolded. "What you need is school. And that's where you're going . . . right now!"

School! Donald groaned. Then he had an idea. If he could go there *alone*, he could use his brains and escape.

He made a face at Miss Baumgrass. "Is that big boiler going to take me to school?"

"No," said the woman in white. "Your conscience will be your guide."

"My *what?*" growled Donald, worried for fear his plans were being spoiled.

"Why, your conscience is your Other You. It's your Good You, Donald, and it will keep you out of trouble." She patted him and handed him some schoolbooks. "Now run along, or you'll be late."

Donald started off. "Conscience? Other Me? Good Me?" he mumbled to himself as he shuffled along. It didn't make any sense.

This morning he'd been only *one* duck. Just the plain Me. Now, with this Good Me, whoever that was, it seemed he was *two* ducks! It began to strike him as funny. Donald laughed out loud.

"Don't you laugh!" whispered an unexpected voice in his ear. It was just like his own voice!

Donald turned. Right at his elbow there seemed to be standing another Donald! He looked exactly like Donald, only he was wearing a long white satin robe. There was a bright little circle floating in the air above his head, and those things on his shoulders looked very much like angel wings.

"Who are *you?*" asked Donald hoarsely.

"I'm your Good Me," whispered the White One. "I'm going to see that you go straight to school."

"Humph!" snorted Donald. "I was going there anyway."

Donald eyed his companion contemptuously as they walked along together. "What a sissy!" thought Donald. "Certainly not *my* type."

"Pssst!" Another voice in his ear! Donald almost jumped out of his blouse.

"Who says you HAVE to go to school?" hissed the new voice. "Skip it, fellow, and come along with me!"

Donald wheeled about. There right behind him was still another Donald, also just like him, only *he* was wearing sharp horns on his forehead and wagging a little pointed devil's tail behind.

"I'm your Bad Me!" said the new one.

Donald was flabbergasted. What a lot of Donalds there suddenly seemed to be!

"Why tag along with that sissy?" continued the Bad Me. "Join up with me. Suppose you and I go swimmin'?" He was a rough one and was already jerking Donald by the arm.

"Swimming! How perfectly dreadful!" The Good Me sprang between Donald and the Bad Me and held up his hand. "*I* say Donald is going straight to school!"

"That's what *you* think!" shouted the Bad Me.

"Oh-oh," thought Donald. "There's going to be a fight. This is a pretty How-Do-You-Do!"

It *was* a pretty How-Do-You-Do. Up the road and down the road and all across the hayfield, the Good Me and the Bad Me fought, with Donald caught in the middle. The Battle of the Three Me's raged and lasted all that day.

It was the Good Me who triumphed in the end.

"That's that," he said proudly, when finally the Bad Me lay flat and panting in a heap. He picked up his bright little circle from the ground, brushed off the dust, and placed it neatly in the air above his head. "As for you," he said to Donald sternly, "*you're* going to school."

But the joke, as it turned out, was really on the Good Me. By the time they reached the schoolhouse, it was almost five o'clock. The door was locked. The pupils, the teacher, and even the janitor had all gone home.

Donald Gets His Start

DONALD laughed and he laughed. Ever since he was born he'd had nothing but trouble, but now at last, here was something really funny! The schoolhouse was locked. His school days were over before they had even started! And the joke was on the Good Me.

The Good Me was standing there stiffly with his hands folded, sniffing and scowling as he watched Donald laugh. Then he sighed and shook his head. "You're hopeless," he said. "I wash my hands of the whole affair." And with that he disappeared, right into thin air!

Donald was alone.

It was too good to be true. No Good Me . . . no nurses . . . no boss of any kind! He was free at last to find a man's job!

He hung his books by their strap on the school's front doorknob and walked away whistling. The world was his oyster. It was waiting and full of pearls.

Parked at the street corner ahead, stood a motor car and trailer.

"Hmmmmm," said Donald to himself. "Just the thing. I'll stow away in that trailer . . . go wherever it takes me. When it stops, out I step and I'll take a job right there."

Donald hid in the trailer.

What luck! There were good things just ahead. The world was wide and wonderful. This trailer might take him anywhere. If it took him to an airport, he'd step out and be a pilot. If it took him to a gold mine, he'd step out and he'd be rich. If it took him to a circus, he'd jump out and train the lions. It might take him to a submarine. It might take him to a ranch. And there was always the chance it might take him to the White House. President! Hmmmm . . . nice work if you can get it.

But the trailer fooled him. It took him only down to Chinatown. When Donald stepped out, he was very disappointed. But he glued on a pigtail and took a job in a Chinese laundry.

He walked uptown, toward the big buildings.

"Hmmm," he thought, "I know what I'd like. I think I'll own a hotel." He walked right into a hotel and said so.

But the man in the hotel said that *he* owned the hotel and he didn't need Donald to help own it with him.

"But, say," he asked suddenly, "can you make cakes?"

"Cakes!" laughed Donald. "Sure! Birthday cakes, pancakes . . . *any* kind of cakes at all!"

They gave him a job in the kitchen mixing dough. But the dough he mixed was gooey, and it stuck up all his fingers. Donald lost his temper, smashed a dish, and lost his job.

It was the same way with the next job. He worked carving statues for a wood-carver named Geppetto. But the wood made him mad; it was too full of splinters. Donald lost his temper, smashed the statue . . . lost the job.

And that's the way it went—job after job, day after day.

Jobs . . . Jobs . . . Jobs . . .

THE JOB in the Chinese laundry didn't last. It was all Donald's fault. Donald lost his temper.

Ironing pink shirts with apple-green stripes wasn't any fun at all. Four pink shirts with apple-green stripes were all the shirts he ironed. The fifth shirt of that color made him mad as a hornet. He ripped it off the ironing board and tore it up in pieces. Then he picked up the pieces and he tore them into pieces.

Then Mr. Fong Chang Wong, who owned the laundry, chased him out of the place with a flat iron.

Donald's first job had lasted only twenty minutes!

"Very unfortunate start," thought Donald. "Now I'll have to start over again."

He tried working in an office, answering the phone. But there was something about that telephone that Donald couldn't stand. It clicked and it buzzed and it burkled in his ear. Donald told *that* phone a thing or two . . . and Donald lost *that* job.

He worked for a circus, trying to train a seal to play the horns. The tune he tried to teach him was "My Country 'Tis of Thee." But the seal he tried to train was a Southern seal and all he could play was "Dixie"! That made Donald awfully mad . . . and *again* he lost his job.

He tried to be a fireman . . . but that day he lost his temper because there wasn't any fire.

Donald joined the police force. He thought it would be lots of fun to chase and capture burglars. But *that* day he lost his temper because there wasn't any burglar.

Somehow, he landed a job as a salesman, selling second-hand automobiles. But his tires blew out and Donald's temper blew out, too.

But Donald's really worst mistake happened thousands of feet in the air. When you're a skyscraper worker, if you're smart you hold your tongue.

Donald made the dreadful mistake of talking back to his boss. He never remembered exactly what happened, but that was the end of *that*.

As a matter of fact, it was almost the end of Donald.

Temper. . . Temper. . . Temper. . .

"This is a pretty kettle of fish!" thought Donald on the day he was fired from his eighty-sixth job! He knew what the trouble was, only too well. This temper of his was ruining his life. Something had to be done and done quickly. But what?

This called for great thinking, and Donald sat down to think it all over. "Everyone tells me," he said to himself, " 'Get hold of your temper.' But *how* do you get hold of something you *can't see?* You can't *slap* a temper; there's nothing there to slap. You can't catch a temper . . . it isn't like a fish. You can't grab a temper by the neck and shake it. And a temper doesn't have any clothes, so you just can't kick it in the seat of its pants."

The whole thing was impossible! Donald shrugged his shoulders. "What a situation!" he sighed. And he walked out into the country to forget his worries by eating watermelons.

He saw a very fine patch of melons on the other side of a fence. He climbed over and started eating. It seemed to help a lot. After the fourth melon, he'd forgotten his troubles completely.

But the fun didn't last long.

"Drop that melon!" said a sudden voice at his elbow. "You know these melons aren't yours!"

"Oh—oh!" gulped Donald. He recognized the voice. It was that Good Me person . . . back to pester him again. He was standing right behind him, looking very stern.

"Aww, let me alone," growled Donald.

"Listen," said the Good Me, "if you *really* want to beat your temper, I'll help you. Take this fountain pen and paper and do as I say."

Donald stared at the pen. "Aww, you're fooling. How can a fellow beat a temper with that?"

"Very simply," said the Good Me. "You just write what I tell you. Ready?"

"I suppose so," grunted Donald. Grudgingly he took the pen and the paper.

"Now write," said the Good Me, " 'I will not lose my temper.' "

Donald wrote.

① I will not lose my Temper (SIGNED) donald duck

2 I will not lose my Temper (SIGNED) donald duck
3 I will not lose my Temper (SIGNED) donald duck

"Now, sign your name. Now write it again," said the Good Me. "Write it till you've written it 500 times. When you've finished, you won't have any temper left at all." And saying this, the Good Me disappeared into thin air.

Donald wrote. . . .

Then something suddenly went wrong.

Donald's temper just exploded. He flung the pen over the fence and ran, kicking, through the fields, kicking melons, kicking pumpkins, kicking cabbages and haystacks, kicking barns and bulls and wagons and everything he saw!

4 I will not lose my Temper (SIGNED) donald duck
5 I will not lose my Temper (SIGNED) donald duck
6 I will not lose my Temp-
(OH OH... PEN SLIPPED)
6 AGAIN I will not lose my Tem-
6 AGAIN I will not lose my Tem-
(OF ALL THE TERRIBLE PENS I EVER SAW!)
6 AGAIN I will not loose my Tem-
BAH!!
I'LL LOSE MY TEMPER AS MUCH AS I PLEASE!!
(SIGNED) donald duck

Up the Ladder of Success

DONALD kicked everything there was to be kicked. Then, completely exhausted, he collapsed in his tracks. He slept right there all night in the middle of the fields.

When Donald awoke, it was dawn. There was something about that dawn that made him feel better. His anger had disappeared. The fields were green; a gentle breeze whispered through the treetops; there was dew on all the daisies. And there was a bluebird sitting singing on his stomach.

Much to his own surprise, Donald felt quite happy. He laughed, and the bluebird on his stomach bumped up and down.

"Something's happened," mused Donald. "I feel like a new man!" He jumped up and shook the leaves out of his clothing. Today was the day! Today Donald Duck would *not* lose his temper!

He hiked straight back to town and west to the place where messenger boys were hired.

"Can you ride a bicycle?" the man asked Donald.

"Sir," answered Donald, "today I can ride *anything!*"

"Very well," said the man. "Here's your bike. You deliver this package just as fast as you can."

Donald jumped on the bike.

But he'd never ridden a thing like that before, and he made the mistake of making his feet go around backward. Zizz! . . . heading down the main street tail-end first!

"Can you imagine that?" chuckled Donald. "A *bicycle* trying to make me lose my temper! Not me! Yesterday, maybe. But not today! I'm too smart!"

Donald peddled so fast that he delivered the package backward more quickly than anyone else could have delivered it frontward. The package took him to a most exciting place.

It took him to a theater.

The manager was anxiously waiting out in front, puffing on a cigar, when Donald dashed up. "Thank heaven you got here quickly!" he said, smiling at Donald and taking the package. "This is Madame Hula's costume. Her act goes on in less than five minutes."

"Madame Hula!" gasped Donald. "The great Hawaiian dancer?" She was the fanciest of all fancy dancers in the world! And to think that *he* had been carrying her costume!

The manager tipped him and hurried back toward the theater. But at the door someone stopped him and whispered in his ear. The manager grew pale. He clapped his hands to his forehead. He looked as though he were going to faint.

Donald rushed up and steadied him by the arm. "Take it easy, old man," he said. "What seems to be the trouble?"

"Trouble?" gasped the manager. "Trouble enough! The theater full of people . . . they've paid to see Madame Hula. And Madame Hula! . . . Oh, it's awful, it's incredible! Madame Hula is—"

"Madame Hula is *what?*" demanded Donald.

"Madame Hula," whispered the manager hoarsely, "can't dance. She's down with mumps!"

In the life of every young man there comes the moment when chance knocks at his door. It is the moment when bold decisions must be made.

Donald saw his chance.

He grabbed the package from the manager's hands, tore off the string, and yanked out the dancer's costume. Off came his own clothes! He jumped into Madame Hula's!

And in his straw skirt, before anyone could stop him, Donald was in the theater and up on the stage.

The band struck up a tune, and Donald began to dance. He wiggled that skirt. He waggled that skirt. He swished and flounced and jounced that skirt in a million wriggling ways. Never before had that skirt ever been so busy.

The audience cheered and shouted. No one even remembered that Madame Hula was down with mumps.

When the great dance was over, the manager gave Donald ninety dollars and a pair of silver cufflinks. It was a wonderful day, and Donald had not lost his temper even once.

Fame . . . and Riches!

Donald's luck had changed! From that day on, one good thing led to another.

For two weeks, while Madame Hula lay at home in bed with mumps, Donald danced in her skirt. By the time she was well again, Donald was as famous a dancer as she.

He opened a new kind of dancing school on Broadway and taught all the prettiest girls in New York. He invented new steps . . . side steps and back steps, tango twists and tap-dance turns that set the town a-talking. Housewives and housemaids and even old professors—*everyone* came to Donald's place, and everyone paid five dollars cash to learn the popular Donald Dip.

It was the same way with singing. He took that up, too, and in no time at all he was singing in operas all over the country. He was starred in a big part everywhere he sang. He sang in Wagner's *Rheinduck* and in the *Master Ducks of Nuremberg*.

But that was too easy. So one night in Chicago he showed them something hard. In the most astonishing musical feat of the century, Donald sang *both* operas . . . the two of them at once!

The people in Chicago couldn't believe their own ears. But, for Donald, it was just as easy as rolling off a log.

From there it was only a quick step to radio, and Donald made still another fortune out of that. With the great soprano, Miss Clara Cluck, he sang every night on coast-to-coast networks. He advertised Soap Flakes, Barley Flakes, and Wheat Flakes. He also sang for Face Powders, Ant Powders, Gun Powders and Headache Powders, House Paint and the kind of paint that ladies buy to paint their fingernails red.

Then, almost overnight, came the greatest triumph of them all! Donald received an air-mail special delivery letter. It was from Mickey Mouse . . . in *person!*

dear Donald Duck,;-

You are Terrific! You are stupendous!! you are super-colossal!!!

what i'm getting at is this ...i need you here as an Actor, and i do mean you!

(Signed) MICKEY MOUSE

P.S. You may name your own Salary.

"This is the tops!" shouted Donald, as he raced for the airport and caught the very next plane to Hollywood.

Within three weeks, he was the most famous Movie Actor in all the world!

What a life! Every morning he rode to the studio in a special limousine. It was as long as a locomotive, and on the door it had his initials in colored electric lights.

"It certainly pays," thought Donald, "when a fellow keeps his temper!"

Gentleman and Sportsman

Donald was rich.

He owned bathing suits and beach umbrellas.

He owned ski clothes by the dozen for winter sports at Sun Valley.

He owned straw hats . . .

and derby hats,

checkerboard hats . . .

and hats for playing polo,

and lots of crazy sorts of hats he wore to masquerades.

Then Donald decided it was time to take up hunting.

"Rich men always hunt," he said, "and I'm as rich as any."

He bought a canoe and a jacket and a hunting cap of coonskin, and he went into the forests after wild, enormous birds. He didn't shoot them. Not Donald! He captured them single-handed and he brought them back alive. He captured almost every sort of bird there was, and he put them into cages and brought them back to give to zoos.

Then, birds began to bore him.

"What I really want to hunt," said Donald, "is something big and dangerous. A man like me should hunt the wily moose!"

Donald set out for the north country, to Canada, the home of the moose. All the way there he made plans about how he was going to catch one. A gun? "Not me!" decided Donald.

Then he had an idea. From an old couch blanket and a pair of paper horns he made a moose disguise. Donald was the back legs, and a friend of his the front.

It was a brilliant disguise and it worked like a charm. Donald just sauntered into the forest, and then he sauntered out. Fifteen real moose mistook him for an uncle and sauntered out behind him. Before they realized he was only a couch blanket, Donald had led them all into a cage.

By this time, Donald was getting very cocky. He boasted that he could catch *anything* by just using his brains. "I can even catch fish," he bragged, "without hook, line, or sinker." And the funny thing was, he did!

He built a fish disguise which he held on with suspenders. Then he studied how goldfish swam, and practiced in his bathtub. In no time at all he could swim in his disguise and flip his imitation tail like any fish in the sea.

Then he went to the sea, and dived in to fool them. He fooled haddocks, mackerels, sharks and eels and cuttlefish—and he even fooled some smelts. When they swam up, he laughed, and simply grabbed them with his hand. On April Fool's Day alone, he caught more than five hundred, and mailed them all home to his friends.

Donald's success as a hunter was the talk of the world. Wherever other hunters gathered round a campfire, they talked of nothing else but Donald's new adventures.

Donald was growing cockier and cockier. "From Africa to Australia," he bragged, "from Iceland to Brazil, there is no bird that flies, no beast that runs, no fish that swims, that Hunter Donald cannot conquer!"

And there wasn't . . . until one terrible day. . . .

It didn't happen in the jungle; it happened right at home. And it wasn't a *live* animal that was Donald's undoing. . . .

One morning, while crossing the room to turn off the radio, Donald slipped and fell . . . right into the mouth of a tiger-skin rug! The tiger had been dead for fifteen years, but its teeth were still sharp, and it bit the Great Hunter in fifteen separate places.

For the first time in years, Donald lost his temper! The Great Hunter flew into a rage. He threw himself upon the tiger rug and tore it limb from limb. He bit and clawed and beat it with such loud shoutings and quackings that the neighbors all rushed out from their houses screaming, "Help! Police!" It took all the neighbors, all the police, and all the Fire Department, too, to save the dead-tiger rug from the Great Hunter.

Down the Ladder of Success

His unfortunate accident with the dead-tiger rug changed the whole course of Donald's career. When you're a famous man and *that* sort of thing happens, the story gets around and everyone laughs.

People snickered when they saw Donald on the street. They laughed behind his back, and called him 'Rug-Rasslin Don.' Yesterday he was famous; today he was just a joke.

And being laughed at was one thing Donald could not stand.

"They can't do this to me!" growled Donald. "I'll show 'em!"

His temper had returned and was growing worse every minute. And the worse his temper grew, the worse grew his luck as a hunter.

He bought a pack of hunting hounds and took up hunting foxes. But even the hounds had no respect for Donald.

Whenever Donald shouted "Go!," they'd yawn and go to sleep.

And when Donald ordered "After the fox!," they'd sniff around, looking for bones.

The foxes thought all this was very, very funny. Whenever Donald came to hunt, they would gather around, just to enjoy a good laugh at the hunter. What a joke! A hunter who couldn't manage his dogs!

This was the last straw. Donald boiled over. He vowed he'd never hunt again. When a fox laughs at a hunter, he thought, that's the only thing to do.

Donald's fame was at an end.

POSTCARD

Dear Brother—
I am sending
your angel nephews
to visit you –
Sister.

Mr.
Donald Duck
Hollywood
Calif.

Temper, Temper, More Temper!

As DONALD's temper grew worse and worse, his friends left him one by one. It was getting dangerous, they said, to have *such* a man around. No one could tell when, or why, or how he would fly off the handle next.

He was no longer invited out to dinners, to masquerades, or even to clambakes. And all the people who had hired him wouldn't hire him any more. Although he had been a rich man, he became a poor one almost overnight.

Donald lost his big home and moved to a little cottage.

There he spent his days and nights alone, trying to keep his temper cool, but it grew hotter and hotter!

He bought a book on self-control and tried to read it in a hammock in his garden. But how could he study a book in the fall, when the apples kept dropping on his head?

It was these little things, not the big ones, that made him most furious: bureau drawers that always stuck and sardine cans that wouldn't open. But the worst thing of all was an unexpected post card.

A visit from *nephews!* This on top of everything else? Sister? Preposterous! He didn't know he had one!

His three nephews arrived that very afternoon. They arrived on their tricycles. Without even pausing at the door, they rode right into the house as fast as they could go.

"So nice to be here, Uncle Donald," they screamed as they shot past him. They peddled straight for the parlor, where they started a fast game of polo.

"This din must CEASE!" bellowed Donald. But the three paid no attention. The polo game went on.

It was the beginning of a nightmare month. Donald had never experienced anything like it.

He tried to send them back to their mother, but Huey, Dewey, and Louie wouldn't go. When he tried to train them by teaching them some simple manners, they set off giant cannon crackers under his very tail.

Then Louie found Donald's expensive cello. He used it for a bow to shoot arrows at Persian vases, which he balanced on his brother Dewey's head.

By the end of the month, when they finally did go home, they had wrecked and smashed and shattered half the things that Donald owned.

Then Donald lost his temper as he never had before. *He* wrecked and smashed and shattered everything else himself.

Back to the Beginning

DONALD slammed the door behind him, and walked out into the deep blue night. He was as poor and friendless as he had been the night he was born. He walked aimlessly into the shadows, letting his feet take him wherever they would. On and on he walked. . . .

The lights of the city faded behind him. There was no sound but the noise of crickets. Now and then a cow mooed.

Donald came to the end of a country road, and turned off into the fields. He was walking up a hillside. Suddenly, he stopped. The place where he was standing seemed mysteriously familiar.

He was back where he had started life so many

years ago. It was the very spot where he was hatched!

Donald stood there alone in the night, and his world was black an empty. He had gone such a long way through life, and here he was back where he'd started.

"Horrid thing, temper!" lisped a voice at his elbow. Donald didn't even turn. He knew who *that* was.

"Hello, there, Good Me," Donald answered sadly. "I suppose you've come to give me another bawling out."

"What's the use," sighed the Good Me. "It never helps a bit. I'm afraid your temper will go on forever."

"Forever?" asked Donald.

"Forever," echoed the Good Me. "It is written in the stars. Look!"

Donald gazed up into the bright stars of night. The Big Dipper, the Dog Star, and the Bear Star—all were there. But, blazing fiercely, right there among them, shone another group of stars—stars that Donald had never before noticed.

"Good heavens!" gasped Donald. "That's me!"

The stars were in the shape of a duck—a duck with his fists up, about to lose his temper!

"You've heard of Lucky Stars," said the Good Me. *"Those* are your *Unlucky* Stars. They were in the skies the night you were hatched. And so, my friend, you'll have a temper always. You'll conquer it at times. Then you'll be successful. Other times you'll lose it. Then you'll have more trouble. You'll be rich some more, poor some more, over and over. So all I can say is Good Luck and Good-by."

The Good Me vanished.

Donald scarcely knew that he was gone. He continued to stare through the night at the Duck Stars. He was fascinated.

Finally he burst out laughing, right out loud!

"Stars! Temper! Good Me! Bad Me! Rich Man! Poor Man! Over and over again! WHAT A WORLD!" laughed Donald.

He laughed so much that he became very hungry. And when a poor fellow gets hungry, he has to go to work. It seemed a crazy way to run a world, but really rather funny, and if other people had to work, then so would Donald!

With no money in his pockets, but new ambitions in his heart, Donald hurried back through the moonlight in the direction of the city.

The Runaway Lamb at the County Fair

DANNY was a little lamb, black all over—as black as midnight. He was in a pen in a great big barn full of mooing cows, ba-a-ing sheep, and grunting pigs.

Danny's master, Jeremiah, patted Danny on the head. "Now, you wait here, Danny," said Jeremiah. "I'm going to look around at the Fair. You be a good little lamb, and maybe we'll win a prize later on, you and I."

Then Jeremiah went away.

"So this is the County Fair," said Danny Lamb to himself. "Ba-a-a, I don't like it one bit! I don't like being shut up in a stuffy little pen like this! I want to find Jeremiah and see the Fair with him."

So Danny Lamb put his little black head down and began to butt against the bars of his pen.

Although Danny was just a little lamb, he was a very good butter. Soon a bar was broken and

Danny was free! There was an open door ahead that led right into the Fairgrounds.

It was noisy out there in the Fair, and there were more people than Danny had ever seen.

They pushed Danny this way. They shoved him that way.

"Ba-a-a! How can I find Jeremiah in this big crowd of people?" said Danny to himself.

But on went Danny Lamb, looking for Jeremiah. In and out of the horse barn. In and out of the poultry barn. Past rows of farm machines, shiny and red in the sunlight.

A little boy blew a toy horn next to Danny's ear. "Ba-a-a," said Danny, and he scampered away.

But not a sign of Jeremiah did Danny see. Danny followed the crowd into another building.

It was full of wonderful smells that tickled Danny's little black nose.

There were stacks of golden pumpkins, there were heaped-up apples, pears, and grapes. There were jars of jam and pickles, and plates of tasty homemade pie.

Right before Danny was the plate that held the prize pie. Danny reached for a bite. But a woman spied him.

"Down, doggy!" she cried, with a slap at his nose.

Danny skipped away before she took a second look. Lucky Danny! For if she had seen that he

was a runaway lamb, his adventure would have ended right then and there!

On went Danny. He saw prize-winning oats and wheat and some blue-ribbon corn. It made him hungry, just to look.

"Ba-a-a," he said.

"What was that?" said a man. "It sounded like a lamb."

But Danny was behind the man, and the man didn't see him. "Ba-a-a," said Danny, and skipped away.

All around the Fair went Danny, looking for Jeremiah. His eyes went wide at the sights he saw. His nose and ears tingled with the strange smells and sounds.

Danny listened to the music of the merry-go-round, to the bells that rang, and to the ticket-seller's shouts.

Danny smelled the taffy apples, and the sizzling hot dogs, and the spun sugar candy in twisted paper cones. Oh, how hungry he was!

The little black lamb's empty tummy told him

it was feeding time, but he did not know the way back to his pen in the barn.

Danny's tummy was right. It *was* feeding time. At that very moment, Jeremiah, with a cane and a cowboy hat and a pinwheel he had won, ran to the barn to give his pet lamb his noonday mash.

But when Jeremiah got there, the pen was empty!

"He's gone!" cried Jeremiah. "My little black lamb has run away!"

"Well, you'd better find him soon," said a man near by. "They're going to pick the prize lamb in a few minutes now."

"Oh, dear," cried Jeremiah. "Where can he be?"

So off ran Jeremiah to hunt for his lamb.

It was a little boy who spied Danny first.

"See the black lamb, Mommy," he cried. "May I take him home?"

"Lamb?" said his mother. "Why, it's a runaway lamb!" People turned to look.

"A runaway lamb!" the cry went up.

The shouts frightened Danny, and he ran. He did not watch where he was going. He just put down his head and ran as fast as he could.

So it happened that he did not see the balloon man ahead, with his big bunch of balloons.

The next thing Danny knew, he was all tangled up in those balloon strings, and the gas balloons were carrying him up, up toward the sky—above the reaching hands, above the whole big Fair!

"There he goes! Catch him, someone!" the people cried.

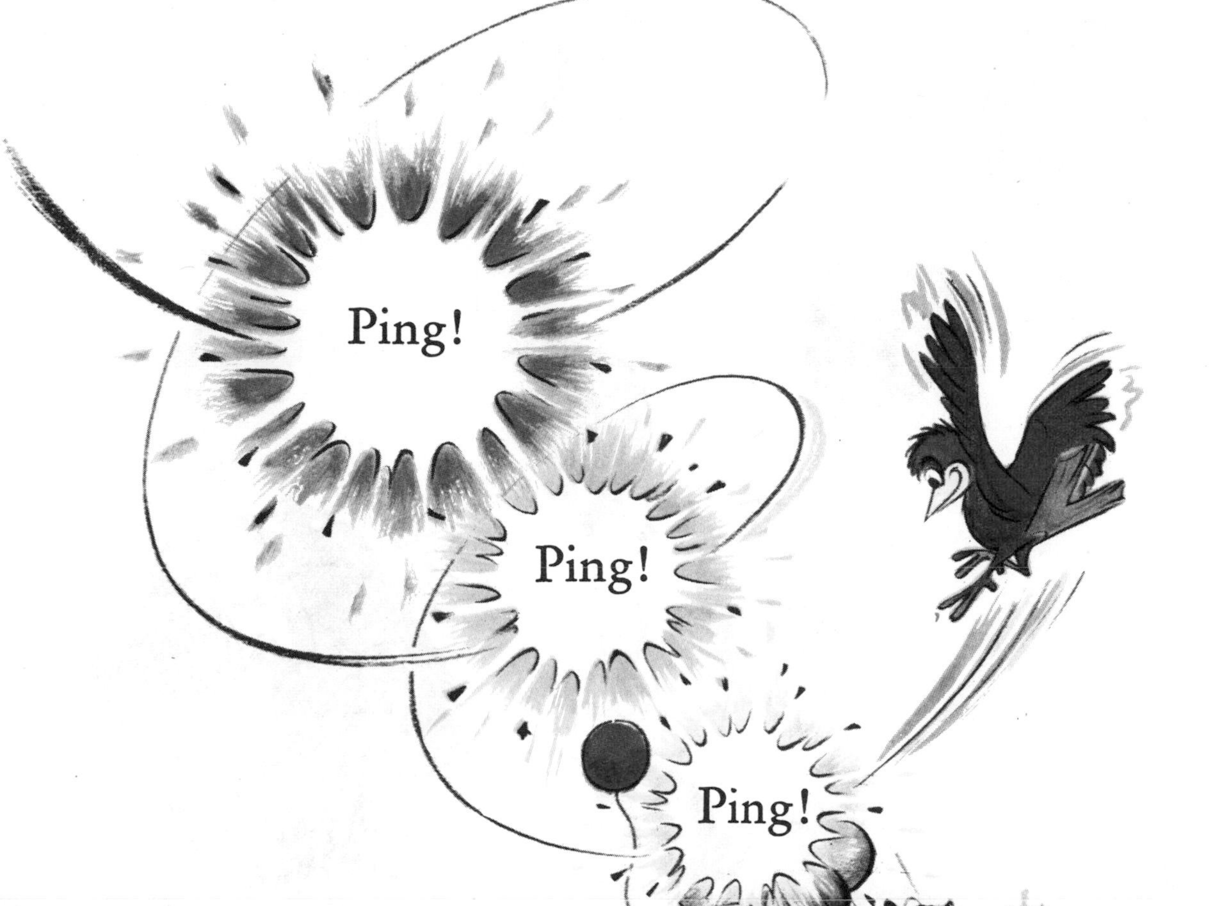

But Danny had floated far out of reach and was bobbing along on the breeze.

"Get a ladder!" a man shouted.

So they brought a tall ladder, and they set it up in Danny's path. Then a tall man climbed way up on top of the ladder, and waited for Danny to come flying by. But a playful breeze turned the balloons aside. The man came down with empty hands, and Danny sailed merrily on.

"The Ferris wheel!" cried someone else. "He's headed that way."

So folks crowded onto the Ferris wheel, just as Jeremiah came along. He had been looking everywhere for his lost lamb.

"Time to pick the prize lamb," called a far-off voice. "Bring your lambs to the judging ring."

"Oh, dear," cried Jeremiah, "now Danny won't have a chance to win!"

"We'll do our best to get him for you," cried the people on the Ferris wheel.

But someone else reached Danny first.

It was a red-headed woodpecker, flying over the Fair to take a look at the sights below.

He spied the balloons, and his eyes danced with fun.

"This looks like good pecking," he said to himself. And he dove at the first balloon with a rat-a-tat of his sharp little bill.

Ping! went the red balloon. It vanished before the woodpecker's eyes. Ping! went the blue balloon and it vanished too.

Down the bird circled, picking off balloons—

Ping! Ping! Ping!

Down flew the woodpecker, and down came Danny, without the balloons to help him fly.

Down he came, and landed right in the judging ring!

"And for the Grand Special Award—" the judge was saying, when Danny dropped down beside him. The judge looked startled, but went on with a laugh—"how can we help giving the Grand Special Award to Danny, the Flying Lamb?"

How the people cheered and shouted! And they lifted Jeremiah into the ring to receive the purple ribbon for his very famous lamb.

"Now aren't you glad you came?" Jeremiah asked his lamb. "Don't you like the County Fair now?"

"Ba-a-a," said Danny Lamb happily. "Ba-a-a, ba-a-a, ba-a-a."

Thumper

IN a forest high in the hills lived many animals. There were opossums and foxes, squirrels and mice. Bambi, the young deer, lived there, and so did Flower, the skunk. There were many birds too, and the wisest of them all was the owl.

But the largest family in the woods was the rabbit family. The mother rabbit had five children, and they kept her busy indeed.

There was Blossom, who had tall, beautiful ears. There was Violet, who had a bushy tail and was very shy.

There was Milly, who was always so hungry that she could never get enough to eat.

There was Frilly, who was very playful. She would rather play than eat or sleep.

And there was Thumper.

Training a big family of rabbits is not easy, but the mother rabbit found most of her children very good. Of course, she wished that Milly would not eat *quite* so much, and she hoped that Violet would stop being so terribly shy. But they were all good about learning manners and obeying.

All except Thumper.

Sweet as he looked, he was a problem!

Every morning the rabbit family went to the meadow and played in the tall grass. Then they went over to a big patch of clover to eat their breakfast.

One day the mother rabbit was watching her children eat breakfast.

"Blossom, come back here and finish your meal," she called. Instead of eating, Blossom was looking into the pond and admiring the reflection of her beautiful, big ears.

Frilly was playing, as usual. "Frilly, you mustn't play with that butterfly until you've eaten two more clumps of greenery," she cried.

Then the mother rabbit noticed Thumper. Nibbling at some sweet flowers, Thumper was not even touching the green leaves.

"Thumper! The flowers are for dessert. What did the wise old owl tell you about eating the leaves first?"

Thumper hung his head, looked at the ground, and thumped his left rear foot. Then he recited what the owl had told him:

Eating greens is a special treat.
They make long ears and great big feet.

"But it sure is awful stuff to eat," he added to himself in a whisper.

Thumper's mother wanted him to eat properly, but *that* was not what worried her most. In the beautiful meadow, she could always make sure that all of her children ate enough greens.

What worried her most was . . . his THUMPING!

Now, all of her children thumped once in a while, beating their strong rear feet against the ground. Rabbits are supposed to thump sometimes, especially when there is danger.

But Thumper thumped about everything.

He thumped when he was ashamed!

He thumped when he was hungry!

He thumped when he was angry!

And he thumped when he was happy!

Thumper really liked to thump.

But Thumper's sisters and Thumper's mother did *not* like his thumping.

"I just can't seem to help it," explained Thumper. "When something happens, I just have to thump."

One day, when the rabbit family was getting ready to go to the meadow, Thumper thumped loudly in his excitement.

"Now, this just *has* to stop!" cried his mother. "I'll have to punish you. Today you cannot go to the meadow with us. Just stay here alone, and maybe you'll learn to control that thumping."

Thumper watched his mother and his sisters hop away. He thumped a few thumps, but then he thought of his friend the owl.

At the base of the tall oak where the big bird had his nest, Thumper thumped as loudly as he could and called, "Hello, Friend Owl."

But Thumper had forgotten that it was daylight and the owl would be sound asleep.

"Stop that infernal noise!" growled the owl, yawning. "What do you mean by waking me out of a sound sleep? If you don't stop that thumping, young man, you're going to get into trouble. Now go away!"

Thumper was very sad. Even the old owl, who had always been his best friend, was angry with him.

The only thing to do, he decided, was to run away from home. Maybe somewhere else he would find friends who didn't mind his thumping.

So Thumper set off, hopping in the opposite direction from the meadow. He had never been very far that way, because his mother had told

him it was dangerous. MAN, who hunted in the forest with his big hunting dogs, lived there.

Thumper didn't know anything about MAN or the dogs, except that all the animals said they were dangerous. But maybe they wouldn't care if he thumped!

After a few minutes, Thumper suddenly heard a strange sound ahead of him. He stopped and listened. Something was crashing through the forest toward him!

Thumper was frightened, so, of course, he thumped on the ground. The hunting dogs heard

the thump and came running toward Thumper. And behind the dogs came the hunters!

Racing homeward, Thumper saw a hollow log and ran into it. He thumped and thumped and thumped, and the log boomed loudly.

Near by, the frog was startled and leaped into the air. Then, when he heard the dogs barking around Thumper's hollow log, the frog was so frightened that he jumped into a nest of pheasants.

"The hunters are coming! Thumper the rabbit warned me!" cried the frog.

The pheasants flew to the oak and woke up the owl. The owl shouted to the crows, and all the birds called to the animals of the forest, "MAN! The hunters are coming! Run to the hills for safety! Thumper the rabbit has given the warning!"

So the animals and the birds of the forest fled to the hills. The hunters and their dogs tramped through the forest for a long time, but all of the forest birds and animals had gotten away safely.

Finally, after several hours, the hunters went home, and the forest was quiet once more.

All the animals returned.

All but Thumper.

Thumper, very frightened by the hunters, still sat inside his hollow log.

The owl and the frog brought Thumper's mother to the log, and then Thumper came out.

The hunters were gone, but now Thumper was afraid his mother would punish him for running away from home. And, in fact, the mother rabbit *was* all ready to scold her son for giving her such a fright.

But the frog and the owl told her how Thumper had warned them of the hunters.

"If it hadn't been for Thumper and his thumping," said the owl, "we would have been in terrible danger."

Then, instead of scolding Thumper, the mother rabbit beamed with pleasure. And as she took her little son home, she vowed that she would never again scold him for thumping too much. All of the birds and animals of the forest agreed with her.

And now Thumper thumps whenever and wherever he likes!

Chip 'n' Dale at the Zoo

CHIP 'N' DALE, two little chipmunks, had just found a new storehouse for their winter supply of nuts. They were having a busy day, for storing nuts was important.

"This big tree is just right for us," said Chip. "It is partly hollow and it has a hole for a door, high above the ground. I'll toss the nuts up to you and you can throw them inside the tree."

"Yes, we can store lots of nuts here," said Dale happily. "There is certainly plenty of room, more than we ever had. So we can eat and eat, and be comfortable, besides."

"We'll need more than this pile to last through the winter," said Chip, thinking of the long months of cold weather ahead. "So let's get these put away, and then look for more nuts somewhere else."

Chip was a bit worried, because he knew they didn't have nearly enough to last the winter. It was not a good year. Most of the trees had fewer nuts than usual. So it was more important than ever that their nuts be kept safe and dry, where the rain or snow would not spoil them. That is why the chipmunks were so happy to find this good hollow tree storehouse.

"Here—catch!"

Chip threw the nuts up, one by one. Dale caught them easily, then tossed them into the hollow tree. Chip saw that Dale was saying something to himself, but he couldn't hear what it was.

"What are you muttering to yourself?" asked Chip.

"I am alphabet-counting," said Dale.

"You are what?" asked Chip.

"I am counting nuts with A-B-C, to help me remember my letters. I will let you know when we get to the Z, but I am not nearly there yet."

"If we have that many," said Chip. He picked up another nut and threw it up to Dale. Then he realized it had felt different. It looked different, too, not at all like an acorn, as it sailed through the air.

"What's this one?" Dale asked, deftly catching it. "It's not the same as all the others."

"Hold it! Don't throw it in the tree," said Chip. "I want to come up and look at it closer. I thought it was different as soon as I threw it."

Chip quickly climbed the tree. The two chipmunks examined the nut carefully. It had a very strange shape, and a thin shell. It rattled when they shook it, and when they opened it they found not just one nut, but two—one for each chipmunk. Best of all, it tasted very good.

"What is it?" asked Dale.

"I think it is a peanut. I heard about them once. I'd like more," said Chip.

"Me, too," Dale agreed.

"Let's look around and find the trees they grow on," suggested Chip. "Maybe we can find a peanut tree."

Of course they didn't find any peanuts growing on trees, because they grow only on vines and ripen underground—but Chip 'n' Dale didn't know that.

The two chipmunks looked at all of the nearby trees, the big ones and the little ones, and the bushes, too. They did not find a thing until Chip ran out on a long, twisted limb from their own tree. It had grown out over a high brick wall.

"Come quick! Look!" cried Chip, as he pointed over the wall. Dale came running, as fast as he could.

"Peanuts!" cried Chip. They could see dozens of peanuts, hundreds of peanuts, yes, thousands of peanuts and peanut shells on the floor of some animal cages. And people were outside the cages, throwing more good peanuts to the animals that were inside. What did it all mean?

Chip and Dale had discovered that their new tree was growing next to a zoo!

There were lots of animals in the zoo, in cages behind bars, or in the open, behind fences that were strong and safe. There were lions and tigers and elephants and monkeys and giraffes and

"Look at that!" cried Chip.
"Let's go!" said Dale.

camels and big bears and seals and gorillas and anteaters and more than you could say in one breath.

"Look at all those peanuts everywhere," said Chip, hardly believing his eyes.

"They must grow in bags around here," said Dale, "because everybody has a bag of them."

"Let's go get some," said Chip. "There are more than enough for everybody."

The two chipmunks dropped down to the ground and looked around.

"Where shall we go first?" asked Dale. "This is a big place."

"Let's go where the most people are. That's where the most peanuts would be," replied Chip. "Follow me."

They heard a heavy rumbling coming from a nearby cage. In it were three bears.

"Papa Bear, Mama Bear, and—that cannot be Baby Bear," said Chip, "unless he grew up considerably."

"I'm glad I didn't taste Papa Bear's hot porridge, the way Goldilocks did," said Dale. "Look at his sharp claws."

"I'm glad I didn't taste Mama Bear's cold porridge either," said Chip. "Look at those sharp teeth."

"Or that Baby Bear's just-right bowl of porridge. He looks as fierce as the others," Dale said.

"I'm scared, just looking at those bears," said Chip. "No nut-snatching here."

They scampered over to the camels, but no one had thrown them any peanuts. The lions and tigers growled and whimpered and purred and almost roared—and looked very interested and very, very hungry when they saw the two little chipmunks.

"These fellows think we'd each make one good bite," said Chip. "This is no place for us either."

"Nope, and no peanuts," said Dale.

"Something is happening over that way," said Chip hopefully. "Listen to the hand-clapping. Let's see what's going on."

They ran toward the new sound, and saw a big pool of clear, cool water. Some large, friendly seals splashed in the pool or sat on the rocks, all looking as though they were enjoying a treat. The keeper was throwing them some things that were evidently good to eat.

One big seal clapped his flippers together. That was the sound of hand-clapping that Chip had heard.

"Maybe we're in luck here," said Chip. "I'll see what the keeper is giving away."

The curious chipmunk hopped down on the rock next to the largest seal. The seal was so surprised to see Chip that he completely missed catching the next fish the keeper threw—or did the keeper throw his next fish at Chip on purpose? Whatever way it happened, the fish knocked Chip over, and he got away from the seal pond as fast as he could go.

"Ugh!" said Chip, rubbing himself off with grass and leaves, to get rid of the fishy smell. "That was no peanut."

There was just one more cage to see—right next to the high brick wall that ran below their tree.

It was like a large, fenced yard, and in it was an enormous animal with the happiest of smiles on its face.

Chip 'n' Dale stared in amazement. This was the biggest anything they had ever seen. Then their eyes opened wider. Because the ground was covered with peanuts, and the big animal wasn't even bothering to pick them up.

"Look at that whatsit," said Dale. "It has two tails, a big one in front, and a little one behind."

"It is an elephant," explained Chip, who knew more about things than Dale. "The front one is his trunk and the back one is his real tail."

"Look how he holds his trunk out when people give him a peanut! He flips it right into his mouth," said Dale, fascinated.

"He won't miss anything if we take some of the peanuts," said Chip. "He's getting enough."

The big elephant swayed back and forth and seemed to pay no attention as Chip and Dale slipped between the bars and scooped up an armful of peanuts. Very quietly they tiptoed toward the brick wall, hoping to reach the overhanging limb of their own tree. They were so excited at their find that they did not notice the elephant was watching them closely. He swung his trunk over toward the tree. Instead of climbing the tree, unknowingly they ran up the elephant's trunk.

Chip jumped over onto the limb of their real tree and was about to throw his peanuts into the hollow storehouse when he heard a sound. It was Dale, tossing his armful of peanuts into the pleased elephant's mouth!

"Hey, what do you think you're doing?" yelled Chip.

"Tossing my peanuts into our tree," said Dale. "What's the matter, can't you see?"

"That's the elephant's mouth!" shouted Chip.

"Mouth!" cried Dale, and he made such a flying leap that he landed on Chip with a thud. Chip's peanuts went flying and fell back inside the wall.

"We're not giving up yet," said Chip grimly.

They watched and waited until the elephant was busy, snatching up peanuts as more people came. Then they hurried down the wall to get another armful, as quietly as they could, making not a single sound.

But luck was against them again. The elephant saw them, and he pelted them with the peanuts in his trunk. They came at Chip 'n' Dale like bullets. The two dropped their loads, and themselves, to the ground. They were a bit scared. What next? But the elephant just turned and walked away.

"We can't let him get away with that," said Chip angrily. "We'll let him know *we* have some spirit, too. Come on, help me."

Tugging and pulling at the limb of the tree they pulled it back, back—and let it go! Whack! It spanked the back of the surprised elephant. This was like a game, and the elephant grinned.

"We've got to think of a way to get some of those peanuts," said Dale.

"Well, they don't really belong to us," said Chip sadly, "so maybe we ought to forget about them. But we'd better put the rest of the acorns in our tree. At least they're ours, because we worked to get them."

They were tired when they resumed that task, and even more tired by the time they were finished. They stretched out on the limb of the tree to rest, and the sound of music floated over to them. It was the band at the zoo.

Chip had an idea. "I know how we'll get some peanuts!" he cried. "We'll work for them—we'll dance. Like this!"

He hopped over to the top of the wall and started to tap dance. Dale joined him, and they danced faster and faster, until both of them were out of breath.

But no one threw any peanuts. The zoo visitors were watching the musicians in the band, and not one person saw the chipmunks dance. That is, hardly anyone, except the elephant and his keeper, and both of them were enjoying the performance.

"Isn't that nice! They must be dancing just for us," said the keeper.

"We're really working for peanuts, but we

aren't getting any," Chip said to Dale. They danced on and on to the music, hoping that the people would see them.

"It's no use," puffed Dale at last.

But the elephant and his keeper decided differently.

"We ought to show our appreciation and give them something," the keeper said, "and maybe they'll dance for us again one of these days."

It is said that elephants never forget, and indeed this one remembered that Dale had given him a whole armful of peanuts, all at once. Maybe some day the chipmunks would do that again.

And that is why, when poor Chip 'n' Dale got so tired they had to sit down and rest—WHIZZ! WHIZZ! a stream of peanuts suddenly came shooting through the air toward them, and landed inside the hollow tree.

"Peanuts! Flying through the air!" cried Chip. "Hundreds of them!"

"Wh-where are they coming from?" asked Dale. "Could it be raining peanuts?"

And then they saw the elephant smiling his big elephant smile, and the keeper standing on the elephant's head, aiming the trunk so not even one peanut fell to the ground. They all went straight inside the hollow tree. Why, there were enough peanuts for a whole year!

"They must have enjoyed our dancing," smiled Dale. "This is the best kind of applause."

"We'll do it again soon," smiled Chip. "This way of working for peanuts is fun."

So it happened that whenever the band played and the elephant trumpeted at them over the wall, Chip and Dale knew it was a signal for them to dance again. And if the elephant was too lazy or too hungry to pick up peanuts one at a

"You left some unfinished business, though," Chip said to Dale one morning as he looked at the big pile of nuts stored in the tree. "Remember?"

"What's that?" asked Dale, munching his breakfast contentedly.

"You were going to alphabet-count our nuts, from A to Z. You started on A, but you never got all the way to the Z."

time, Chip and Dale would scamper over the wall and pick up an armful of peanuts—and plop them into the elephant's mouth all at once. It was a fine arrangement all around. Of course they all became the best of friends—the elephant, the keeper, and Chip 'n' Dale.

"Yup, I remember," said Dale. "Should I try to do it now?

"No," laughed Chip, "we didn't go from A to that Z, we went from A to Zoo—and I think that's a lot better!"

Don't you think so, too?

The Little Red Hen

A Swinging Fairy Tale

ONE DAY the Little Red Hen went looking for treasure. She had heard about the miller's son who had found a sack of gold under a rock in the road. She had heard about the wise old man who gave the poor shepherd boy a golden goose. She had heard about the leprechauns with their bags of gold under thorn bushes.

So she decided to get some of this loot for herself. With her little wicker basket under her arm, she went forth. By the end of the day she was scratched from the thorns, tired of speaking to dull old men, and she had muscle strain from lifting rocks out of the road. And did she find any treasure? You bet she didn't.

On the way home, however, she did find a grain of wheat on the road. "Oh-ho," she cackled to herself. "This is an omen. I will plant it and reap it and grind it and bake it and have some bread for my tea. And somewhere along the line a handsome prince will come by and eat the bread and I'll move into the palace." At this stage of the game, she was willing to settle for head cook in the castle, in case the prince already had a princess.

So she picked up the grain of wheat and carried it home.

Next day, bright and early, she went to the field to plant the grain of wheat. On the way to the field she saw Gus Goose asleep under a spreading maple tree.

She went up to Gus and asked, "Will you help me plant this grain of wheat?"

"Not I." replied Gus, opening his eye barely enough to see whom he was talking to. "Sorry, Little Red Hen, but I've just returned from my vacation, and I'm resting up."

"Well, if that's the way you're going to be, I'll have to plant it by myself," she said. And she marched on toward the field.

Pretty soon she found Donald Duck, sitting cross-legged on the grass playing his bongo drums. *Trippity-thud-trippity-boom* went the bongos. Donald looked up. "High, Chickie-baby, what's the scam?"

The Little Red Hen didn't know what he was talking about. Besides, she thought he had her confused with Chicken Little (which indeed he had). She said, "Will you help me plant this grain of wheat?"

Trippity-thud-trippity-boom! "I don't plant seeds, I *eat* them," Donald replied.

The Little Red Hen knew the handsome prince would never come by if she didn't plant the seed, so she walked on toward the field. Pretty soon she found Donald Duck's three nephews, Huey and Dewey and Louie. They were sitting on the ground, close together. She approached them and said, "Will you help me plant this grain of wheat?"

"Shhhh," said Louie. "We're listening to the dragon fights on our transistor radio. No time for planting right now—the dragon is ahead of Saint George on points."

"Then I will plant it myself," she said. And she walked to the edge of the field. There she dug a small hole with her trowel, dropped in the seed,

patted down the rich brown earth, and went away. She knew the hot sun and the warm rain would make her seed grow.

The seed did grow, and soon the time came for the Little Red Hen to reap the wheat.

On her way to the field she passed Gus Goose. He was still asleep. "Will you help me reap my wheat?" she asked.

"Sorry, Little Red Hen," Gus answered. "But it was a long hard vacation, and I haven't caught up on my resting yet."

she walked up smiling and said, "Oh, boy, am I going to have fun! I'm going to reap my wheat."

"Have your fun," said Dewey, looking up from the radio. "Saint George finally has the dragon on the ropes, and we couldn't leave now, even if we wanted to."

"Then I will reap it myself," she said as she moved away. Arriving at the field, she took out her scythe and reaped the lone stalk of wheat.

Once she had reaped the wheat, she had to take it to the mill to be ground into flour. So she

"Then I will reap it myself," she said.

Next she came to Donald Duck, who was pounding on his bongos. "Reaping time," she called.

"Dig, Chickie. But not now. I'm practicing a riff."

Trippity-thud-trippity-boom went the bongos. The Little Red Hen said, "I don't know what a riff is, but I don't think it has anything to do with reaping wheat." Which indeed it hadn't.

Nearing the field, she saw the three Duck nephews. Again they were grouped around their transistor. Deciding to try a different approach,

went to Gus Goose and asked, "Who will help me grind my wheat?" But Gus was resting up from his morning nap and didn't answer.

She went to Donald Duck and asked, "Who will help me grind my wheat?"

Donald replied, "This is no grind, this is groovy." And the bongos went *trippity-thud-trippity-boom.*

Again, the Little Red Hen didn't understand what Donald was talking about. She was puzzling over his strange answer when she heard the Duck nephews' transistor radio. "Who will help me grind my wheat?" she asked.

"Not now," Huey said. "The dragon and Saint George have joined forces and are beating up on the referee! Sit down and listen. Wow!"

The Little Red Hen didn't like the sound of that at all, so she scurried away to the mill. Mickey Mouse was glad to grind the wheat, and she left the mill with just enough flour for a fine loaf of bread.

She wandered around asking, "Who will help me bake my bread?" But nobody was interested, so she did it herself. When she took the loaf from the oven, she put it on the window sill to cool.

At this moment who should come strolling down the lane but Gladstone Gander, who was known far and wide as one lucky duck. He was in costume to try out for the lead in *The Student Prince,* soon to be presented by the Duckville Summer Hiking and Theater Society.

He smelled the bread cooling on the window sill, and he said to himself, "Gladstone, you lucky duck, some kind soul has put this loaf of bread on the window for you to eat. How lucky can you get?" He took the loaf of bread and sat down to enjoy it.

But the Little Red Hen didn't see Gladstone Gander. Thinking that her loaf of bread was safe, she ran to her friends. "Who will help me eat my bread?" she asked.

Gus Goose leaped up from his resting place. "Vacation's over," he announced happily. "Time for a little old-fashioned bread eating."

Donald Duck was in the middle of a *trippity-boom* when he heard Little Red Hen call out.

He dropped the bongos immediately and ran toward the house. "Scoobie-doo, baby, I'm with you," he said, and though the Little Red Hen didn't quite understand him, she thought he was saying nice things.

The Duck nephews heard the glad words above the blare of their transistor, and they turned it off. "Dragon fight's over," they shouted. "Time for some bread and jam."

Soon they were all at the Little Red Hen's house—all except the loaf of bread. "Where is the bread?" they all asked together.

Then they all saw Gladstone Gander licking his fingers. Donald pointed to Gladstone. "There is the luckiest Duck in the valley."

"In the *world*," added Gus Goose.

The Little Red Hen was overjoyed. Her bread had been eaten by a prince. She recognized him immediately.

"You," she said, "are a prince. You have come to give me treasure—rubies and diamonds and sapphires and emeralds."

"Who?" Gladstone asked. "Me?"

"Of course you. You're a prince, aren't you?"

"As a matter of fact, I'm an out-of-work actor," said Gladstone.

Everybody looked at Gladstone, then they all looked at the Little Red Hen. They all wondered what she would do. After a while she shrugged and said, "Well, you can't win 'em all."

The Gingerbread Man

A Swinging Fairy Tale

Minnie Mouse was busy in her new air-conditioned, all-gas-and-electric, Green Ribbon kitchen. It had stainless steel table tops, walnut paneled walls, non-skid tile on the floor, non-glare glass in the windows, hidden fluorescent lighting, a teakwood spice cabinet and a complete set of all the new uncrackable and unmeltable mixing bowls. Considering the equipment she had to work with, she could have cooked a gourmet dinner for any gourmet—even a king.

So what did she cook? A gingerbread man. A lone, solitary gingerbread man. It had two raisins for eyes, a cherry for a nose, and three currants for buttons down his front. As a matter of fact, it was a handsome gingerbread man, as gingerbread men go. And as gingerbread men go, this one went!

It happened after Minnie had set him to cool

on the maple-grained plastic no-stain table top, while she was wiping up crumbs from the Self-Help Eye-Beam oven and putting the pots and pans in the Jiffy Aide combination dishwasher-dryer. One minute the gingerbread man was there, and the next he wasn't. He had pushed open the see-through odor-proof two-way kitchen door and rushed out into the garden like a Notre Dame halfback. Minnie saw him running down the path.

She knew he wouldn't last long in the outside world, so she cried, "Stop! Stop!"

As he ran away, the Gingerbread Man sang:

"Run run run,
"As fast as you can;
"You can't catch me
"I'm the Gingerbread Man."

Minnie put her hands on her hips and stamped her foot. "We'll see about *that*," she snorted. And she started after him.

Sprinting down the road, he came upon Mickey Mouse's nephews, Morty and Ferdy. Minnie called to them, "Help me save the Gingerbread Man." Morty and Ferdy were on their way to try out for the local Pop Warner football team, and they took the proper stance to tackle the Gingerbread Man.

But he speeded up like Gale Sayers, gave them a swivel hip, and scooted between them, running to daylight. As he ran away, he called:

"Run run run,
"As fast as you can;
"You can't catch me—
"I'm the Gingerbread Man.
"I ran away from Minnie
"And I can get away from you."

Morty and Ferdy, the would-be linebackers, were humiliated. "Stop! Stop!" they yelled. But the Gingerbread Man didn't stop, any more than Jim Grabowski would stop if some shrimpy rookie yelled at him.

The Gingerbread Man ran farther down the road. Pretty soon he came to Chip 'n Dale. The two perky chipmunks were passing an acorn back and forth like a football, when the Gingerbread Man ran by.

"Hi, Gingerbread Man! Wanna run pass patterns?" asked Chip.

But the Gingerbread Man didn't. He sang:

"Run run run,
"As fast as you can;
"You can't catch me—
"I'm the Gingerbread Man.
"I got away from Minnie
"And those two scrub tacklers
"And I can get away from you."

The chipmunks looked down the road and, sure enough, there were Minnie and Morty and Ferdy, all chasing the Gingerbread Man.

"Looks like fun," said Chip. So they joined in the game, whatever it was.

Soon they were running through the woods. Of course, they weren't the only ones running in the woods. The Three Little Pigs were running for their very lives. Behind them was the Big Bad Wolf. Practical Pig, who happened to be in the lead, shouted, "OK, guys, play number 21-53-B." At that moment his brothers slowed down enough to let the wolf grab their curly tails.

Then one pig ran on the right side of big pine tree, and his brother ran on the left side. The Big Bad Wolf was too greedy to let go of either tail, so—

BONK!

He hit his head on the tree, and half a dozen pine cones fell to the ground. He let go of the pigs' tails and rubbed his head. He tried to run again, but he slipped on the fallen pine cones. This gave the pigs time to run home to their little brick house and slam the door and bolt it.

At that moment the Gingerbread Man ran by their cottage. Practical opened the window and yelled, "Hey, Gingerbread Man, you're getting into wolf country. Come on in here. We'll help you."

The Gingerbread Man wasn't about to believe Practical, either. Instead, he shouted:

"Run run run,
"As fast as you can;
"You can't catch me—
"I'm the Gingerbread Man.
"I got away from Minnie
"And those two scrub tacklers
"And that pint-sized Joe Namath
"And I can get away from you."

Practical was astounded that anybody would doubt his sound advice. He yelled, "But you don't know about the Big Bad Wolf. He's tricky. Stop! Stop!"

The Gingerbread Man had heard the word "Stop" so many times that he knew only one thing—when anybody yells "Stop," all good Gingerbread Men should keep going!

The pigs stared at each other in astonishment. "We can't let him go any farther, or he's done for."

The other two pigs agreed, so they threw caution to the winds and took off after the Gingerbread Man.

The Gingerbread Man led them deeper and deeper into the woods, and soon he came to a river. Sitting at the edge of the river was the Big Bad Wolf. He was holding a damp cloth to his aching head when the group appeared on the trail. There was the Gingerbread Man, followed by Minnie, Morty, Ferdy, Chip 'n Dale, and the Three Little Pigs. At first the Big Bad Wolf didn't believe what he was seeing. "What's this?" he asked—"the Cleveland Browns doing roadwork?"

By this time the Gingerbread Man was getting tired. He thought the Big Bad Wolf looked like a kindly old codger, so he decided to seek his help.

"Kindly Old Codger," the Gingerbread Man

said, "I must escape from those single-minded people. You appear to be a Nice Person, so would you please take me across the stream?"

"My pleasure," sneered the Wolf. "I am here to help—heh-heh-heh."

So the Gingerbread Man jumped on his back, and the Big Bad Wolf started swimming.

On the bank of the stream, everybody was very unhappy.

"We tried to warn him," said the Three Little Pigs.

"We were a fraction of a second too slow," complained Morty and Ferdy.

"Him make great split-end," said Chip.

Minnie was disgusted with the whole thing. "Well, back to my Stay-Crease Dry-Drip Never-Fail kitchen stove, with the solid bronze casters," she said.

And they all turned sadly around and went home.

All except the Big Bad Wolf, who was swimming slowly across the stream. He was in no hurry.

Presently the Gingerbread Man said, "Mister, I am getting wet."

"Then jump on my head," said the Wolf.

After a while the Gingerbread Man said, "Mister, I am getting wet even on your head."

"Then jump on my nose," said the Wolf.

So the Gingerbread Man jumped on Wolf's nose. Which was his last mistake.

Gobble. Crunch. Smack.

In a minute the Big Bad Wolf had eaten him up.

Which is what should happen to all Gingerbread Men.

Chicken Little

A Swinging Fairy Tale

Chicken Little lived with her mother and father, Mr. and Mrs. Samuel J. Little, in a pink house at the edge of a large oak grove. She was kind of a dumb kid, and she was flunking math, geography, and science. She didn't do much but sit around and daydream.

This was OK with her mother and father. Mr. Little was away most of the day, spraying his oak trees, and Mrs. Little stayed in the house and tidied up. She cleaned out closets, cupboards, wine cellars, gardening sheds—anything that had a speck of dirt in it. So when Chicken Little chose to sit outside and dream the Big Dreams of Tomorrow, both her mother and father were glad to be left alone.

Chicken was sitting under an oak tree one day, dreaming about becoming a princess and wearing a crimson silk dress, when a tiny acorn fell on her head.

Now, if Chicken Little hadn't been flunking science, she would have known that acorns come from oak trees, and they fall off all the time. But she didn't know this, and instead she thought the sky was falling. She jumped up and said to herself, "Oh my, the sky is falling! I must go and tell the king!"

But first she went to her mother to get permission to see the king. Mrs. Little was busy cleaning out under the sink, and she had no time for her daughter. The little girl said, "Mother, Mother, the sky is falling! I must go and tell the king!"

Her mother said, "That's nice, dear. Be home in time for dinner." And so Chicken Little set off down the road.

If Chicken Little hadn't been flunking geography, she would have known that the road to the king's palace was to the left, under the freeway, and straight up the hill. But she didn't know this, so she ran down the path to the right, in the wrong direction.

She ran into the forest, and the first person she met was Donald Duck. Donald was out with his

bow and arrow, trying to shoot some game for dinner. But he hadn't found anything. In fact, he had lost three arrows—and his temper. He was very angry.

He saw Chicken Little running toward him. "Hi, Chicken," he said. "Seen any moose or elk or anything I can shoot for dinner?"

"No time for that," she answered. "I'm in a big hurry."

"How come? Where are you going?"

"I'm going to tell the king the sky is falling."

"Sky falling?" gasped Donald. "No wonder I haven't been able to hit anything with my bow and arrow."

"Yes," said Chicken Little. "I bet the sky kept getting in the way."

"Obviously," Donald reasoned. He added, "How do you *know* the sky is falling? Tell me—are you *sure?*"

"I saw it with my eyes. I heard it with my ears. And a piece of it fell on my head."

"Well," said Donald, "I'll come with you and we'll tell the king together!" So they went running down the road.

Soon they came to Goofy. He was lying in a hammock, taking a snooze. He opened one sleep-filled eye and gazed at them. "Duh, what's up?" he asked.

"Not up. *Down.*" Chicken Little said excitedly. "The sky is falling!"

Though Goofy is not noted as a great thinker, he did a little thinking. And looking. He stared upward at the sky. "It looks as far away as it usually does," he observed. "How do you know it's falling?"

"I saw it with my eyes. I heard it with my ears. And a piece of it fell on my head."

"Dad-gum, then you must be right. If I were you, I'd go and tell the king."

Donald Duck piped up, "That's exactly what we're going to do. Do you want to come with us?"

"I guess so. I was getting tired of sleeping anyway."

So Goofy got out of his hammock, and the three of them went off to tell the king.

They hurried through the woods, and soon they found Mickey Mouse sitting on a log reading a book. Now Mickey Mouse is a pretty smart cookie, and not one to fall for any lame-brain story about a falling sky.

"Hi there, Goof," he said to Goofy. "Where ya going?"

"To tell the sky the king is falling," said Goofy.

"No, Goofy," Donald Duck corrected him. "To tell the *king* the *sky* is falling."

"You've got to be kidding," said Mickey.

"No, Mick. Ask Chicken Little. She'll tell you."

Mickey asked her, "How do you know the sky is falling?"

Chicken answered, "I saw it with my eyes. I heard it with my ears. And a piece of it fell on my head."

Mickey was doubtful. "I haven't read anything about it in any of my books. In fact, I never heard of such a thing.

"Of course not," Donald explained. "This is the first time. This is something *new*."

Mickey still wasn't so sure they were right, but he thought it wouldn't hurt if he were to go along

to see the king. So he joined in, and the four of them trotted off through the forest.

Soon they passed a little cottage, and smoke was wisping from the chimney. There, standing in the doorway, was Minnie Mouse. Before anybody could say anything, she spoke up. "Why, you're in time to help me with my cake."

"But we're in a hurry, Minnie," said Mickey, "the sky is falling and—"

"It can wait!"

"Wait for what?"

"For me to finish my cake," Minnie replied. "I'm about to mix everything together, and I need a few strong right arms."

Before they knew what had happened, Minnie had herded them together in the kitchen. "It's an extra big cake," she explained, "so I need to double the recipe."

And she set Donald to breaking eggs, Goofy to sifting flour, and Chicken Little to doubling the amount of baking powder. Unfortunately, Chicken Little was flunking math, and she mumbled to herself, "Let's see now. Two times three is . . . *ten!*" So she put ten teaspoons of baking powder in the batter.

When the cake was ready to go in the oven, Donald and Goofy and Mickey and Chicken Little said good-bye to Minnie.

Minnie was surprised that they weren't staying. "Where are you going in such a hurry?" she asked.

Chicken Little answered, "To tell the king the sky is falling."

Minnie was surprised. "How do you know the sky is falling?"

"I saw it with my eyes. I heard it with my ears. And a piece of it fell on my head."

"Oh, dear," said Minnie, "then maybe I'd better

go along. I can use an oven at the palace and save on the gas bill." So she joined them, with her cake batter in a bowl which she carried under her arm.

They hadn't gone more than a quarter mile when they met the Big Bad Wolf. He was prowling through the bushes looking for the Three Little Pigs. When he saw Chicken Little and Donald and Goofy and Mickey and Minnie with her cake batter, he forgot about the pigs.

Wiping the pine needles off his hat and putting on his best manners, he asked, "Why hello, you-all. Where are you going on this warm day?"

"To tell the king the sky is falling," said Chicken Little.

"The sky? Falling? Well, I declare. How can you tell?"

"I saw it with my eyes. I heard it with my ears. And a piece of it fell on my head."

"Yes, I can see that," murmured the sly old wolf. Brightening, he suggested, "Why don't you-all come to my house for a mint julep and a bit of refreshment?"

"But we've got to see the king," said Chicken Little.

"Ah, little one," cautioned the wolf, "the palace is a long way off, and if the sky falls right away, you'll need the protection of a sturdy roof."

"I guess you're right," Chicken Little agreed.

"Then let's haul out for my place," the wolf said, "and wait to see what happens."

So they did. Chicken Little, Donald Duck, Goofy, Mickey Mouse and Minnie—they all went to the Big Bad Wolf's shack in the woods.

No sooner had they entered the house than the Big Bad Wolf slammed the door shut and locked the heavy-duty padlock. Then he ran around to the window. "Why don't you put the cake in the oven to bake. I'll mosey down to the General Store for some candles, and we'll all have a dandy party."

Chicken Little clapped her hands in joy. "Oh, good! I like parties."

"Hmmmm. So do I," the wolf muttered to himself. He slammed the window shut and jogged down the lane to the store. He thought to himself, "My, what a fine dinner I'm going to have. Chicken, Duck, AND a cake. Oh, boy! My birthday isn't until August, but I think I'll celebrate tonight."

He was far away when the sky darkened and BOOM! Minnie's cake blew up. The door of the house fell out, the windows fell in, and the roof sailed somewhere into the next county. Scrambling out came Chicken Little, Mickey Mouse, Minnie Mouse, Donald Duck and, last but not least, Goofy.

Minnie was very sad. "I don't know what could have happened to my cake. I measured everything so carefully." Alas, poor Minnie would never know that Chicken Little couldn't add. She had put enough baking powder in that cake to level the Taj Mahal.

In the excitement of the Big Bad Wolf's shack blowing up, they all forgot about the sky falling. Chicken Little ran home to her mother's clean house. Goofy ran back to his hammock. Mickey ran back to his book. And Minnie ran home to tear up that cake recipe.

And it's just as well they never got to the palace, for the king wasn't there. He was out for the day, attending the royal ball game.

And the Big Bad Wolf? What of him? He came back and saw his house flat on the ground. And he held his face in his paws and wailed, "Oh, my! The sky *did* fall—right on top of my house!"

Duck in Boots

A Swinging Fairy Tale

TODAY EVERYBODY knows that Scrooge McDuck is without doubt the world's richest duck. His vaults filled with gold, his swimming pool filled with money—these are common sights along the highway. His stinginess, his penny-pinching—these are common topics of conversation around the world.

But the McDuck family wasn't always rich. There was a time when Scrooge's great-great-great-grandfather was penniless. In fact, he had nothing to call his own except a nephew named Donald.

"Wak," said Donald one day. "We shall soon die of hunger, Uncle Scrooge, for I know of no way to earn a living."

Scrooge of old, much like Scrooge of today, did not give up easily. "No," he said, leaning on his cane, "I have an idea. Maybe not a good idea, but an idea. Get me a sack and a pair of boots."

Donald thought that hunger pangs were affecting Uncle Scrooge's brain. "Sack? Boots?" he muttered to himself. But he hunted in the attic until he found an old burlap sack and a splendid pair of shiny boots. He gave them to Scrooge, who set off into the woods. When he came to a clearing he put down the sack. (Fortunately for Scrooge the sack had some juicy carrots in it, otherwise the story would have ended right here.)

Soon a fat rabbit came by and sniffed the carrots. As the rabbit sniffed the carrots, Scrooge popped him into the sack and tied it up.

Then, whistling merrily, he walked down the road to King Mickey's palace. So important did

he look in his shiny boots that the palace guards took him straight to the king. Scrooge bowed low.

"Sire, my master begs you to accept this small gift."

"And who is your master?" asked King Mickey, delighted at the plump rabbit.

"The Marquis of Carabas," said Scrooge, repeating a name he had heard once in a fairy tale.

Bowing low again, Scrooge went away.

After that he returned every day with a gift for King Mickey, who grew more and more impressed with the generosity of the so-called Marquis of Carabas.

"Sir Scrooge, you must bring me your kind master, for I long to meet him," said Mickey.

One day Scrooge learned that King Mickey was going on a journey with Princess Minnie. Scrooge ran home as fast as his boots would carry him.

"Quick, Donald! The king will be driving by in his carriage. Run to the river, take off your clothes, and jump in!"

"Why should I jump in the river?" asked Donald, quite reasonably.

"This is no time to ask silly questions," said Scrooge.

"Silly?" squawked Donald. "That river is cold."

"Never mind," Scrooge said, pushing Donald into the river. SPLASH!

"Glub, glub—wak . . . wak . . . WAK!!" yelled Donald.

At that moment King Mickey drove by in the royal carriage.

Scrooge ran toward the carriage, crying, "Help! My master, the Marquis of Carabas, is drowning. Some thieves stole his clothes and threw him in the river."

At once the carriage stopped, and Donald was pulled, dripping, from the river. Mickey, de-

lighted to meet the Marquis at last, insisted on opening up the royal clothes trunk. Soon Donald, handsomely dressed in silks and satins, bowed before the king.

"Sir Marquis, allow me to drive you to your castle," said Mickey in his best King's English.

"I will run ahead and prepare the way," said Scrooge quickly, and he was off in a flash.

Scrooge came to some peasants named Huey, Dewey and Louie working in a field.

"Tell the King that this land belongs to the Marquis of Carabas," said Scrooge. Huey, Dewey and Louie giggled but said they would obey.

Scrooge ran from field to field, telling all the workers the same thing.

At last he came to a huge castle, the home of

Madam Mim. He knew she had power to work magic.

"Hi there, Mim," said Scrooge.

"Go away," said Madam Mim rudely. "I'm expecting visitors for dinner." She made a grab at Scrooge, but Scrooge skipped nimbly out of the

way and thunked her, clump on the shin with his cane.

In a purple rage (her favorite color), Mim turned herself into a roaring lion.

Hanging by his cane from a chandelier, Scrooge said, "It is all right for you to turn yourself into a big lion. But I bet you eight million dollars you can't turn yourself into a tiny beetle! You are not clever enough for that!"

"Oh, yes I am," said Mim, and in a flash she became a tiny beetle—a ladybug, to be exact. Scrooge dropped to the floor, picked up a glass bottle and popped the ladybug inside.

Madam Mim scratched in vain on the smooth glass, trying to get out, but she could not. "Maybe in a few centuries I'll let you loose," said Scrooge. "Your magic power should wear off by then!"

At that moment the royal carriage arrived. "Welcome to Carabas Castle," said Scrooge. "As you can see, a feast is prepared for you."

When King Mickey finished dinner, he said, "My dear Carabas, you have wonderful lands and a beautiful castle. And you serve the best roast pork this side of the Big Bad Wolf. It is a shame that you have all this, and your good friend Scrooge McDuck has nothing. Because he is such a good friend of yours, I hereby proclaim that Scrooge McDuck shall be named Lord McDuck with the best harvest lands in the kingdom."

"If you don't mind," said Scrooge, "I'd rather somebody else had the good harvest lands. I'll settle for those worthless, rocky mountains where nobody can till the soil."

King Mickey agreed. And that is how the Scrooge McDuck fortune got started. All it took was a sack of carrots and a pair of splendid boots —oh, yes, and a nimble brain to match the boots. (At least a brain nimble enough to know those untillable mountains contained mines rich in both silver and gold.) And if your brain is nimble, maybe you can do the same.

The Golden Goose

A Swinging Fairy Tale

GRANDMA DUCK was a no-nonsense type of Duck. She ran her farm like a tight ship, so to speak, with no goofing off. The routine was simple: Up at 5:30, milk the cows, slop the pigs, weed the garden, feed the chickens, pasture the sheep and THEN . . . breakfast!

Fethry Duck didn't realize what he was in for. He went to Grandma's for a week of relaxation away from smog, noise, hustle and bustle, and, above all, work. He was really dragging one day when Grandma Duck clapped an axe in one hand, a picnic basket in another, and told him to chop wood for the stove.

"You've gotta be kidding, Grandma," said Fethry, nervously tugging at his turtleneck sweater. "I mean, already my blisters have blisters. Two swings with this axe, and my hands will dissolve."

"Stuff and nonsense, sonny," said Grandma. "A little exercise will firm up those shoulders."

"What shoulders?" asked Fethry. And he was right.

"Well, anyway, I need some wood. And *you're* elected," Grandma stated, and that was the end of the matter.

"Where do I chop this wood?" asked Fethry, resigned to a fate worse than.

"At that close batch of trees over there," she

answered, pointing somewhere toward the north.

So it was that Fethry set forth to chop wood. He walked along the north side of the east forty and the east side of the north forty, and over the ridge, down the valley and along the stream until he arrived, an hour and a half later, at "that close batch of trees over there."

By this time he was quite hungry, and he set out Grandma Duck's picnic lunch. He was about to take the first bite when a funny little old man appeared. The little old man looked closely at Fethry and at Grandma Duck's spread of goodies, and he asked, "Will you share your food with me?"

"Why not?" said Fethry, for though he was a little scatterbrained, he had a good heart. The little old man sat down and proceeded to put away a goodly share of the sandwiches, cakes, pies, tarts, cheese, fresh fruit, and homemade apple cider.

When he had finished, he leaned back, patted his stomach, and said, "You were kind to share your meager lunch with me. You have a good heart, and you shall not go unrewarded."

Fethry was examining his blisters and studying the axe handle, so he wasn't really paying attention. But he did hear the little old man say, "If you will look under that gorse bush, you will find a reward."

Fethry looked under the bush, and there he found a goose with feathers of pure gold.

"This goose could be valuable," Fethry thought to himself. He turned to thank the little old man, but the man was gone. Thinking that Grandma Duck might be interested in this new type of goose, happy-go-lucky Fethry trotted off in the direction of the farm.

Fethry may have had a good heart, but he had a terrible sense of direction. First thing he knew, he was lost. He walked and walked, and eventually came to an inn. The sun was beginning to set, so Fethry figured he'd better spend the night at the hotel and continue the search for Grandma Duck's farm in the morning.

Now it so happened that Scrooge McDuck was also spending the night at this particular hostel. Scrooge, as everybody knows, is the world's richest Duck. What was he doing at this modest wayside inn? "I didn't keep all my money by staying at the Ritz, Charley," was the way Scrooge expressed it.

Scrooge was sitting in the lobby with his copy of the Wall Street Journal, when Fethry Duck entered. Scrooge sniffed and sniffed again. Gold! He could detect it anywhere. He put down his newspaper and saw Fethry with the goose under his arm. Scrooge's eyeglasses popped clean off his nose.

A Golden Goose!

Scrooge longed to touch it!

But Scrooge was a gentleman, and he knew that proper people did not go up to strange geese and lay hands on the feathers. Scrooge, therefore, determined to wait until dark, when he could

caress the golden plumage without being seen.

That night he crept into Fethry's room. The goose was sleeping on the floor, and Scrooge crawled forward and put his hands on the feathers. What a wonderful feeling! Pure gold.

Scrooge tried to pull his hands away, and couldn't! He was stuck fast to the goose. When Fethry awakened in the morning, he found the world's richest Duck unable to separate himself from the Golden Goose.

"Are you in the habit of stealing into other people's rooms in the middle of the night to touch their geese?" Fethry asked.

"Shut up and unglue me from this thing," Scrooge snapped.

"How?"

"Go and get Huey, Dewey and Louie. They all belong to the Junior Woodchucks, and Junior Woodchucks know everything."

So Fethry bounced downstairs and found

Huey, Dewey and Louie. The three boys were building a color television camera from bits and pieces of old glass and aluminum soft drink containers. Fethry watched them a while, then asked, "How did you kids learn how to do that?"

Huey said, "Our Junior Woodchuck Guide. It tells how to do everything."

"Then you better take it upstairs to my bedroom. Your Uncle Scrooge has troubles."

Quickly the boys forgot about the camera ("We can build it tomorrow instead," they explained) and went to aid Uncle Scrooge. But alas, their Junior Woodchuck Guide had nothing about parting rich uncles from Golden Geese.

So they wrapped their arms around Scrooge and tried to pull him loose. This was a bad idea. First, it didn't work; second, the nephews found themselves stuck fast to Scrooge McDuck!

"We can spend the rest of our lives here in this hotel room," Scrooge complained. "So we'll have to go in search of a goldsmith or a chicken plucker or somebody with a chisel."

Fethry agreed, so they all trooped out of the inn and set off down the road. Soon they ran into Daisy Duck, who was out shopping. They immediately pleaded with her to free them from the Golden Goose.

"It's easy," she said, and she tugged at Huey. But no sooner had she touched him than she also became attached to the Golden Goose.

As they continued their trek, they were spied by the Beagle Boys. For years the Beagles had been trying to steal Scrooge's gold, and here he was, in broad daylight, walking down the road with a Golden Goose. The temptation was too much for the Beagles—they rushed forward and grabbed the goose from Scrooge. But they, too, became stuck to the feathers. Frantically they tried to pull away, but to no avail.

By this time it was pretty difficult walking. Either the three Beagles or else Scrooge, Huey, Dewey, Louie and Daisy had to walk backwards. Fethry, who owned the goose, couldn't get near it. He walked along the edge, herding them in the proper direction. And everybody was getting desperate.

Now it happened that their route took them by the Royal Palace. And in the palace lived a king and his daughter. The king was a happy soul, but the little girl refused to laugh. The king had tried everything to bring a trace of a smile to her lips, but nothing worked.

The court jester brought a frown. The king of TV comics brought a scowl. And that pair of goonies who set five new records in Las Vegas—they brought a bored yawn. Even Clarence the Cross-Eyed Lion was a failure.

The king was in despair. As he tried, for the thousandth time, to figure out what to do, he heard happy cries from the royal nursery. He rushed inside, and there was the princess, laughing her head off. The king looked out the window, and he saw the silly group of travelers which had brought such joy to his daughter.

Immediately he sent for Fethry Duck and his companions. When they were gathered in the Royal Throne Room (with the princess still giggling to herself), the king thanked them all.

"What can I do for you people, who have brought such joy to my daughter?" he asked.

Before Fethry could answer, Scrooge McDuck spoke up. "Do you know anybody who can separate us from this idiotic Golden Goose?"

"Certainly. *I* can," replied the king. He waved his hand in the air, and immediately they all came loose, tumbling and falling over each other.

Scrooge was amazed. "How did you manage to do it?" he asked.

"I can do anything. How do you think I got to be king?"

"In that case," said Fethry, "you keep the Golden Goose. It wouldn't do me any good anyway—I'd only get stuck with it."

"Thank you," said the king.

"My pleasure, kingie," said Fethry.

The king then ordered the Beagle Boys clamped into the Royal Jail, he promoted Huey and Dewey and Louie to Junior Woodchuck First

Class, and he invited Daisy and Scrooge to stay for dinner. He invited Fethry, too, but Fethry said, "Sorry, king, old buddy, but I've got to get back to Grandma Duck's farm." And he left the castle.

He was back at the farm before nightfall (having been given detailed directions by the Royal Mapmaker). He walked into the farmhouse, and Grandma Duck was there to meet him. She had just finished re-roofing the barn and digging a new root cellar.

"Where's my wood?" she demanded.

"Now, Grandma," Fethry began. "It's like this—"

"Are you going to give me a cock-and-bull story about some little old man with a Golden Goose?" she said, stamping her foot.

"Why, yes, now that you mention it."

"You can just forget it, sonny. I've heard that one before. Now tomorrow morning, I want you to chop that wood, or nobody gets any dinner."

And next day, that's exactly what Fethry did.

Donald Duck, Prize Driver

"WELL, what did you learn in school today, boys?" Donald Duck asked his nephews one evening.

"We're studying safe driving, Uncle Donald," said Huey, Louie, and Dewey Duck.

"Good idea," said Donald. "That's what this country needs. You boys just watch your Uncle Donald. You'll see what safe driving is!"

"How did you bash your fender, Uncle Donald?" asked Huey.

"We noticed it outside," said Louie.

"Now there was a stupid driver," said Donald. "Turned right out in front of me. I was coming along at a good clip, minding my own business. Boy, was I burned up! I told him a thing or two."

The nephews nodded at one another.

"Driving too fast in traffic is bad," said Dewey.

"Anger causes accidents," said Louie.

"Always figure the other driver is not as smart as you are," said Huey. "Be ready for him to make a mistake."

"Now listen, you fellows," said Donald. "I was driving a car before you were born. You don't have to teach me! I'm going over to call for Daisy now. Do you want to trust my driving and come along or not?"

"Sure, Uncle Donald. We'll come," said the boys. They all hopped into the back seat. And they got out pencils and papers.

As Donald flipped the starter, he glanced at his watch.

"Gosh, we're late!" he said. "Have to make up a little time."

The first stop light turned yellow as they came up, but Donald sneaked on through. One, two, three, the boys made notes on their pads! But Donald did not see that.

When he tried to turn onto the busy highway, traffic was racing by. No one would wait for him.

"Doggone these drivers," Donald fumed. "They never think of the other guy." And at last he stamped his foot on the gas and swung out in front of an oncoming car so it had to slam on its brakes. "That'll show him," Donald said. The boys' pencils all went back to their pads.

"Now," said Donald, "we can make some time." So down the busy highway he zoomed, swishing from one lane to another, back and forth across the road. The boys had to hang onto each other.

"Wow! This is too fast!" they cried.

"So you want to go slow," cried Donald in disgust. They were in the left lane now, the fast lane, but Donald crept along. Cars lined up behind them. Drivers tried to swing out around them. What a traffic jam he caused!

Z-z-zing! came a siren. It was a police car.

"Sorry, sir," said the policeman. "This lane is for faster traffic. If you want to drive slowly, please keep to the right on busy highways."

He saluted and went back to his car.

"Well!" said Donald Duck, surprised. With a sheepish smile, he started up again. And they went on to meet Daisy Duck.

Back home the three boys went into a huddle.

"Why all the gloom, boys?" Donald asked.

"Well, we entered you in a contest at school for the most courteous driver in town," said Huey.

"You did?" said Donald. "Say, that's great!"

"Yes, but look at your record on this trip," said Louie.

"Sneaked through a yellow stop light," Dewey pointed out.

"Took a chance because you were angry," Huey added.

"Wove from lane to lane on a busy highway," said Louie. "And jammed up traffic by driving too slow in the fast lane."

"You have all the answers, don't you?" Donald snapped. "But take a look at the things I do right. I keep my brakes adjusted and my lights working right. And I don't pass on hills and curves."

"Yes, we know, Uncle Donald," the nephews sighed. "But for us to win the contest, you have to be the most courteous driver in the PTA. And you're a long way from that."

"Oh, I am, am I?" cried Donald. "Well, I'll show you! I'll show the whole PTA!"

Next day, as Donald was driving the boys home from school, he saw some cars waiting to turn onto the busy highway. So he slowed down and let some of them in.

He drove at the speed of the rest of the traffic, staying in one lane most of the time.

He was careful in parking to get close to the curb, and not to slide over the line into the next parking space.

And when he parked the car on a hill, he turned the wheels in toward the curb so the car would not start to roll back down the hill.

"Courtesy doesn't take much time," the boys were quick to point out. Donald politely opened the door and bowed as they stepped out.

And as the days went by, Donald found it was fun to be polite. He liked to see the ladies smile when he stopped to let them cross the street.

He liked to see the truck drivers wave in salute when he had let them make a left turn.

When he saw cars waiting to turn, as he was coming toward them, he stopped to let them go.

He always signaled carefully when he was going to turn or stop or slow down.

Soon along came a meeting of the PTA, where the boys took part in a safety drill.

"By golly," Donald whispered to Daisy at his side, "those kids are the best of the lot!"

Next the school principal introduced Police Chief Horsecollar.

"The Chief will award the prizes in the courteous-driving contest we've been running here in town," the principal explained.

"It's a pleasure to be here," said the Chief. "I guess you can see it's been some time since I was here learning my three R's. But folks, we're never too old to learn. And the biggest lesson we need to learn today is: In driving, it pays to take time to be polite.

"Tonight it is my pleasure to award the prize for the most courteous driver in town to—"

Donald smoothed his hair and straightened his tie, all ready to stand up.

"—Mr. Mac Turner, father of Sandy Turner of this school."

"Thanks," said Mr. Turner from the platform. "I drive a truck for a living. And anyone who drives all the time can tell you it pays—really pays—to take time to be polite."

"Now," said the Chief, "we have another prize to award. An even more important one, because it proves we can keep on learning, even when we're grown up. The prize for the driver who has *improved* most in driving courtesy goes to the uncle of Huey, Louie, and Dewey Duck—Mr. Donald Duck!"

"Folks," said Donald from the platform, "I used to think it was smart to be speedy. But I've learned it's a lot more fun, and smarter, too, to take time to be polite. The credit really belongs to my teachers, though. They did all the work. Huey, Louie, and Dewey, come and take a bow."

Huey, Louie, and Dewey came to the platform. And they took it—one, two, three!

The Country Cousin

There was once a little country mouse who lived in a cornfield. Abner—that was the country mouse's name—had a neat little pantry well stocked with seeds and grain, bits of cheese, and whole beans and peas. He was warm and snug and well fed, and content with his life.

But he had a cousin who was an elegant city mouse. Now this fine fellow would not let Abner rest until he agreed to come to town for a visit.

"I'll show you what life can really be," said Monte, the city cousin.

So Abner closed up his little house and started off one day for the city. With an extra pair of clean socks and a toothbrush slung over his shoulder in a red bandanna handkerchief, and his trusty umbrella tucked under his arm, Abner felt ready for anything the city might offer.

In town, he had no trouble finding the place Monte had described. It was just as Monte had said, a fine big town house with stone walls which stretched up and up and up, farther than Abner could see. He was looking about him wide eyed when the door opened and Monte appeared.

"Come on in," said Monte sharply. "We can't stand around in the streets here in the city. It's much too dangerous."

Abner obediently followed his cousin into the house and through a series of dim passageways. When they stepped out into a fine big room, Abner's eyes grew wide again. For there, right

beside him, set out on a neat little wooden platform, was a large and tasty looking chunk of cheese.

"Hey!" said Abner happily. "This is swell!"

Monte, who was leading the way, spun around at Abner's words.

"Stop!" he cried. "Leave that alone!" And he slapped down Abner's hand just as it touched the cheese.

Zam! the trap slammed shut, whistling past Abner's fingers.

"Never touch cheese you find lying around!" said Monte very sternly.

Abner nodded meekly, and followed his guide on shaking legs.

"There!" said Monte proudly as they came into the next room and hopped onto a big table. "Feast your eyes on that!" added Monte.

He swept an arm out over the great white expanse of a dining room table laden with food. There were fruits, cheeses, and mounds of jello. There were cakes and breads and great puddings, and so many other good things to eat.

"Ooh!" said Abner, in pure delight. But he did not dare touch a thing, for fear of traps.

"Go ahead," Monte told him. And to show the way, he snapped off a corner of cheese and munched daintily at it.

Abner waited no longer. He sampled the cheese, too. It was delicious cheese! Abner broke off a larger piece and tucked it away as fast as he possibly could.

"This is great, Monte," he admitted. "This is the life, all right!"

He dipped into a bowl of cream and smacked his lips in delight. He marveled at a great mold of jello. Next he came to another jar of what looked like darker cream, and he scooped up a big mouthful. But it was mustard, hot mustard! and tears rolled down Abner's cheeks as it sizzled his insides. He gulped down a glass of water at one swallow, but that only gave him the hiccups.

Poor Abner stumbled across the table top. His eyes were red and watering from the hot mustard. And Abner's whole body was shaken with great coughs.

Suddenly Monte shouted, "Look out!" But it was too late.

Abner had lurched against the rim of a plate. And as he clutched at it, the plate started rolling crazily across the table top, carrying poor Abner with it. It scooped up Monte, too, as it whirled and twisted along. Then over the edge of the table it went, plunging down toward the floor far below, landing on the floor with a crash!

In a flash Abner snapped open his trusty umbrella, which he always carried. He grabbed Monte's coat tail in his other hand, and together they floated to the floor, unharmed, after the plate crashed down.

But now a new danger awaited them! With eyes gleaming hungrily, the cat approached on padded paws!

"This way!" shouted Monte, and he dived for his mouse hole and safety. But Abner, in his haste and fright, ran in the opposite direction. As Monte peeked out of his mouse hole, he saw Abner heading out the door, inches ahead of the cat's bared teeth and snatching claws. And that was the last Monte saw of Abner.

Down into the street raced Abner, with the cat close behind.

Zip! a huge tire whistled past in front of his nose. Wh-whip! another sped close behind him.

Whoo-OO-oo! shrieked a siren.

Clang-g-g! snarled a noisy bell.

Rattle-rattle! went a heavy truck above his head.

Poor Abner raced along with his heart in his mouth. He was swerving this way and that way, as danger rushed at him from all sides! Poor Abner! He was running as fast as he could. And as he ran, he clutched his trusty umbrella in his right hand.

Not until he found himself in the open countryside once more did he dare stop to catch his breath and mop his dripping face. Then he began walking slowly down the country road toward his cornfield.

"If that's the city," he vowed, "no more of it for me! I'll stay in my cornfield where I can have a long life and a happy one!"

Donald Duck, Private Eye

"HELP!" cried Minnie Mouse. "Mickey, my jewel box is missing. I can't find it anywhere. Someone must have stolen it."

"Now, now," said Mickey, "keep calm, Minnie. I will help you find it."

Together they searched Minnie's house . . . upstairs, downstairs . . . and even in the garden. There was no sign of the jewel box.

"Oh, dear," sobbed Minnie, "what shall I do?"

"There is only one person who can help us," answered Mickey, "and that person is Donald Duck, the great Private Eye. I will go to him at once."

Donald was in his office, and as usual, he was busy.

"Donald! Donald! Wake up!" said Mickey. "Minnie's jewel box is missing. We need you to help us find it."

Donald opened a sleepy eye.

"I'll take the case, Mickey," he said. "I'll search the underworld tonight, and find the jewel box in no time."

It was midnight when Donald entered the underworld. His coat collar was pulled high and his cap was pulled low to hide his face, and he carried all his detective tools.

It was dark and spooky, and glittering eyes watched him from under lowered curtains. Donald was so busy searching for clues that he didn't notice a huge figure hiding in the deep shadows.

As Donald moved further into the darkness, a huge shadow tiptoed silently after him.

"I'll find Minnie's jewel box," Donald said aloud, "or my name isn't . . ."

"Donald Duck, the great Private Eye," a loud voice boomed out.

Donald leaped into the air, dropping his tools. The voice went on:

"That's not a very good disguise you have there, Donald."

And, as the moon came out from behind a cloud, Donald saw that the voice belonged to Black Pete.

"Everybody can recognize you in that outfit," added Pete kindly. "Better try another one."

"I will," said Donald, "and nobody will ever see through it."

The next morning, Donald looked through all his books about disguises, but he didn't find any that he liked. Then he happened to look in a mirror."

"Say," he chuckled, "I've found the answer."

"First," he said, "I'll fluff up my feathers and add a hair ribbon . . . then I'll put on a blouse and skirt . . . and . . . OUCH! . . . a pair of tight high-heeled shoes! Now nobody will know me from *Daisy Duck.*"

He smiled proudly as he walked out the front door.

His three little nephews were playing marbles on the sidewalk.

"Hello, Unca Donald," they all shouted.

Donald stopped short. He was very surprised.

"I guess my disguise isn't quite perfect," he thought. "I'll have to try a different one."

Back he went to his disguise closet. He took off the hair ribbon, and he pulled an old-fashioned blouse over his sailor shirt.

Next, he added a pair of steel-rimmed eyeglasses.

"There," he said, as he put on a white wig, "nobody will know me from *Grandma Duck*. Now to search the underworld for Minnie's jewel box."

Just as Donald was coming out of his front door, Goofy walked by.

"Hello, Donald," said Goofy gaily. "Are you going to a fancy dress party?"

Poor Donald!

"How did Goofy see through my disguise?" he asked himself. "If *he* recognized me, everybody else will, too!"

"This makes me angry," grumbled Donald, as he peeled off the blouse. "But I'll fool everyone yet. I'll leave on the glasses . . .

. . . then I'll slip on this old smoking jacket . . .

. . . and, with a few odds and ends of whiskers, nobody will know me from . . .

. . . my own rich uncle, *Scrooge McDuck!*"

Just then, Mickey and Minnie Mouse came running down the street, at the head of a happy parade.

"Oh Donald," they called, "we won't need your help after all. We've found Minnie's jewel box."

Minnie's nephew, Morty, had borrowed it to keep his fishing worms in.

"I'm glad you found the jewel box," sighed Donald. "But how did you all see through my disguises? I thought they were perfect."

"This Uncle Scrooge disguise was *almost* perfect," laughed Mickey and Minnie. "But you forgot two things that Uncle Scrooge would never be without."

"That goes for your Daisy Duck disguise, too," chimed in Huey, Dewey and Louie.

"We thought you *were* Daisy until we noticed something was missing."

"You almost had *me* fooled," chuckled Goofy. "Then I saw something you were wearing that didn't look like Grandma Duck."

Here are the real Daisy, Grandma and Uncle Scrooge in their own clothes.

Do *you* know what was wrong with Donald's disguises?

Donald forgot:
Daisy's *long black eyelashes,*
Grandma's *old-fashioned high-buttoned shoes,*
Uncle Scrooge's *spats.*

Lucky Puppy

Lucky Puppy lived with his father, Pongo, and his mother, Perdita, and with all his sisters and brothers. The people who belonged to them were Roger and Anita and Nanny Cook. There were Penny and Lenny and Salter and Pepper, Jolly and Rolly and Patch and Latch. There were Spot and Dot and Blob and Blot and Blackie and Whitey and—where's Lucky? Here is Lucky, in front of the television, watching his favorite, Thunderbolt. Whenever Penny and Lenny wanted to dig holes or Salter and Pepper wanted to chew bones or Patch and Latch wanted to chase tails or Jolly and Rolly wanted to jump at

Nanny Cook's apron strings, or Spot and Dot wanted to play hide and seek or Blob and Blot wanted to growl at the mirror, or Blackie and Whitey wanted to take a nap, Lucky never wanted to. He just wanted to sit in front of the television watching his favorite, Thunderbolt.

Or he practiced television tricks. "I'm going to be a television star myself," said Lucky Pup.

Well, all the other puppies learned puppy tricks. Soon they could sit up and roll over.

They could dance and shake hands, jump for a treat and walk politely at heel. But not Lucky. He was too busy dreaming of being a television star. One day he decided he was ready to be in a television show. So he slipped out of the house and he ran down the street. He ran around a corner. And there he stopped. He was lost. He did not know his way to the television place. And he did not know his way home. Poor Lucky. He walked and walked and walked. He tried to show people his television tricks. But they did not understand. "He doesn't seem to know any puppy tricks," was all the people said. Finally a policeman came along. He looked at Lucky's license tag. And he took Lucky home. There were Penny and Lenny and Salter and Pepper and Jolly and Rolly and Patch and Latch, Spot and Dot and Blob and Blot and Blackie and Whitey, all doing puppy tricks for treats. But not Lucky. Lucky was all tired out. He crept straight into his basket. And he went straight to sleep. He even slept through the Thunderbolt Show which the other puppies watched. But next morning Lucky was up first of all. "Time enough for television later," he said. "Now I am going to learn my puppy tricks." And he did!

The Practical Pig

ONE DAY the Practical Pig was busy working on an Important Invention. His two brothers wanted him to stop and play, but he kept right on working. They even made fun of him.

"He's making another old wolf machine.
The craziest pig we've *ever* seen!"

But the Practical Pig paid no attention to them. He just went on with his Invention.

"To work all day is fun for him—
But not for us! Let's take a swim!"

The Practical Pig shook his hammer warningly.

"Don't go swimming, do you hear?
The pond's not safe! The WOLF is near!"

But the two foolish pigs laughed and ran straight to the pond. "Last one in is a pork sausage!" they squealed happily.

Splash! The foolish pigs were having a grand time in the water. "You're a pork sausage!"

They teased each other.

"Who's afraid of the Big Bad Wolf?" they sang. But the Big Bad Wolf was watching them from behind some nearby cattails.

"Pork sausage nothing," he muttered. "Pork pie!" He dressed himself as a mermaid, waded into the water, stretched out on a rock and Looked Lovely. He played on a lyre, which is a very poetic instrument. He even sang. "MERMAID!" cried the thoughtless little pigs. And when the pretty creature threw a red rose into the water, they fell for it. In fact, they even *dove* for it!"

But when they came up again, the foolish pair found themselves *caught* in a heavy net.

This was no mermaid, but their enemy, the grinning Wolf! He carried them off to his home in the old mill.

But the villain was not satisfied with having two of the Three Little Pigs in his power. He wanted to get ALL of them.

His Bad Little Wolves were hungry and impatient. But he made them wait. Papa had plans! He wrote a letter . . .

"Don't dare eat till I bring the other one back," he warned his greedy children.

"We won't," they promised. But the minute Papa Wolf was gone they stuffed the two pigs into a big pan and surrounded them with dough.

"You'd better mind your papa," the frightened pigs reminded them. "You'll be sorry!"

"We'll be sorry? Ha ha ha!" The bad little wolves danced around and showed their teeth. *"Ha ha ha!"*

Meanwhile the Wolf, dressed as a messenger, knocked at the door of the Practical Pig's house. But his letter did not fool the Practical Pig.

DEAR BRUTHER
WE ARE IN TRUBBLE
CUM WITH ~~ME~~
BEARER
LUVINGLY
YUR BRUTHERS

The Practical Pig had plans, too. He wanted to see if his new Invention would work. Now was his chance! So he pulled a lever and pushed a button—the signal for his Important Invention to start working.

MACHINERY ROARED. The Wolf was pulled in, seated in a chair and strapped down. The Invention did it all. He tugged and pulled, but he couldn't get away. Then the Practical Pig asked the Big Bad Wolf a question. "WHERE ARE MY BROTHERS?"

"Never heard of them," snarled the Wolf.

Wham! Lights flashed, whistles blew. An indicator on the wall registered "LIE."

A scrubbing-brush washed out the Big Bad Wolf's mouth with foamy soapsuds.

At the same time the Wolf got a good hard *spanking.*

Now you know! The Practical Pig's Invention was a Lie Detector! It punished the Wolf harder each time he told a lie.

At last he panted, "I'll tell! They are in the old mill!"

The indicator registered "TRUTH" at last. The Invention shot the Wolf right out through the chimney. The Practical Pig grabbed his shotgun, ready to go to the rescue of his foolish brothers.

Meanwhile the little fellows were hot and miserable in their pie-crust blankets, as the hungry little wolves pushed them toward the fire. Then . . .

"We forgot the pepper!" But they used too much pepper, and the pigs sneezed themselves clear out of the old mill. They were free!

Home they ran, right past the Practical Pig on the doorstep.

"Didn't I tell you not to go swimming because the Wolf was near?" the Practical Pig asked crossly.

"Oh," the two Foolish Pigs chorused sweetly, "we did not think of swimming!"

Oh, no? *Wham!* The Lie Detector reached out for the hairbrush and the Pigs. The two storytellers were spanked soundly.

"This hurts me more than it does you," the Practical Pig told them.

Wham! He dodged. But it was too late. The Lie Detector always worked!

The Brave Mice and the

It seems to me that not enough credit is given to mice for the great advances that have been made in the world. Now take me, for example. I'm a mouse. Pretty insignificant, some people would say. But if it hadn't been for me Columbus might never have discovered America.

Does this sound fantastic? Well, it is—but it's true, all the same.

It all started with Cigam, the official wizard at Cinderella's court. (In case you didn't realize it, no royal court is really complete without a wizard or soothsayer, or at least an alchemist.) Cigam wasn't a very famous wizard, or even a very good one, even if his name spelled backward did mean "magic." As a matter of fact, hardly anyone believed in him. But he was there, tucked away high up in the north tower, with his bats and his books and his bottles and jars of strange things like

Magic Cheese

newt's dust and mandrake root. Sometimes one of the maids would creep up the windey stairs and ask Cigam to mix a love potion for her. But Cigam's love potions had a strange way of working out. They're still talking in the kitchen about the time the cook used one to . . . but that's another story.

As I was saying, Cigam was pretty well forgotten, except by a few of us mice who liked to drop in on him from time to time for a thimbleful of tea.

One evening, Gus and I were having a little chat with Cigam when he brought up the subject of the enchanted cheese. "It's a wonderful cheese," he told us. "I've been saving it for years and years, waiting for a brave, adventurous spirit to try it. And you're both brave and adventurous spirits."

"What does the cheese do?" I asked. I must admit, I'm a little suspicious of cheese that anyone has been saving for years and years.

Cigam leaned closer to the table, where Gus and I were sitting on a large crock of mummy

dust. "If you eat the cheese while I say an incantation, you'll be transported to any time and place you desire."

"Really?"

"Really!"

"You mean time-travel?"

"Absolutely."

"We could go back to the court of Cleopatra?"

"Without a doubt."

"Or to China with Marco Polo?"

"Yes, indeed."

"Suppose you don't say the incantation right?"

Cigam looked pained and ran his hand through his beard, startling a bat that seemed to have taken up housekeeping there. "Of course I'll say the incantation right," he said. "I've been practicing every night for five years!"

"Hmm." I thought about it for a minute. "How do we get back from the court of Cleopatra, or wherever we go?"

"That's the easiest part," Cigam assured us. "After three days, the charm wears off and you're back."

"You sure?" Gus squeaked.

"Don't worry about a thing." Cigam patted him on the back with one finger, nearly knocking him off the jar of mummy dust. "You're clever and resourceful mice, and that's why I've chosen you. Shall we try for ancient Egypt now?"

I remembered that the old Egyptians were

very fond of cats and said, "How about China instead?"

"All right, all right. Just make sure you notice everything you see, and if you should happen to meet any magicians, try to find out something about their incantations. Those old Chinese magicians were the best."

Cigam doddered off to a big, deep cupboard that stood in one corner of the tower, took out a moldy, old cheese dish and showed us the cheese. Surprisingly, it looked like very ordinary, yellow cheese.

"A crumb will be enough," Cigam said. "Hold it in your hand and when I stamp my left foot three times, eat it."

So we each held a crumb of cheese and Cigam stood in the middle of the room, spun around three times and said:

"Hum-didy, hibidy, hickory, doc!
Hi-didy, why-didy, mouse up the clock!"

Then he stamped his foot three times and we swallowed the cheese.

The next thing we knew, the tower was gone and we were sitting on the floor in one corner of a long, gray stone room. At the other end of the room were two big chairs, thrones really, with a red and gold canopy over them.

"This not look like China," Gus whispered.

Some men dressed in strange clothes, long stockings and short pants and funny coats, stood around near the thrones. Then a boy wearing a uniform or livery of some sort, obviously a page, blew a blast on a trumpet and yelled: "Their Majesties, King Ferdinand and Queen Isabella!"

Ferdinand and Isabella! That Cigam was some magician! He tried to send us to ancient Cathay, and we wind up in Spain in about 1490!

The men around the throne bowed and in came the king and queen. He wasn't much to look at, but she was pretty spectacular, all covered with diamonds, emeralds and pearls from head to toe.

"The Italian sea captain, Señor Christoforo Columbo," yelled the page. And in he came, Chris Columbus himself, looking very much like his pictures in the history books.

Well, he bowed to their majesties and started telling them about how the world was really round, not flat as everyone thought, and how by sailing west he could find a new trade route to the Indies and how wonderful it would be for their majesties to help such a noble venture and one thing and another, and let me tell you he was just about the worst salesman I've ever heard. He couldn't have convinced me of anything—not anything! He droned on and on about ocean currents and shipping by sea rather than by land and cargo stowage and gross tonnage per cargo hold and every so often he would stretch out a big map of the world, or a globe, and show it to the king and queen. Isabella got more and more bored and King Ferdinand simply went to sleep.

"He never gonna discover America that way," Gus remarked. I agreed.

At last, the audience was over and Columbus trailed himself out.

"C'mon," I said to Gus. "We gotta help."

That night, when Queen Isabella came into her chamber, there was a note on her dressing table next to her jewel box. It told her that Columbus would never discover a trade route to the Indies, but that he would find a great new continent—a "New Spain"—and that she would sell her jewels to buy ships for him, and pay a crew to man the ships.

That's all the note said, but it was enough. The queen jumped up and screamed for the guards. She said that someone had gotten into the room to leave the note. They searched, and of course since they were looking for a person, they didn't ever think to peer up on top of the bed curtains where Gus and I were watching.

After things quieted down and the queen went to bed—and to sleep—I scooted down the bed curtains and pinned another note to her pillow. It was more of the same. In the morning when she woke up there was more screeching and scurrying and another scene with the guards.

And so it went for two days. Notes on the breakfast table, notes in the sewing basket, notes for lunch and tea and dinner. Gus and I were

getting writers' cramp. And all this while we had to watch out for the cat.

That's right! A cat! A big yellow tomcat who was very nippy on his feet. We were a little out of practice, because Cinderella didn't allow cats in *her* palace, so that big tom almost caught us a couple of times. Once Gus had to take refuge in a teapot and once I escaped the cat only by diving into the ornamental fountain in the royal garden and swimming underwater for quite some distance.

When the third day dawned, we knew our time was running out. Cigam's spell would wear off soon and Isabella still hadn't consented to outfit Columbus for his trip to the new world, even though the mysterious notes were beginning to make an impression on her.

It was time for desperate measures!

Columbus was to have another audience with their majesties at eleven, so Gus and I took up separate stations behind the portraits in the royal portrait gallery. We knew the queen would have to pass through the gallery on her way to see Columbus in the throne room.

Promptly at eleven, she came. And that dratted cat was following her. But we did our duty.

As she passed the portrait of King Ferdinand's great-great uncle on his mother's side, Gus yelled out, "You'll be the greatest queen in history if you help Columbus."

Isabella stopped dead and stared at the portrait. And the cat went up to the wall and sniffed very suspiciously under the picture. At that moment, from behind the painting of King Ferdinand's father, I called, "Sell your jewels and you'll be famous forever."

She wheeled around and ran over to my hiding place, the cat just behind her, and Gus quickly scampered to the portrait of Isabella's grandmother's brother, a dark gentleman with a large beard. Just as the queen reached my side of the room, Gus called out once more. We kept this up with the cat and the queen both getting more and more frantic until we heard the voice of the page in the throne room. He was announcing the arrival of Columbus. The queen put her hands up to her head, looked around rather wildly at the pictures and said, "All right! All right! I'll do it," and she ran into the throne room.

"Hooray," cheered Gus, and fell out from behind a very bad picture of Isabella's uncle.

The cat saw him and started to leap.

"Look out!" I squeaked.

At that exact instant, the portrait gallery wavered and shimmered and grew dim. The cat faded, in mid-leap, and Gus and I were back in the tower with old Cigam. The spell had worn off in the nick of time!

Cigam was very disappointed when he heard where we'd been. "I can't understand it," he kept saying. "That spell was just right to send you to China. Maybe I need more practice."

"Never mind, Cigam," I told him. "The spell was a dilly."

And it was. Because without Cigam's spell, and the efforts of two brave mice, would Columbus ever have discovered America?

The Brave Mice and the Invisible Menace

CIGAM the Magician is the end—the absolute living end. For years he's gone along as a complete failure. His love potions make people hate each other. His ulcer cures give folks the stomach ache. His wart removers will remove just about anything but warts. He can't even forecast the weather. So you could have knocked Gus and me over with the well-known feather when he actually proved himself as an alchemist.

You see, Cigam used some magic cheese to send Gus and me back to ancient Egypt to get a piece of philosopher's stone. This stone, carefully guarded and kept on an altar in an old temple, makes it possible to change lead into gold—provided you've got the right formula. Cigam claimed he had the formula, and we got him the stone. He was all set—so he said—and he went to work. "I'll make my mark as an alchemist," he kept muttering. We left him in his tower and went off to bed.

Lo and behold if we didn't go up the next morning to find Cigam, even shaggier than usual, with a large burn in the front of his best robe, and completely surrounded by gold!

"I've done it," he chortled when he saw us. "I've made gold! I'm a success at last." And he did a sort of shuffling little jig.

Gus touched a piece of gold in a dazed sort of way and asked what I thought was a clever question. "What ya gonna do with it, Cigam?"

"Do with it?" Cigam crowed. "Do with it? Why I'll . . . I'll . . ." He stopped and looked confused. Obviously he hadn't thought that far ahead.

I suppose, when you come right down to it, Cigam didn't really want to be rich. He'd always had everything he needed at Cinderella's palace —a good home, steady job, plenty to eat, lots of time to putter and nobody to bother him very much. Gus's question caught him short; he didn't know *what* he was going to do with the gold. "I'll buy a new robe," he finally announced.

"Then what?" I asked.

"Why then I'll . . . I'll . . ."

He was still pondering when we heard a loud scream from the courtyard below. We rushed to the window and looked out in time to see the Captain of the King's Guard stagger around in a circle and fall to the ground in a dead faint.

"Shades of Zebulon!" Cigam yelled. He snatched Gus and me up, popped us into his pocket and ran downstairs, his bony old legs taking the steps two at a time. In the courtyard we found the Captain of the Guard coming to.

"He's gone—disappeared!" the captain yelled, pointing at the drawbridge, which was down.

"Who's gone?" asked the Keeper of the Imperial Coffee Urn, who'd just run out from the pantry.

"The postman!" said the captain. He pointed again at the drawbridge.

"Hmph!" snorted the cook. "So the postman went away. What's so exciting about that. The man's daft."

"But he didn't just go away," the captain explained. There were actually tears in his eyes. "He walked out of here across that drawbridge, the way he does every morning after he's delivered the mail to the Imperial Secretary. He nodded to me, the way he always does, and then he walked across the drawbridge and he disappeared. Just on the other side of the moat, he vanished into thin air. It was as if he'd been swallowed up by some . . . some . . . SOMETHING!"

With that the brave Captain of the Guard forgot that he was the winner of the bronze oak leaf for courage in battle. He began to cry.

A fuzz-faced young second lieutenant was about to lead the captain away to the palace infirmary, convinced that the man had popped his top, when we saw the milkmaid from the nearby farm coming up the road. She was coming to deliver milk to the palace kitchen. For some reason everyone in the courtyard stopped and watched her approach. We could see her clearly. That is, we could see her until she got within about three feet of the moat. She put her foot out to take a step and the foot vanished as if it had been cut off! Without noticing that she seemed to be minus one foot, she took her step and slid into nothingness. It was like watching a person walk through a door into another room, except that there wasn't any door and there wasn't any other room. There wasn't anything except a drawbridge, a moat and an empty road.

Betsinda the chambermaid screamed. The cook went pale. The Keeper of the Imperial Coffee Urn said "Hmm-Ha!" and pulled at his mustache.

"Disappeared!" muttered the captain. "Just like the postman."

The second lieutenant, with a wild sort of look in his eye, drew his saber and charged at the drawbridge yelling "Villains! Stand and fight!"

He got across the drawbridge all right, but the minute he set foot on the other side he, too, vanished. *Pouff!* Cut off in mid-charge.

The days that followed took on a nightmare quality. Needless to say, no one tried to leave the castle via the drawbridge. The second assistant dishwasher in the imperial kitchen did slip out through a small gate in the north wall. He, too, disappeared completely in the twinkling of an eye, giving a case of hysterics to the scullery

maid who'd been watching. So we knew that the "Zone of Disappearance," as the Court Chamberlain called it, extended all the way around the palace.

The King posted a guard on the parapets to warn travelers and townspeople away. And believe me, after the disappearance of the postman and the milkmaid, they didn't need much warning. No one—but no one—came near the palace. We were cut off—besieged as if an army had been camped around us.

With food enough on hand for a week, we weren't too uncomfortable. But after the third day everyone grew very nervous. The cook snapped at the butler. The butler boxed the footman's ears. The footman had a spat with the upstairs maid, who, in turn, pinched the poor parlormaid severely.

It was on this third day that everyone remembered Cigam. No one understood the strange thing that had happened; wasn't it logical to ask the Official Court Magician to deal with it? The Chamberlain was the first to approach Cigam to see if, in some of the old books of magic lore, there might be a key to the secret that seemed to threaten the palace. The Chamberlain was almost immediately followed by the Lord Chancellor of the Privy Seal, and after the Lord Chancellor came the Keeper of the Royal Bedchamber.

Poor Cigam! He didn't know any more about

what was going on than anyone else. I'll say this for him, though—he put up a good front. He took to looking wise—or at least as wise as Cigam can ever look, which isn't very—and he muttered things like, "It takes time," and "I'm on the trail of a very potent spell." His visitors would go away trying to be patient. There wasn't much else they could do.

It was our cat—our wonderful loyal vegetarian cat—who discovered that someone was patrolling the "Zone of Invisibility." The cat came to us on the evening of the third day and squeaked. (I mentioned, didn't I, that the cat never mewed? He squeaked. He thought he was a mouse, you see.) It was plain that he wanted to show us something. We followed him out across the courtyard and up to the drawbridge. There we stopped. But the cat went on and on until he'd almost crossed the bridge and we were sure we'd see *him* vanish any second, like the postman and the milkmaid. But not our cat. He was too smart! He stopped at the far end of the bridge and looked at the road and squeaked again. Then we saw what he saw. Footprints!

I don't mean old, dead footprints just lying there—footprints that might have been made by someone passing that way last week. These were brand new footprints. As a matter of fact, they were being made right there before us. We saw, one after another, the imprints of feet pressed into the dust of the road. And we heard clearly the tread of unseen feet. An invisible person was walking around the palace!

We took our news to Cigam. He wasn't much help. He only became more confused trying to decide whether it was an invisible postman or an invisible milkmaid who was picketing the drawbridge.

Again, the cat helped us find the answer. He wandered into the kitchen and fell into a perfectly enormous canister of flour. He came yowling and scurrying into the pink throne room, white as a ghost from the flour.

"He looks funny," Gus commented as the cat started to clean himself.

He did look funny. You'd never have been able to tell he was a black and gray and white and orange cat. He looked like a ghost of a cat.

A ghost!

It was then that I got one of my most outstanding ideas. I know that my career has been practically studded with outstanding ideas, but even for me, this one was a gem. Suppose we sprinkled our invisible pacer with flour. Wouldn't it stick to him, just the way it had stuck to our cat, and make him visible to us?

With me, to think is to act. Within half an hour I'd mobilized all the mouse reserves in the palace. Every able-bodied mouse was called to an emergency meeting in the east ball room. Speaking rapidly, I outlined my plan to them and, clear-headed mice that they are, they saw the logic of my idea immediately. Soon every mouse was armed with a small paper sack filled with flour (the cook protested, but we got Cigam to threaten to cast a spell on her and she kept quiet after that!). Out we marched through the huge double portals of the palace. It was a thrilling sight! Hundreds of brave mice, each with a mission. We crossed the courtyard, then marched over the drawbridge to the very edge of the moat. Above us, high on the parapets, Cigam watched.

We stopped, just short of the "Zone of Invisibility," and we waited. But not for long. Soon we heard footsteps approaching. Then we saw them planting themselves on the ground, one after another. A rose bush on the edge of the moat stirred, though there was no wind. The invisible one was there!

I shouted "Go," and every mouse hurled his sack of flour into the air about five feet above the ground. The sacks burst; there was an immense billowing white cloud. Then the flour settled and we saw him!

The invisible one was a man—but what a strange man! He wore a weird flowing robe and had a crown on his head, the like of which I'd never seen. In his hand was a long staff. As the flour cleared, he realized what had happened. He saw us and pointed with his staff.

We did not wait another moment on the drawbridge. Helter skelter, we swarmed back into the palace. But we'd accomplished our mission. We knew what the invisible menace looked like!

In Cigam's tower, we found the old magician shaking like a leaf.

"You see him, Cigam?" Gus said.

Cigam groaned. "He's a priest of ancient Egypt. One of those who were keepers of the Temple of Isis, where the philosopher's stone rested."

Cigam groaned again. "I know why he's here. He's come across the years to get back that piece of the philosopher's stone we have. There must be some magical condition we don't understand that keeps him from entering the palace and taking the stone, but it also keeps us from leaving. Oh, what will I do? I've brought this terrible curse down on everyone here!" And the poor old soul began to weep.

"Give him back the stone!" I suggested. I mean, even Cigam should have been able to figure this out.

Cigam agreed. "That's what I'll have to do, before anyone else disappears. It was nice to be able to make gold. There isn't another magician alive today who can do it. But I'll give back the stone."

"Never mind, Cigam," I comforted him. "You can make yourself famous even without the gold."

"How's that?" Cigam said.

"Don't tell anyone you've got a piece of the old Egyptian's stone. Just say you've got the answer to the invisible menace—which is true. Then go out there tomorrow morning in front of the whole court and leave the stone on the other end of the drawbridge. The Egyptian will go back to Egypt and we'll go back to living normally and you've got it made in the shade."

So, early the next morning, Cigam put on his best robe, draped it carefully to hide the burned place, and marched across the drawbridge with the philosopher's stone in a little golden box. The entire court, watching from the parapets, saw him put the box on the drawbridge, but only Gus and I saw the lid of the box open, then close. Then the box slipped into invisibility.

Suddenly it began to rain people. First the postman dropped out of thin air onto the palace lawn. Then the milkmaid, the second lieutenant, and finally the dishwasher. None of them were hurt, but none could tell anything about where he'd been for three days.

That was the end of the invisible menace. From that day forward anyone could go or come freely. I'm sorry to say that Cigam's magic gold disappeared. In its place was just so much lead. But Cigam didn't really care. He'd never wanted to be rich; he'd wanted fame and prestige, and now he had them. Because everyone thought he'd been able to drive the menace away by his great magic. Cigam was smart enough never to tell anyone the truth about the whole affair. And until now, so were Gus and I.